A STRANGER LIGHT

Gloria Cook titles available from
Severn House Large Print

Keeping Echoes
Never Just a Memory
From a Distance
Listening to the Quiet
Moments of Time
Pengarron Dynasty
Pengrarron Rivalry
Touch the Silence

A STRANGER LIGHT

Gloria Cook

Severn House Large Print
London & New York

This first large print edition published in Great Britain 2007 by
SEVERN HOUSE LARGE PRINT BOOKS LTD of
9-15 High Street, Sutton, Surrey, SM1 1DF.
First world regular print edition published 2006 by
Severn House Publishers, London and New York.
This first large print edition published in the USA 2007 by
SEVERN HOUSE PUBLISHERS INC., of
595 Madison Avenue, New York, NY 10022.

British Library Cataloguing in Publication Data

Cook, Gloria
  A stranger light. - Large print ed.
  1. Harvey family (Fictitious characters) - Fiction
  2. Cornwall (England : County) - Social life and customs -
  Fiction 3. Domestic fiction 4. Large type books
  I. Title
  823.9'14[F]

  ISBN-13: 978-0-7278-7620-1

Printed and bound in Great Britain by
MPG Books Ltd, Bodmin, Cornwall.

To my dear nephew Shaun,
his wife Sara, and Carl, Bethany
and Megan, with my love

One

A late snow came at mid-morning, quickly transforming gardens, fields and trees into a white winter land. It gave the place a Christmas-card magic, but also brought the threat to outlying farms and homes of difficulty in reaching the village of Hennaford. It sent Faye Harvey scurrying along the narrow ribbons of lanes, and finally up the short, now slippery, hill to the small draughty school, where she knew the antiquated heating would be struggling and the teachers eager to see the pupils safely on their way home before the snow grew worse.

She arrived with her head bent down as the biting cold wind thrust heavy snowflakes into her face and body. In a full-length fur coat and fur hat, fur-lined boots and leather gloves, Faye was notably smarter than the local mothers were. It wasn't her own children she had come to fetch – her son, Simon, was three years old. It was the three orphans, once war evacuees, under the guardianship of herself and her uncle, Tristan Harvey, whom she was anxious to get home to the warmth and comfort of Tremore House.

'A bit parky, isn't it?' a young woman remarked to her as she emerged from the porch of the girls' entrance with her daughter. Susan Dowling stamped about in insubstantial lace-up shoes to warm her feet. Her coat, made from an old grey blanket, as so many outdoor garments had been out of necessity during the war, and her darned wool stockings and cotton paisley headscarf were not up to the job of protecting her from the cold.

Faye glanced at Susan's hands and was pleased to see she had knitted gloves on, and that six-year-old Maureen was wrapped up well and had her stick-thin legs inside thick tights and rubber boots. As the second largest land and property owner in Hennaford, Faye was Susan's landlady, but she hardly knew her. Susan was known for keeping herself to herself

'Let's hope it doesn't freeze tonight,' Faye said. She resisted the comment that here in the relatively mild climate of Cornwall, the snowfall was much lighter and far less dangerous than was typical in some states of America, the continent where she had been raised, and in Scotland, where she had lived for a few years. She had been born at Tremore House, but during her eighth year her American mother had left her father. Her soft transatlantic accent set her a little apart.

8

As did the fact she was an unmarried mother. Faye felt something of an oddity, an outsider, and despite having more family on the other side of Hennaford, she was often lonely.

Susan nodded. She had the habit of trying to be inconspicuous and tended to agree with everyone. She had moved to Hennaford on her marriage. She was a war widow, one of three women in Hennaford who had suffered the loss of their husbands before six years of Nazi tyranny had been brought to an end the previous year. She neither complained nor sought pity, and she had gained the villagers' respect. People thought of her as a 'dear young maid' and were moved to feel protective towards her and her 'poor little chile', and to offer her baskets of produce and pass-down clothes, which she accepted graciously. Faye recognized the coat she was wearing as previously being a blanket on her housekeeper Agnes's bed. 'It said on the wireless we'd have snow today and I'd wondered if it would be wise to send Maureen to school, but you can't wrap them up in cotton wool, can you?'

'No, it's best not to,' Faye said, pleased that Susan was keeping up a conversation and not excusing herself and going on ahead with Maureen. She received Pearl Smith, who was in the same class as Maureen, and already clad for the journey home, from the young female teacher. Tiny Londoner Pearl seemed twitchy as she grabbed Faye's hand, and Faye put it down to the weather. A glance over the thick stone wall that separated them from the boys' playground showed Pearl's older, boisterous, twin brothers were on their way out of the battered wooden gate.

'Shall we walk back together, Mrs Dowling?' Faye ventured, eyeing the darkening pinky-grey sky. The wind was whining on a low note and the atmosphere was forbidding.

'It would be a good idea to stick together,' Susan said. She reached for Maureen's hand but her daughter ran on ahead with the twins. 'Don't go on too far,' she called after the skimpy girl.

'Be careful, boys,' Faye warned. She wasn't overly worried. The snow was up to their ankles and small drifts were formed against banks and walls, but they should reach their homes without problems. As they cautiously made their way down the hill, the three children ahead deliberately made themselves slide, screaming with laughter, while gathering up snowballs.

'Maureen's such a tomboy,' Susan said.

Faye heard the note of pride in her voice. Susan seemed to have no one in the world except the daughter she obviously adored. 'Aren't you going off to play with the others, darling?' Faye encouraged Pearl.

'No,' Pearl pressed her face into Faye's arm as they crunched and occasionally slithered over the snow. Susan held out a hand to her and the little girl took it eagerly.

Faye smiled. It was nice to do be doing something companionably with another adult, another woman, that was. After the terrible letdown she'd had from Simon's father, she was in no hurry to consider a new romance. There was always a lot of male interest in her, she was fine looking, with a fabulous figure, with an unselfconscious poise that made her stand out, and she had the freshness of her twenty-one years. 'It will be a different story the instant Pearl's inside the door. She'll run straight to my uncle. Her Uncle Tris,' she explained to Susan. 'He indulges her. He wanted to come and fetch her himself but I pointed out that he'd look a bit of a fool.' Women had played a vital part in the war but many rules were still set firm – children were considered the women's domain.

She noticed Susan was shivering. If she didn't have enough warm clothes, what else might she be lacking? Lance Dowling had enlisted at the outbreak of the war and had given his all for the country, and it fell on everyone's shoulders, her own most of all, as his widow's landlady, to ensure Susan and their little girl were at least sufficiently provided for. Faye felt herself flushing with guilt. She knew Susan took in sewing and worked in the potato and harvest fields, but it was unlikely to cover all her needs. 'Please don't think I'm intruding or anything, but is all well in the cottage? Please don't hesitate to ask for repairs or anything else to Little Dell. I am responsible for your comfort. Since I turned up on my father's doorstep two years ago I've been fully occupied with Simon, and then Pearl and her brothers, and I'm sorry to say I don't really know how Tremore's tenants are faring. Is there anything I can do for you?'

Faye's worries that Susan might be offended weren't realized. She replied, 'Your father called on me just after I got news of my husband's death and he checked the roof and everything himself. He arranged for a new fireplace in the front room and a slab in the kitchen. He was very kind. Of course, everyone worries about their pipes bursting in this weather.'

Faye could imagine her patriotic father rushing to give Susan support. She had a mixture of sad memories of Ben Harvey. His autocratic, bitter ways had made him unpopular, and for years he had rejected her, but she took comfort in that he had wanted to make amends and had died a hero's death while on secret service in France. They turned off into Back Lane where snow obscured the ditches and had been blown into small drifts in field gateways, fields that belonged to Faye. Tremore House would be reached first, and Susan and Maureen had another half mile to go on alone. Faye was worried. Little Dell was isolated, situated off a short, rough track with only another deserted Tremore property tucked up on a wooded slope above it. How would Susan get help if she or Maureen were hurt or ill or needed help in the dead of night?

'Do light all your fires when you get home and keep them burning. I can arrange for some logs to be sent over.' Extra coal was out of the question. Rationing still had a tight grip on the country, and would remain so for a few years yet, it seemed. The Labour government, elected in the previous year, had told the country to expect things to get worse before they got better.

'I get firewood scavenging in the woods, but I'd welcome some proper logs. Thank you, um ... Miss Harvey,' Susan mumbled at the end. She felt uncomfortable referring to Faye as Miss, Faye being a mother. She admired Faye's courage for admitting she wasn't married, but it was quite a scandal.

There was always speculation about Simon's Harvey father. A top-ranking officer, a businessman, a showbiz star perhaps. Knowing that Faye had come over by herself from America to a boarding school in South London to train for the ballet, an unrealized dream, and then evacuated to Scotland, where she had eventually worked as a secretary on a highland estate, the favourite assumption was a Scottish laird. The gossips of Hennaford didn't know they had hit on the truth.

'It's all right to call me Faye, if you'd like.' She hoped Susan would agree: she was warming to her and it would be good to make a friend. It would be a pity if, after the war had seen off so many outdated structures when people of all walks of life had pulled together, their backgrounds got in the way.

Susan took a moment to answer. 'And I'm Susan.' Faye got the feeling she had something on her mind.

They reached Tremore House. The twins and Maureen were nowhere in sight. Susan gazed up and down the lane then along the drive up to the grand house. 'Maureen, where are you? Come along now, sweetheart! We mustn't dawdle in this weather.'

'It's a shame that you really ought to be going on, Susan,' Faye said. 'Otherwise you and Maureen could have come inside for a hot drink.'

'That would have been nice. You're very kind.' Susan looked down shyly at the white-blanketed ground. 'Um, Faye...'

'Yes?' Faye replied keenly. 'Is there something I can do for you?'

'Well, I wondering, I mean, I've heard that Agnes is retiring at the end of the month and that you don't intend to replace her with a live-in housekeeper. Will you be doing the housework yourself from then on, or are you thinking of getting a daily help, or something? If you're going to advertise a job and give interviews, would you consider me?'

'It's the very thing my Uncle Tristan and I have discussed,' Faye was delighted that Susan found her approachable. 'Agnes's room will be needed for my little boy, you see. He's currently in the guestroom, which we would like to be returned as such. Of course I'll consider you, Susan. As soon as the snow has thawed, why don't you come to the house and we'll talk it through?'

Susan had a pale face, which was marked at the moment with a red nose and cheeks from the cold. Her hopeful smile made her look as young as a schoolgirl. 'I'll do that! Thanks a lot.'

Pearl was still in between them and she suddenly shrieked and howled as a series of snowballs hit her on the face, legs and back and front. 'Stop it!' she screamed lustily at the perpetrators, her brothers and Maureen. She was trying not to cry, but she wailed, 'I want Uncle Tris!'

'Boys!' Faye cried. 'That's enough. Don't you dare throw any more.'

With bloodcurdling shouts, the twins, balaclava helmets off, mufflers in disarray, sodden from head to foot from rolling in the snow, leapt out from behind snow-laden bushes in front of the two women and Pearl. Maureen, similarly dishevelled, appeared from somewhere behind them.

'Come here, Maureen!' Susan was horrified. 'Say sorry to Pearl at once.'

'We didn't hurt her. She shouldn't be such a baby,' Maureen said, standing her ground and poking her tongue out at Pearl.

'Maureen! Oh, Faye,' Susan stuttered. 'I'm so sorry.' She was worried Faye would change her mind about giving her an interview for the job.

'It's just playful fun,' Faye replied. She wagged a finger at the obstinate Maureen, a clear leader of mischief, a willful button of a child. Her multi-coloured pixie bonnet was hanging by its ties and her flaxen hair was in wet straggles. 'But you've upset Pearl, young lady, and you really should say sorry to her.'

Faye was taken aback by the cheeky grin she received in return. 'All right then,' Maureen cheeped. 'Sorry Pearl.' She tore off a wet knitted glove and hooked her little finger. 'Friends?'

Pulling her hands free from the women, Pearl went forward, and using her teeth she peeled off a glove and hooked her little finger through Maureen's. 'Friends. But you'll have to give me some sweets next time you get some.'

'Pearl!' Faye chided, then observed wryly. 'A pair of scallywags.'

Susan heaved a sigh of relief. 'I'm glad you think so.' Fat flakes of snow were thudding against her face. 'We really must hurry along, Maureen. Quickly now. I'll come to the house as soon as I can, Faye. Hopefully tomorrow, if the snow doesn't last.'

'I'll look forward to seeing you, Susan. Take care and stay warm.'

Susan was forced to wait because Maureen was whispering something into Pearl's ear. Pearl was looking devastated. Was Maureen alarming her? Even frightening her? She owned some of her father's forceful ways. 'Maureen!'

Faye too was concerned about Maureen's intentions. 'What's going on? Girls?'

Maureen stared at her mother then at Faye. 'I want her to tell you something.'

Pearl poked her in the back and looked mournful. 'I don't want to say. They'll think I'm a scaredy-cat.'

'If you're scared of something, Pearl, it's only sensible to tell a grownup,' Faye said, reaching her quickly. 'Uncle Tris and I are here to protect you. We won't think you're silly or anything.'

'Yeah, what is it?' Len and Bob said together, adopting protective stances.

Tears gathered on Pearl's eyelashes and she hung her head. She was now clinging to Faye.

Facing Maureen, Susan put her hands on her shoulders. 'This could be serious. You must tell us.'

'It was a stranger, a man,' Maureen said, jittery herself now. 'He turned up at school during milk break and asked Pearl a lot of questions, like he knew her. Pearl's scared that he's come to take her and the twins away.'

Two

The next morning, Susan dropped Maureen off at school, then made her way to Tremore House. The snow had eased off the moment she'd got Maureen safely home the day before, and after a bitterly cold night the thaw was setting in and the lanes were running with icy water. She trusted Faye's word about providing extra logs, and had kept a fire in all night in her little front room, her bedroom, and in the kitchen slab. Maureen often shared her bed, and they had cuddled up together with a sense of security, and Susan had been grateful not to spend another February night shivering through the small hours, worrying that Maureen might catch a cold. Her lovable, feisty little daughter was all Susan wanted or would ever want, and she loved to fuss over her, which she didn't really need to do often, for Maureen was confident and robust, with a cast-iron constitution. When Lance had been killed in action on French soil, prior to the Dunkirk withdrawal, it had relieved Susan of the worry that her beloved baby might grow up witnessing his heartless tendencies. Lance had not been a brute with his fists, but bit by bit he had been taking total control of her.

The sky was murky and heavily shadowed with rain clouds, the wind keen and harshly cold, but Susan was in a light mood. She might be poor, constantly having to juggle money to pay the rent and buy food, but she was at ease with her lot as a widow. Lance had promised her the heavens, and she, a down-trodden teenaged girl, had believed him and thought she'd loved him. He had been burly and fearless and had impressed her with his smart-talking ways. No one knew where he had come from and he wouldn't say, and to her impressionable mind he had seemed beguilingly mysterious. His past was a secret Susan had no desire to delve into. He had been a lodger of her mean-hearted mother. Like herself, he'd hated her mother's grasping ways – the lazy, greedy woman who'd worn the same dress, wrap-around apron and hair net every day, and had packed paying guests into every available space in her run-down, unsanitary three-bedroom house in Truro. Susan had shared a mouldy mattress in the box room with her mother, with little room for her clothes and scant personal possessions. She had been forced to hand over all her wages as a shop assistant at a greengrocer's. Lance had kept one of his promises, to get her away from home. The day of their on-the-cheap wedding, he'd told her to pack their things and they had caught the next bus from Truro to Hennaford. Her expectations of a happy life in the tiny, isolated Little Dell, carrying the baby she had conceived on her wedding night, had been quickly and ruthlessly shattered by Lance's inexplicable, festering silences. When he did speak, it was to tell her what she must do and to demean her at every opportunity. She no longer held hopes or dreams, except to see Maureen grow up to be happy and fulfilled, and to definitely not marry young but to get herself a well-paid job and to make something of herself. To be independent as she now was. She supported them as a seamstress, and any other job she could find. Life ticked on, and with the kindness shown by the villagers she and Maureen rarely went without the basic necessities.

She was confident she would secure the job of daily help at Tremore House. She had met up with Tristan Harvey, after he had escorted the Smith children to school, and he had intimated as much. If all went well and she gained a permanent position, things would be really settled. 'I appreciate your plucky little girl in bringing to light about the stranger who frightened Pearl yesterday, Mrs Dowling,' he'd said. A typically tall, black-haired Harvey, he'd smiled down on her. 'The headmaster and Miss Brice saw no one loitering about themselves but they're keeping all the children under close observation today, just in case. I'm about to ask round the village if anyone saw this individual. A thin chap in a long heavy coat and a dark hat, with a strange light in his eyes, the girls said. It all sounds ominous. I'm considering informing the police.'

'I hope it proves to be nothing to worry about, Mr Harvey,' Susan had said. 'Who do you think it might be?' Susan never spent more than a few moments talking to men, specially unattached ones like Tristan Harvey, whose wife had died in a road accident during the war. Lance's manic jealousy had seen to that, but she felt comfortable with this gentleman. Mr Harvey had been an officer in the Great War, and his late brother the local squire, but he never put on airs and was open and friendly. He had a kind face, adorned with a neat moustache sprinkled with silver, as was his thick hair. His was a face she felt able to look into. She had never dared look directly at a man when Lance had been alive. As a committee member of the Royal British Legion, and an official of other ex-servicemen's charities, Tristan Harvey had arranged for her to receive all she'd been entitled to as a war widow, and she owed him her gratitude.

'Well, if it's above board, perhaps he's a

relative of the children,' Tristan replied, adding vehemently, 'He will not be able to take them away. I'm their legal guardian.'

Susan had thought it typical of his goodness to be so concerned over three orphans while having a grown-up family of his own.

She rounded a deeply curving bend in the road, which then went back on itself for a few yards. Here in the hedgerow was a sharp dip, made by children scrambling over to play in the field on the other side, and it gave a view of the lane she had just left behind. She took fright. She saw a man matching the description of the stranger who had scared Pearl at the school. He wore a dark trilby hat and was striding along with his head down. Susan froze to the spot. Then he looked up and saw her. 'Oh, hello there,' he called. 'I was wondering if you...?'

Susan gasped. She wasn't about to find out what he wanted and forcing her feet to move she hurried off. She'd go straight to Faye and tell her she had seen the stranger.

'Please wait!' he called again.

He carried on talking, but Susan didn't stop to listen. She trusted few people, and this man was an apparent threat to the children taken in by the Harveys. She ran all the way to Tremore House, spattering her legs with mud. Her headscarf fell round her neck and her wavy ash-blonde hair was quickly tangled by the fresh wind. She was out of breath when she reached the house. She hammered on the door. 'Faye, hurry!' she shouted through the letterbox. 'Open the door!'

She heard running. Faye yanked the door open. Her son came toddling in her wake. Faye went back to Simon and snatched him up in her arms. 'Susan! What on earth's the matter? Come in.'

'No! It's him, the stranger, the man who scared Pearl. He's coming this way!' Susan thrust out her arm to indicate the way to the village. 'If you come with me now we can face him together.' Her instinct to protect the young superseded her fright.

Agnes, the lank, white-haired housekeeper, had rushed from the kitchen in her apron to find out what the commotion was about. 'Take Simon.' Faye pushed the startled boy into her arms. She pulled on a raincoat and took two old umbrellas out of the hallstand. 'Right, let's find out who this man is.'

'If he's turned round we should still catch him before he reaches the village,' Susan said, panting, running along slightly after Faye, who had the advantage of not being puffed out. Like Faye, she was wielding an umbrella like a weapon.

'He'd better have a good explanation,' Faye shouted over her shoulder. 'He had no right to upset Pearl like that.'

It took only a couple of minutes for them

to face the stranger in a straight stretch of the lane. He stopped in the middle, bearing a look of shock as they ran at him. Faye slowed down for Susan and they approached him together, close enough to see him blinking. 'Ladies?' he said, lifting a crooked arm as if he might need to ward them off.

'Who are you?' Faye demanded. 'Why were you at the school yesterday?'

'What? Well, I...' He went still and then something strange happened, his eyes appeared to be vacant.

'Speak!' Faye shouted.

The man was about thirty, of a good height but woefully skinny; his overcoat was large enough for two of him. He seemed to have slipped into a trance. Faye glanced at Susan and whispered, 'What do you think his game is?'

'Be careful,' Susan hissed.

Faye went forward a few more steps. The man was gazing right at her yet he was not seeing her. She prodded her umbrella in his chest. He made no reaction. Nothing. 'He doesn't seem to be with us, Susan.'

Susan came to her side. She fluttered her hand in front of the stranger's eyes, which were pale brown and large within a haggard sallow face and heavily under-shadowed. He didn't blink. 'He doesn't know we're here. He's switched off for some reason. Do you think he's ill?'

Faye lowered her umbrella. 'You watch him. I'll see if he's got any identification on him.'

With Susan ready to make a swipe at the man, Faye moved to his side and gingerly reached inside his coat pocket. 'Nothing in here. The coat is good quality.' She rummaged in the other pocket. 'Cigarettes, lighter. House keys. Ah, train tickets. Let me see ... he's travelled down from Surrey and got off at Truro station. Pearl and the twins don't know anyone from Surrey. This is all very odd.' She stepped in front of the stranger and gazed into his eyes. They were glazed over. She was still cautious, but now that he seemed helpless and definitely wasn't a tramp or a thug, she was beginning to feel sorry for him. Feeling more like an intruder, she gently put her hand into the inside breast pocket of his coat and pulled out his wallet. 'This should tell us who he is.'

Taking her sight off him, Susan read his identification card. 'Mark Richard Fuller. His address is there, and a telephone number.'

There was a photo of a young woman, much creased and faded, as if well thumbed and looked at often. Even in its poor state she came across as striking and lovely, with a formidable presence. Faye turned the photo over. There was a name on it, Justine. Next she found a note, which she read aloud. 'It says his next of kin is his wife, Justine. We could give her a ring, find out exactly what he's up to. He doesn't look the sort to get up to funny business, but we can't be too careful. Well, we just can't stay here like this. He doesn't look strong enough to give us any trouble. We'd better take him to the house. Perhaps I should call for the doctor. I'll phone the shop. Uncle Tris is bound to have gone there first to ask if anyone's seen a stranger, but if he's already left, I'll get the Eathornes to go after him and send him home. Is this all right with you, Susan?'

'Yes, fine. Poor man.' She was peering at him closely. 'He did wrong yesterday, but, well, there's something about him ... he's certainly not capable of hurting anyone.'

'Yes,' Faye agreed. She snapped her fingers in front of Mark Fuller's face. Nothing. 'We'd better take his arms.'

'Ohh.' Mark Fuller moaned softly, but there was a pitiful edge to it. Susan and Faye quickly dropped the hands reaching out to him. They watched as he shook his head and slowly came out of his stupor. He rubbed his eyes then looked to left and right. 'Where...?' Putting his head straight he saw the two women and looked utterly bewildered.

Faye and Susan kept their umbrellas low at their sides, but stayed vigilant in case he proved trouble. 'Hello. Mr Fuller, isn't it?' Faye kept her voice soft.

'What? Um ... yes.' He rubbed his temple and pulled a hand down over his face. 'Oh ... I'm in the little village, aren't I?'

'Yes,' Susan said. 'Do you know exactly where you are?'

'Cornwall. Hennaford. I came down here to ... to find some children.' His expression changed to one of enlightenment, the laxness in his body went and he straightened his back, an obvious military stance, and he was in control of himself. 'The Smith children, originally of North London, and billeted here during the war at the house of a Mr Benjamin Harvey. Their father served under me in the Far East. I'm very sorry, I've made an awful hash of things. I can see I've caused you both great alarm. I'm former Lieutenant Mark Fuller, of the Royal Artillery. I was with Corporal Vincent Smith when he died. I promised him if I got back in one piece I'd look up his children, see if they were all right. I'm staying at the pub. Mrs Brokenshaw told me this morning that Mr Harvey was killed on active service, and the way to Tremore House. I was on my way there. I should have asked yesterday.' He looked embarrassed, 'Are either of you two ladies Miss Faye Harvey?'

'I am. And this is my friend, Mrs Susan Dowling,' Faye said. She was relieved Mark Fuller offered no danger to the children, but she grew serious. 'Yes, Mr Fuller, you did

28

make a hash of things. You shouldn't have gone to the school and spoken to Pearl without first consulting me or my uncle. You scared little Pearl. She had no idea who you were.'

'And you're angry with me, and rightly so,' Mark's face fell, making him look years older and washed out. 'I can only say how sorry I am. I get a bit vague at times, although that's no excuse for what I did yesterday.'

'You seemed ... unwell just now,' Susan said carefully.

'Was I? Oh yes. My apologies again. Um, injuries. Prisoner of war...' He looked away.

Faye felt sorry for confronting him so strongly. 'There's no need to apologize for that, Mr Fuller. You look all done in. Would you care to come to the house and recover with a cup of coffee with us?'

'Well, if it's no imposition.' He smiled briefly at the two women and it lifted away some of the weariness from his face. They walked off, Faye and Susan either side of him, protectively, feeling they might need to nudge him along if he went off into a trance again, both attempting to hide the umbrellas behind their backs. As if it had suddenly dawned on him, he said, surprised, 'You're not English, Miss Harvey. I was told the Harveys had been the landowners in Hennaford for generations.'

Faye gave him a brief account of her

history, leaving out Simon. 'The family history is varied and confusing. My Aunt Emilia lives on the other side of the village, and my Uncle Tristan used to live at Newquay, but he's handed his house over to his step-daughter. He came to live with my father during the war, and after I came down from Scotland we took in the Smith children together. I'm sure the children will be interested to learn all they can from you about their father, Mr Fuller. You will be careful what you say?'

'Oh yes, of course.' His voice was steeped in sorrow, in anguish, and the women got the impression that despite his lapses in memory, the details of Vincent Smith's death were harrowingly engraved on his mind.

'I'm sorry, that was thoughtless of me,' Faye said. 'Actually, it's very good of you to come down all this way to see the children.'

'It's good of you to give me the opportunity to see them. I'd have come a lot earlier, but I've not been many weeks out of convalescence. I came across a photograph Vincent Smith placed into my keeping, and then it took some time to recall who the children were. It's how I recognized the little girl.'

'We noticed you live in Surrey, Mr Fuller,' Susan said. 'You have a family there?'

'Only my wife, Justine. Actually, we've grown apart, have just agreed to separate.'

Susan looked for more sorrow on his gaunt face. It was evident, but there was also something that might indicate resignation. Coming to terms with the irreversible changes the war had made to their lives was the only way some people coped. He was trembling and had grown grey and was sweating. She was pleased they were closing in on the house. The journey down from Surrey had obviously been too much for him. 'The war has made so many of us victims.' It was the usual sort of thing to say, although she didn't include herself in the comment.

Minutes later they were in the drawing room, where a log fire crackled cheerily under a magnificent fireplace. Mark was revived by coffee and Agnes's fruitless cake. He drank and ate absently, and Faye and Susan got used to his vagueness, which descended upon him at pitiless intervals. During those times the women came to an arrangement that Susan would come in each weekday, between school hours, and do the cleaning and laundry and some baking, at three pounds, five shillings a week. Faye was hoping Susan would become a friend as well as an employee. Susan, although pleased Faye had introduced her to Mark Fuller as an equal, had no thoughts of relinquishing her habitual aloofness. She was enjoying the surroundings, grander than any she had been in before was enough for her. The house, a former steward's cottage had been greatly extended, including a balcony, and changed to modern lines by Ben Harvey nearly thirty years ago. The decor was light, giving the illusion of even more space. She was making a mental list of the basic things she would now be able to afford for Maureen, and how she could make their little home more comfortable.

'Poor gentleman,' Agnes observed when she came to collect the coffee tray, as Mark once more became unaware of his environment. 'He'd be something of a fine-looking man, I believe, if he got a bit of flesh back on him, don't you think?'

Faye gazed at him. 'Perhaps. I suppose so.' She agreed with Susan's observation about him in the lane that there was 'something about him'.

She glanced at Susan, who merely shrugged. She wasn't interested in a man's looks. Lance had been handsome in a roguish way, one of the reasons her youthful mind had been captivated by him, which in turn had made her truly a captive.

Agnes tutted. 'You young women have no sense of romance. A mysterious stranger turns up to do a good deed and you both sit there like a couple of maiden aunts.'

The moment she left the room, Faye burst out laughing. 'She should talk! She's been a maiden aunt all her life. And it's not as if he's actually single.' She studied the silent Mark, wondering if his mind was stuck somewhere, hoping it was nowhere grim. He didn't seem distressed, but she wondered if he got horrific flashbacks of battle or his incarceration. If so, it would be the horrors and inhumanity of a Japanese labour camp – Vincent Smith had died during the building of the Burma-Thailand railway, known as the Railway of Death.

Tristan Harvey came bowling into the room. 'I've found out all about that chap! Oh, is this him? He's off and away, I see. Ruby Brokenshaw, in the Ploughshare, told about his mental lapses. She's quite concerned about him, and had tried to get him to stay put and ask us to visit him there instead. He'd said, it wouldn't be polite. So the mystery's cleared up. The children will be delighted, I should think.' He turned to Susan and gave her a gracious smile. 'Good morning again, Mrs Dowling. Have you ladies come to an agreement about the domestic arrangements?'

'We have, Uncle Tris,' Faye said. 'Susan will start tomorrow, working with Agnes, who will show her the ropes.'

'Excellent. Well, that's a relief all round. Now, when Mr Fuller comes to, I shall be glad to make his acquaintance.'

Susan got to her feet. She had declined to remove her coat on entering the house, and after pushing her headscarf into a pocket she had tidied her hair with her hands. She had no idea how appealing she looked with tresses of lush ash-blonde hair falling on her shoulders. 'If you'll excuse me, I'd like to run along. I have things to do at home.'

'Feel free to come and go as you please, Susan.' Faye offered to see her to the door, but Susan insisted on seeing herself out.

'She's very nice. We're lucky to be getting her,' Tristan said, flitting to a window where he'd get a view of her in the lane through the garden gate. 'She's a bit of a dazzler too.'

'Uncle Tris!' Faye was astonished. Hopeful women pursued him, but this was the first time he'd shown interest in someone. Her uncle's leanness, while so many middle-aged men tended to become portly, his thick hair and gentle looks, made him engaging and attractive.

'Oh, I know I'm old enough to be her father but, well,' he straightened his tie light-heartedly, 'Susan Dowling's worth more than a second look, even though she's totally unconscious of it.'

'I don't think she'd appreciate any sort of male attention,' Faye said doubtfully. Not even from a man as courteous and as genuinely pleasant as her uncle was. 'She's seen off more than one potential suitor.'

'And of course, she'd never consider an old chap like me, anyway,' Tristan went on

34

jovially, dismissing the idea.

Leaning forward in front of Mark's chair, he watched the younger man surfacing from his other world, whatever it might be. 'Now let's see if this chap is well enough to return to his lodgings.'

A moment later, Mark keeled over and Tristan caught him before he hit the floor. 'Faye! We'd better call the doctor.'

Three

Mark found himself in a strange place, staring at two women who were strangers, and both carrying infants. Where the hell was he? And who were these flame-haired women? He closed his eyes. Opened them again. Sometimes when he did this the apparition would disappear. But the strangers were still there. These women were real and they were staring back at him. He got a horrible dragging feeling in his guts, the same sickly sensation as when he'd discovered before that he was inadvertently trespassing. Now, for goodness sake, where had he wandered off to? He looked down at himself hastily; thank God, he was dressed but his clothes were crumpled, as if he'd slept in them.

'Hello, you must be Mr Fuller,' one of the women said in a pleasing Cornish accent. She appeared to be the elder of two statuesque sisters.

'I'm sorry, you have the advantage of me,' he said, desperate to know who these women were. He couldn't have made an enormous mistake, for they didn't appear to be angry with him, but he didn't relax. It didn't make things easier. Or less frightening.

'That's because we haven't met before,' the woman said, and she and her sister were smiling at him. Kind, understanding smiles. The kind of smiles Mark had seen before and he didn't like them. They were the smiles reserved for the ill and infirm and they reinforced the reality of his suffering, his lack of health and his reduced situation. 'I'm Emilia Bosweld, and this is my daughter, Lottie Harmon. We've just arrived to visit my niece, Faye, and have just let ourselves in. Is she about?'

'What? Your daughter? Oh, but I thought ... Faye?' Sweat trickled clammily down the back of his neck as he tried to recall the name Faye. Then it came to him. Thankfully his memory usually came back quickly. He looked around. He was at the bottom of the stairs in Tremore House. 'Faye. Miss Harvey. Oh, yes. But what am I doing here? I remember her and Mrs Dowling bringing me here. Why didn't I return to the pub? What day is it?'

'Mr Fuller.' Faye was there. His thin, bewildered face broke into deep relief. 'I'm sorry you've been worried. Come through to the drawing room and I'll explain. And you'll be able to meet my uncle.'

Mark followed Faye, with the two mothers following after him into the drawing room, the last place he remembered being in the day before.

A lanky, casually-dressed man leapt up from a leather armchair beside the roaring fire and came forward, full of welcoming smiles. 'Take my seat, Mr Fuller,' Tristan said quietly, and Mark was glad the other man had nothing hearty about him, and didn't attempt to look at him often, or assume to coddle him. Here was a man who truly understood him, and he was right in his assumption that Tristan Harvey had held rank in the First World War and had suffered during it.

Mark was grateful the Harveys kept thundering fires, for after enduring the steaming heat of the jungle, the cold weather bit into his bones. But he wished there wasn't so many people in the room. The infants were now toddling about on the brick-red Tabriz rug. One of them used Tristan Harvey's knees to pull itself up on its feet. Mark would hate it if the child did this to him. He didn't like being touched. For the three and a half years, he had sweated and stank in captivity; his skin had been cropped with sores and scabs. It was still tender in places and prone to outbreaks of stinging rashes. Sometimes he was convinced he must smell like a corpse, and he had seen so many dead and decaying men, hundreds of them, and the stench of death all too often returned to him. He didn't like people near him, even Justine during her thrice-weekly visits to the convalescent home. After his discharge he had insisted on sleeping in another room. She had been very good about it – it was a good thing she was able to move on with her life. Mostly he just wanted to be alone. Right now, he needed to know why he was still in this house.

'You keeled off the chair you're sitting in,' Tristan began. 'It gave us a bit of a fright, but the doctor said you were exhausted and dehydrated, nothing more serious. You slept right through, except for a couple of times when you woke and sipped some water and ate a little bread and soup.'

Mark didn't remember the sequence of events. 'It was very kind of you and Miss Harvey to take so much trouble, and to call a doctor. You have my gratitude.' Without the hospitality of these people, and the kindness of Susan Dowling yesterday, he might have ended up in any sort of sticky situation. He suddenly broke into a cold sweat, and wished again that the well-spaced room wasn't teaming with people. He was feeling hemmed in and jittery. He coped by trying to focus on what the room was like. It had lots of mirrors and reflective ornaments, and the latest in radio and gramophone. Justine would like it here. Their home – her home now – had been newly built before the war and she had taken great pride in providing it with 'Plan' furniture, bright ceramics, and anaglypta wallpaper in autumnal shades. Mark cared nothing for interiors; he was an outdoor man and he glanced out of the tall windows, where the long, broad expanse of garden was turned over and an elderly gardener was planting early potatoes. Food shortages, while the country lumbered back on its feet, necessitated little flower growing.

As if coming out of one of his dazes, he noticed there were *three* infants on the rug, playing with wooden alphabet bricks and tin cars. One had a fluff of fair hair – Lottie Harmon's child – the other two had black mops. 'Oh...' He raked a hand through his hair, thoroughly puzzled. Was he going mad?

'I hope you're not being overwhelmed, Mr Fuller,' Emilia Harvey said. 'The boy nearest you is my son, Paul. He's just turned two years old. The fair-haired boy is my grandson, Carl, who's a year younger. And the little boy now running about is called Simon. He's Faye's. Lottie and I didn't expect to find you still here or we would have come another time.'

Mark glanced warily at Simon, eldest of the children and adventurous. He hoped he and the others didn't get noisy; he couldn't stand a lot of noise. 'Another evacuee?' he looked at Faye with admiration.

'No.' Faye coloured slightly, as she always

40

did when explaining Simon's parentage, while hiding, for her confused guest's sake, the defiance she also kept about it. 'He's my son.' Mark nodded, but his admiration didn't seem replaced by anything else, such as shock or prudery, as Faye was often confronted with. It bothered her for Simon's sake, and she would have been disappointed to get such a reaction from Mark.

Mark thought nothing of it. Justine was a hospital almoner, she had mentioned how she had helped many an unfortunate girl left to bear the brunt of bearing a baby by a serviceman boyfriend who had not made it back, as he presumed, by the impression he had of Faye, was the case. She was certainly no floozie. And what the hell did it matter, a child out of wedlock, after all he and the world had seen? 'When might I get to meet the Smith children?'

'They're at school now, of course,' Faye said. 'You'll be able to see them this afternoon.'

'I couldn't possibly impose on you for such a long time,' Mark said.

'Of course you may. You've done a jolly decent thing undertaking such a long journey while not really being up to it to tell the children about their father,' Tristan said. He understood Mark's intention. There was a special bond among men who went into battle together and suffered together, and

41

whether an officer or an ordinary squaddie, a man burned inside to complete the last wishes of a dying comrade. 'And, well, it's not as easy as that, old chap.'

'What do you mean?' Mark was alarmed.

There was a tap on the door and Agnes and Susan came in with coffee and biscuits. Mark was agitated to have to wait for his answer. Faye noticed and felt for him and she aimed him an encouraging smile. Emilia and Lottie saw his discomfort too and they glanced at each other.

Lottie said thoughtfully, 'I think I'll take the children upstairs to play. Hot drinks, and all that. If you stay on in Hennaford, Mr Fuller, perhaps you'd like to come across to Ford Farm. Take a peaceful look about the fields and meadows with my brother, Tom.'

'Yes, perhaps. Thank you, Mrs Harmon.' Mark wasn't sure how long he was staying in Hennaford, how long it would take for him to be well enough to travel up to Surrey – he had to go back sometime to the suburban semi to make amicable arrangements with Justine about the divorce. The prospect of strolling around fields and meadows wasn't daunting, but he didn't want to meet another stranger.

'I'll help you take the children up,' Emilia said. 'Then I'll come back down for coffee.'

As the room was emptied of little people, Mark was able to breathe easier. Faye smiled at him again and he managed to return in kind.

Tristan had jumped up when Agnes and Susan had arrived. He took the coffee tray from Susan and placed it down on the occasional table beside Faye, who would pour. 'How are you finding things, Mrs Dowling? We're not too off-putting for you, I hope.'

'I'm finding my way around, Mr Harvey,' she replied. It was kind of him to ask. She had just seen to his room. He was neat and tidy. It had only taken a minute to make his bed, and his pyjamas had already been folded and placed under the pillows. No shoes or clothes were left lying about. The things on his dressing table were in precise places, the mark of a military man. The many photographs of his late wife and children pointed to him being exactly what he was known for, a caring family man.

'So you're enjoying your first day?' Tristan smiled down on her.

'Yes, I am.' Susan dropped her eyes.

Tristan realized he was monopolizing her and she was embarrassed. He returned to his seat with vague feelings of disappointment. He rebuked himself, but for what? He had done nothing wrong. He had merely been welcoming. He would have done the same to any young woman starting work here. So why did he feel he'd just behaved like a foolish middle-aged man? Why was he embarrassed? He would be careful from now on in regard to Susan Dowling.

Mark was recalling that Faye had mention Susan Dowling was a friend, but she had just become a new member of her staff, and there was a formality about her. She didn't look at anyone for longer than a moment, not even Faye.

Susan and Agnes left for their own elevenses, and Emilia returned and passed round the mock butterscotch biscuits, and Faye poured the coffee. Mark took a biscuit, hoping the plate would come around again. From the days of starvation, when food and survival had been uppermost on his and fellow prisoners' minds, there remained a burning desire to eat and eat, even if he felt sick and didn't have an appetite. Wasting food was a crime to him, and he'd scrape up every last crumb and mop up every spot of liquid. Justine had understood his scavenging, ravenous ways, and at home she'd fed him with as much as the rationing allowed. Justine ... there was something he was supposed to do. 'Oh, damn!' he suddenly blurted out. Then, horrified, 'Oh, forgive me. I forget I'm not in the company of servicemen.'

'Don't worry,' Faye said. 'What is it?'

'Would you mind if I phoned my wife? We're still close, you see. Justine will be fearful by now. She tried to talk me out of coming down here and I promised I'd contact her every day. I have a large notice in my overnight bag to remind me.' It had been his idea; he'd argued he was unlikely to forget because he had to freshen up twice a day, but his hazy mind had seen off the plan, just as Justine had feared it might. Hell! He must need a shave. He must look a mess. It was an effort not to shed tears of humiliation.

'There's no need,' Faye said. 'Uncle Tris and I discussed what was best to do about you and we took the liberty of phoning Mrs Fuller. She was very grateful. We reassured her that you'd arrived safely at your destination, that you'd found out where the children lived, and that we'd be taking care of you for as long as it's needed.'

'You're taking care of me? Here?' Mark looked from her to Tristan.

'That's what I was about to mention. I brought your things here yesterday. Ruby Brokenshaw, the landlady of the pub, wishes you well, but she's a little bit concerned,' he said diplomatically. 'About your tendency to wander off. We thought it better all round if you stayed here. You'll want to spend time with the children, after all. Mrs Fuller is going to send down more of your things.'

'I see. You're very kind, but I—' Mark broke off. How could he tell these kind people he was horrified at the thought of staying where there were so many children?

Inevitably, there was a lot of noise and bustle in the pub but he could shut himself away in his room. Mrs Brokenshaw had agreed to serve his meals there.

Faye read his mind. 'We'll ensure you have plenty of space and peace and quiet. The children are very excited to meet you, but we promise we won't let them overtax you.'

'It will all be for the best,' Tristan said. He was pleased Mark had to stay – he had no other choice – and he thought he might be able to help Mark come to terms with some of his suffering. Tristan had been hit by a shell and nearly killed on Flanders soil, and although left with a stiff left ankle, he had not been scarred mentally like Mark. If he could do anything at all to help the young man's recovery, he'd do it. Mark had come here to perform a worthy task. It was something to keep him going. And then what? Tristan knew men like Mark were prone to feel a nuisance; some were overpowered by depression and felt a handgun to the temple to be an honourable way out. He wasn't about to let that happen to Mark.

'We want you to stay, Mr Fuller,' Faye said earnestly.

'Lottie and I, and the rest of the family, will be careful when we call again, Mr Fuller,' Emilia said gently. She was reading Tristan's mind. She had seen his torment when married to his brother, Alec, the squire of

46

Hennaford. It had taken Tristan a very long time to recover. 'Lottie and I will be leaving now.'

'Well, all I can say is thank you. You must have my ration cards, of course, Faye,' Mark said. 'But please don't leave on my account, Mrs Bosweld. Could I be excused instead? I'd like to take a bath if that's possible, and then take a rest.'

Faye was delighted to have him agree. She had never felt she'd really done enough for the war effort. To care for this badly-treated former officer was the least she could do. And Mark Fuller was appealing and honourable. She wanted to learn more about him. 'I'll show you up. And where the bathroom is.'

'That would be a good idea.' At last Mark smiled. 'I probably wouldn't find my way.'

He bid Emilia 'goodbye' and followed Faye out into the hall. Susan was busy with a feather duster, softly singing *As Time Goes By* to herself. Faye was warmed through that she had made two people feel happy and settled.

'Everything all right, Susan?' she said.

'Everything's fine, thanks.' Susan paused.

'I'm showing Mr Fuller up to his room. He's going to take a bath and a rest.'

Susan looked at Mark and smiled into his weary face. Poor man, he looked as if all he wanted was to sleep for a week. 'Would you like a hot water bottle, Mr Fuller?'

Faye could hardly believe her reaction to the kindly gesture: to feel intensely jealous that it wasn't she who had made this offer and she had to force a smile of her own not to reveal it. Mark wasn't exclusively her invalid or anything else to her, and even if he was, where did she get this ridiculous attitude? 'A good idea, Susan. Agnes will show you where they're kept.'

'Thank you, Mrs ... um, Dowling,' Mark had difficulty drawing up her name, while politely stifling a yawn.

Faye glanced at him to see if he was gazing at Susan in a similar doe-eyed manner to how her uncle had done in the drawing room. This was getting silly. Mark was edging towards the stairs. Faye told herself that she would concentrate only on his needs for shelter and food, and what his temporary presence would mean to Bob, Len and Pearl.

Nonetheless, she took possession of him and walked closely up beside him.

Four

Tom and Jill Harvey burst into the back kitchen of Ford Farm together, making the stable door creak and slam behind them. He grabbed her round the waist and hauled her off her feet. She shrieked and beat on his chest in play. They were always larking about, kissing and embracing, touching and loving. Every day was the same since they had fallen in love and married, shortly after Jill had come to work here as a member of the Women's Land Army. Their insatiable love affair was rivalled only by the intense romantic passion shared between his mother Emilia and his stepfather.

Tom put Jill down and brought her body in close to his, then closer still, swaying provocatively against her while nuzzling his cold face into her neck. 'After breakfast, I'm going to take you upstairs and make love to you until you tingle all over,' his rich voice dropped to huskier tones as he made the erotic promise.

'I should think so too.' Jill was always as sensually alive for him as he was for her, already tingling through every scrap of her slight form, wonderfully alive to the burning desire in his strong rangy body. She adored her good-natured husband, and his sometimes dignified ways and sense of fair play, and his velvety dark eyes and quick friendly smile. He was the only Harvey male not to have inherited raven-black hair but the rich red-brown of his mother's, and Jill loved to tease her fingers through it. She wrapped her arms possessively round his neck and kissed his mouth long and hard.

The farmhouse kitchen door was thrown open. 'Oh, for goodness sake, give it a rest you two!' Lottie cried, hands her hips. 'Come in and get your breakfast like ordinary people do and don't make so much noise about it. You'll start the dogs off again, and I'm in no mood for chaos this morning.'

Jill dropped her arms and made a puzzled face at Tom. Some of the pack of Jack Russells had slipped inside with them, but although eager for their breakfast of scraps, none was being a nuisance. She crept into the cosy warmth of the vast kitchen and sat down meekly, as was her mild, unassuming manner, on the form at the huge table. Emilia, presiding at the head, gave her a smile but kept it brief.

Lottie was in no mood for amusement. At the foot of the table was Emilia's husband, Perry Bosweld, the astonishingly handsome stepfather Lottie adored. He shrugged his shoulders, as bewildered as the others as to the cause of Lottie's present exasperation. The house usually bustled with contented speech and activity, but everyone, including Edwin Rowse, Emilia's father, Midge Roach the cowman, and Tilda Lawry, the house-keeper, kept a strained silence. Lottie was inclined to be prickly and vociferous, and sometimes awkward, but lately she had given way to outbreaks of prolonged irritation. It sliced through Tom's easygoing nature and he had endured enough. While Tilda served bowls of steaming porridge, he pointed his spoon across the table at his sister. 'What the hell is the matter with you now?'

'Tom, language,' Emilia warned. She had seen Tom's vexation building up for days and she was worried there would be a quarrel. Lottie could vent a hurricane when she got started. It would alarm Paul and Carl, who had been fed and were now glugging down bottles of warm milk in their high chairs. Lottie refused to talk about her reasons, even to Perry, whom she was usually eager to share things with, but it could only be be-cause she was missing her Texan husband Nate, whom she had met while Cornwall had been packed with American servicemen during the enormous build-up for the D-Day landings. It was a pity, for she had so much to look forward to. Nate had got his discharge, and because he had no family of his own, rather than Lottie emigrating as a GI bride he had sold his ranch and was soon to join her to settle down in Cornwall. They were planning buy a farm of their own.

Jill pulled Tom's hand down and took the spoon away. 'Shush, Tom.'

'No, darling, I won't shut up, and Mum, never mind about my language. She,' Tom pointed at Lottie with his forefinger, 'bawls people out for no good reason and I'm not prepared to put up with it any longer. Lottie, what is it? Tell us.'

'It's all right for you!' Lottie tossed back, showing her teeth like a snarling dog.

Whiskery Edwin Rowse, sitting stooped with his battered tweed cap on the remains of his donkey-grey hair, tapped her shoulder. 'Steady, maid.' He was a quiet plodder, un-ruffled and satisfied, and had a close, caring relationship with his grown-up grandchild-ren, but his usual common sense couldn't make out Lottie's problem.

'Oh, Granddad, no one understands!'

Perry, dark and of chivalrous charm, glanced at the little boys but they were suck-ing away on their bottles, oblivious to the tension. 'Tell us darling, what is it that we don't understand?'

Lottie gave him a glowering look, some-thing she had never done before, hating the despairing look he aimed up the table to her mother, but she was just as impatient with him. She was used to claiming a lot of Perry's attention, but he, as a leg amputee in the Great War, a former Army surgeon, spent much time nowadays supporting fellow sufferers from the more recent battles, and he'd been too busy to read her misery.

'Lottie, shall we go somewhere on our own?' Emilia offered in her most maternal voice. She was aching to know what was causing her daughter such distress that it had rendered her unjustifiably rude.

'What good would that do?' Lottie barked back.

'Can I do anything for you?' Jill ventured over her cold porridge.

'You're the last person I'd ask!' Lottie snapped.

'Don't you dare speak to Jill like that!' Tom was appalled and furious. 'Apologize at once or I'll wring it out of you.'

'You'll do—' Emilia was broken off before she could add, *'no such thing, Tom,'* for Lottie jumped up off her chair. Tom had risen to his feet and was about to rail further against Lottie, but Emilia silenced him with a raised hand. Tom managed the farm, but his father had bequeathed it to her. And with her stately bearing and resolute manner, it was she who was in charge. She gazed at her daughter with vexation. Lottie might feel she had a justifiable grudge and wanted it aired, but this wasn't the way to go about it. It

53

spoke of her immaturity at nineteen years, despite her being a wife and mother. 'Go on Lottie, let's hear exactly what you have on your mind. I'm sorry about this, Midge, do get on with your breakfast.'

The little, leathery-skinned cowman did just that, helping himself to milk and a sprinkle of sugar. He cocked his ear to listen to what Lottie had to say. Emilia – Mrs Em to him – had not suggested he leave the room, and it did not occur to him to make a withdrawal. He was as much a part of the set up here as was the solid, functional Victorian furniture and the three generations of family.

Faced with her mother's stern face, and Perry and Jill's and her grandfather's bewilderment, and Tom's fury, and old-fashioned Tilda's anxious hand-wringing, Lottie saw with a sinking heart that she had let her grievances get out of hand. It was really none of their fault. It was Nate's. He should be on a transatlantic ship on his way to her for good, but instead he had chosen to visit his former ranch hands and say goodbye to them. She hadn't seen him since Carl's christening, the only time he had seen his son, when he had got a twenty-four-hour pass. Shortly after that his unit had returned to the States. His absence had made them miss out on a wonderful opportunity. A month ago a farm of two hundred and forty acres had come on the market in a nearby hamlet, Taldrea. It would have been perfect, near enough for her to keep easy contact with her family. She had phoned Nate and asked if he would allow Tom to put in a bid on their behalf, but Nate had said he wanted to be there to choose their new home for himself. Lottie's prayers that the farm wouldn't sell quickly had gone unanswered. A retired major had snapped up the farm. She was furious and left feeling rejected. Nate should be eager to be with his family. She and Carl should be his first priority.

She lowered her eyes and intended to lower her voice, but it came out steeped in resentment. 'It's just that I'm surrounded by happily married couples and people who are getting on with their lives, and until Nate finally arrives my life is on hold.'

Her explanation did nothing to make Tom less riled; he had missed her mournful notes. 'Oh, that's typical of you, Lottie. Nate's giving up everything for you, his ranch, his friends, even his country. You're so selfish. You should be counting your blessings that he survived the war, that you're not widowed like Susan Dowling. You should take a leaf out of her book. She doesn't harp on about her fate but shows quiet dignity. Our own brother was shot down in his plane and denied his future. And don't forget those who are still suffering, Jim Killigrew, for instance, trying to run his building business with only one arm, and what about the chap staying at Faye's? He went through every sort of torture under the Nips yet he took it upon himself to come down to see the Smith kids at the earliest opportunity. You saw for yourself what a mess he's in.'

'I know all that,' Lottie cried. 'And don't you dare accuse me of being selfish. It was Mum's intention to leave the farm to both of us but I've forsaken my half so you and Jill can have it all one day. You and Jill are already settled. When you start a family you'll have everything, so Tom Harvey, don't you dare preach at me.'

'OK, OK, I take your point,' Tom said, less irate. 'But do you have to be so damned cantankerous? Carry on like this, when Nate does arrive and he'll turn straight round and return to Texas.'

A shrill sound escaped Lottie's throat. Before she could utter another word, Perry got up crossly from the table, lifted Paul out of his high chair and banged out of the room. It wasn't unusual for his stepchildren to squabble, and Lottie was normally the instigator, but it was the first time he had felt compelled to desert a meal table. Emilia had watched him and their son disappear. She said forcefully, 'Right, that's enough, you two. A lot of hurtful things have been said and I'm ordering you both to stop before one of you goes on to say something unforgivable. Lottie, you and I will discuss your concerns later. In the meantime, you will both apologize to everyone here for disturbing their peace, and later to Perry. Eat up, the country still needs feeding, and as far as the running of this farm is concerned we're all in it together.'

She watched grimly as her son and daughter mumbled apologies, then turned and went to the den to Perry and Paul.

Perry was bouncing Paul in his arms, making him chuckle as he made funny faces.

'Sorry about that, darling,' Emilia said, putting her arm round his waist.

'You're no reason to say sorry, Em, darling.' Perry brought her into his embrace. 'I hope Nate sets out for Southampton soon. Perhaps we should suggest to Lottie that she travel up alone to meet him. They could badly do with a proper honeymoon.'

'Oh, you don't think trouble between them is inevitable, do you?'

Perry's deep blue eyes displayed surprise. 'Don't you?'

Emilia sighed and snuggled into him. 'I know what you mean. We're getting crowded here now that there's three separate families with their own ideas and needs. And Lottie is feeling let down by Nate's decision not to join her at once. And Lottie being Lottie, she'll not rest until she's hammered her point home to him.'

Five

Faye looked down on Mark's sleeping form in one of the twin beds in the guestroom, and was pleased to see he was peaceful and still. He was on his side, stretched out, his breathing coming effortlessly. She had crept into his room yesterday morning to check on him and found him sleeping fitfully, twitching and groaning. The bedcovers had been heaped on the floor and he was shivering with cold. She'd rushed to cover him up, tucking the blankets in and smoothing the candlewick bedspread over them, hoping he wasn't suffering harrowing flashbacks of his incarceration.

It was only five months since he and the pitiful number of survivors, out of thousands of British and Australian troops, and other nationals and natives had been liberated from the labour camps. How long, if ever, would it take him to get the horrors and deprivations out of his mind? She felt compassion for him, how could she feel otherwise? But there was something more burning away in her heart. She wanted to care for Mark, to comfort him and cherish him, show him how grateful she was for his sacrifice and how she admired him. Last night Mark had told her uncle he had fought against his medical discharge. For a career soldier it was a terrific blow. What would he do with his life now? Her uncle was worried about him. 'There was a sense of shame for the men put under surrender at Singapore, but there was no other option,' Tristan had said. None of it was fair to Mark, and Faye wanted him to feel his life was worth living, and she was furious with his uncaring wife. Justine Fuller should have done more for him

Mark had been under her roof for three days now and didn't rise until late. Everyone was careful to allow him a quiet breakfast and not to engage him in long conversations. Then he'd sit beside the drawing room fire, listening to the radio, or browsing through the newspaper. His wife rang each evening at six o'clock and he'd spend a short while in friendly conversation with her. No one asked him what she'd had to say. The only questions put to him, apart from inquiries if he was comfortable and had had enough to eat, were by the Smiths.

On their arrival home from school, after being drilled by Tristan that they mustn't overwhelm Mr Fuller, the children had filed eagerly into the drawing room, keeping a pensive hush, to hear about their father's death. Tristan and Faye had sat in the background in case any of the children needed a comforting hug, or Mark's mind switched off.

Mark had stood up to greet them and sat down again when the children were settled in a tidy row on a sofa, Pearl in the middle, all holding hands. Faye noticed he had studied their avid little faces. He smiled. 'You boys are very much like your father, and you, Pearl, are the image of your mother. Vincent showed me a family snap in Singapore, he used to bring it out and show all the men and boast about how proud he was of all of you. You've all grown very nicely. Your parents would be delighted to know you now have a loving home.'

'Was our dad one of your mates?' Bob asked, leaning forward over his grubby knees.

'Not at first, I was an officer over him. But after we were captured things levelled out a bit. Vincent was quite a comic. He lifted the spirits of the men. He was a very efficient black-marketeer, but he never kept anything for himself but traded with the natives for medicines for the sick, and there were a lot of sick men. He liked to act and fool about and make people laugh. I expect you remember him like that, always happy, making others happy too.'

'Yes, that's our Dad,' Len said proudly. 'He

60

used to joke like Bob Hope. Did he kill many Japs?'

'No. None of us did really. The British surrendered in 1942 and were taken to British barracks which the Japs renamed Changi because they were near the infamous Changi jail. The barracks had been a wonderful site with all sorts of amenities including cinemas, tennis courts and yacht clubs, but before the surrender British forces had destroyed the water supply and everything so the Nips couldn't enjoy the comforts, so it wasn't all that nice for us.' This was an understatement. The degrading conditions, the deaths by beatings and disease prepared none of the men for the hell that was to come. 'Then after a while we were taken on a long march through the jungle to various camps to help build a railway.' They were forced to trek through pitiless terrain, straining under the weight of heavy equipment, then to live in squalor, and work as slaves, even the sick, on rations barely enough to sustain an infant. Death had snatched lives away in droves every day. Mark would never tell another human soul about what had really gone on.

He grew serious and looked into each child's face. 'Do you know anything about how your father died?'

Bob shook his head. 'Mum wrote to us just before she got killed in an air raid, that she got a telegram telling her that he'd gone up to heaven.'

A shadow fell across Mark's face and Faye knew he would hold back the true facts. 'Well, a lot of men got sick. You know how at school there are outbreaks of mumps and measles? It was a lot like that in camp. Men got fevers and sometimes it was quite serious and they'd die. It was what happened to your father. There was a doctor and a hospital' – *called the death house*, he didn't say, *just a bamboo hut* – 'and after a short stay in the fever ward Vincent died very peacefully. The padre and I were with him. I promised him if I got the chance I'd come and see you, tell you all how much he loved you and wanted you to have a good life.'

'We've got that,' Len whispered. Like his twin and his sister, his eyes were wet with tears as the loss of both of his parents and the family home bit into him.

Pearl let go of her brothers' hands and approached Mark shyly. She had a deep pocket in her skirt and she took something out of it. It was a photograph. A copy of the one Vincent Smith had shown him. 'That's them, our Mum and Dad. Mum gave us this before we was evacuated. Uncle Tris got us each a copy. I take mine everywhere.'

'Do you, sweetheart? That's lovely.' Mark had to fight back a burst of emotion. The photograph brought back vivid memories of the time at the base before the surrender, and the harrowing and tormenting ones after that, and the true nature of Corporal Vincent Smith's death. A guard discovered him trading cigarettes for medicine with an old Burmese woman. The cheroot the tiny woman had clamped between her lips had been kicked out, smashing her jaw, and she had been bludgeoned to death with rifle butts. Her agonized howls had reverberated round the camp for hours. Mark shut off the terrible images of Vincent's unspeakable, drawn-out end, staked out in the blazing sun and tortured. If he allowed it to invade his mind, he would not be able to present a calm front to the children.

The twins got down off the sofa and went to him. 'Thanks for coming to us, Mr Fuller,' they said together.

'It's an honour to have done this for you all and for Vincent.' Mark bent forward and kissed the top of Pearl's head. The boys put out their hands and Mark shook them. Then as if drawn by invisible threads the four joined together in a hug.

Tristan swallowed the lump building up in his throat. Faye had to wipe away the tears searing her eyes. 'Now children, you know that Mr Fuller is not very well. Why don't you run along to the kitchen where Agnes will have your tea ready.'

The Smiths trooped out, but not before they'd received a few gentle words and a kiss from their guardians. 'We can't thank you enough, Mark,' Faye said. 'As the years pass by for the children, you coming here like this will mean so much to them.'

'It means a lot to me.' Mark's voice had grown cracked and dry. He was drained by the effort, but he had done his duty, he had kept his promise to his comrade, and some of the downheartedness lifted away from him.

Mark retired for a nap, and woke forty-five minutes later. He was always sluggish and confused first thing; sometimes the rumbling of the trains on that dreadful railway, which had usually run at night to avoid allied bombers, echoed mockingly through his mind. This time he felt warm and cosy and instinct told him he was safe. Keeping his eyes closed he enjoyed the snug weight of the covers over him and breathed in the fresh smell of clean sheets. He was wearing a pair of pyjamas he'd kept for home leave. They were two sizes too big for him now, but it was a luxury to have anything on his scrawny form that wasn't tattered, crawling with stinging bugs, and soiled and soaked with sweat.

He listened to Susan singing downstairs, and thought about Justine. Mark was philosophical about the breakdown of his marriage. His father and Justine's had served at the same Army postings, so they were life-long friends. They had been greatly fond of each other and always would be. On one occasion, he a young officer then, after they'd had too much to drink they had fallen into bed and had enjoyed a lustful relationship. When Justine's mother suggested they get engaged they had gone along with it – it was the usual thing to do, get married and raise a family.

Justine had not been a typical officer's wife. She had refused to live in married quarters, saying she had seen enough of them, and had plumped for a new suburban semi instead. Her job as a hospital almoner was important to her. He hadn't minded. His career was uppermost in his mind and he'd not desired the rounds of drinks with other officers and their wives. When he'd been posted to Singapore, she had only joined him for the odd month or so, for holidays. Thank God she had not been there when Singapore had been surrendered. Women and children had also suffered horrendously in Japanese internment camps. Knowing Justine was relatively safe at home had kept him going during the horrors.

Susan's voice carried to him: 'There'll be blue birds over the white cliffs of...' He wasn't feeling too frail this morning, he'd take a stroll round the garden and if his energy held up he'd look over Faye's farm. As he stretched his long thin taut limbs and got out of bed, he smiled at thoughts of Faye. Like Susan, she was a thoroughly nice, caring woman. Both were attractive. He smiled to himself: for all his weaknesses he must be in some sort of good nick to have noticed that.

Putting on his dressing gown, he slipped along to the bathroom. It was infinitely nicer being a guest here than at the convalescent home. He had received every kind attention there, and also on his release into Justine's care. Justine, the good old thing, had taken three weeks off work, but he'd hated being an invalid.

'You don't have to stay at home with me, Justine,' he'd stressed, although he'd been desperate in those early days to have her with him.

'You were at death's door, Mark,' she'd replied. 'If you hadn't been liberated when you were I'd have lost you.' Strange, how affectionate they were, how much they cared for each other, yet were planning to put an end to their marriage. He missed Justine, as one missed a best friend. There could have been more between them. Perhaps they had never given their marriage the chance to work. She had no new man in her life and said she wasn't looking for anyone, and he as sure as hell wasn't interested in anything of the sort. He had to reclaim himself as the person he'd used to be, if that was possible, before considering any such new alliance. He must talk to her, see if they should think about starting again on a fresh note. He wouldn't mind that at all. He and Justine had a lot in common. She shared many of his thoughts, so perhaps she was thinking along the same lines too.

He had learned, as one only could in a POW labour camp, to take one day at a time, and right now he was enjoying the stay at Tremore House. He stripped off and sank down into the hot water in the porcelain bath. There was just the Government-ordered few inches, but ah, such luxury. In No 2 camp, Sonkurai, he had dreamt of soaking himself in hot clean water, breathing in healthy steam rather than the lung-clogging stuff of the jungle, to smell clean skin instead of unwashed bodies and the putrid flesh of tropical ulcers and gangrene. He soaped himself all over and washed his hair, the smell of the coal tar soap as sweet as roses after breathing in the stink of bodily functions and death for so long. On liberation, his horribly greasy hair had been shaved off to remove the bugs and filth. It had grown back nicely. Justine liked his soft waves. Justine. His mind drifted. He recalled her gorgeous figure ... fine mantelpiece of a bosom ... shapely legs ... laughing voice ... intelligent and fun ... miss you, Justine. He floated off to sleep.

Susan was giving Bob and Len's room a good 'bottoming'. Agnes's age and rheumatism had lately denied her doing this sort of thing. The boys' room needed a thorough clean-up. The cheeky scamps were hoarders, and from under their twin beds she dragged out old biscuit tins and boxes of stones, leaves, horrible dried up insects and sweet wrappings – some obviously picked up from the ground. There were slingshots, and bows and arrows made from hazel sticks. There was also a box of blobs of something indescribable that smelled offensive and could only be animal droppings – she would put everything back after she had brushed and polished the wooden floor but this collection would have to go. She wiped down the window sill and cleaned the glass and did all the other extra cleaning, then, satisfied she'd done the room justice without encroaching on the boys' right to have the room their own way, she gathered up the cleaning materials and rubbish and left. There was only Mr Fuller's room and the bathroom to see to now. She had heard him running the water for an earlier-than-usual bath and assumed that by now he would be downstairs. She would finish upstairs before going down for her morning break. She broke into singing again. It was many years since she had felt this cheerful. She liked working here, everything was perfect, and when Agnes left next week she was looking forward to setting up her own routine.

As soon as she entered the guestroom, she saw Mr Fuller had not yet dressed. His dressing gown was not on the hook behind the door. He must still be in the bathroom. She frowned. He had been in there a long time. She hadn't heard a sound when passing the door just now. Suddenly afraid for him she hurried there and tapped on the door. 'Mr Fuller? Are you all right?'

There was no answer and she tried the door. It wasn't locked and she thanked goodness, for he was slumped in the bath. 'Mr Fuller! Mark!' She went to him and shook him. His skin was cold and clammy, and for one terrible moment she thought he was dead. Then one of his eyelids flickered. She got down on her knees and splashed cold water on his gaunt face. 'Mark, wake up. Wake up!'

Next instant she was looking into his startled eyes. 'Ohh … what?' he mumbled groggily. 'Oh, Mrs, um … what's happened?'

'You fell asleep in the bath. You're freezing. You must get out.' Susan reached for a towel. 'I'll help you.'

Becoming aware of the situation, Mark blushed fiercely, and it made his sallow complexion patchy and peculiar. 'Th-there's no need to trouble yourself, Mrs, um...'

'It's Susan. Your limbs will be rigid and you

might slip. I'm afraid Mr Harvey has gone with Agnes to move some of her things into the cottage. Don't worry, I'm quite strong.'

Mark coloured hotly again. 'I wasn't thinking about that.'

Susan knew he was horribly embarrassed about his nakedness, mainly for her sake. 'I've been a married woman. The only thing that matters is that get you warm and dry.' She pulled the plug to let the water drain away, tossed the towel over her shoulder, and after getting to her feet was ready to support him.

'Yes, of course.' Mark could have died of mortification. He had suffered many a humiliation as a prisoner of war, but this was somehow worse. Never had he felt so stupid, useless and such a nuisance. He put his hands on the sides of the bath and after a couple of tries managed to lever himself on to his knees. He felt dizzy, and the effort made him hang his head and take a couple of deep breaths. Susan was close at his side. When he tried to stand, she held on to his arm to steady him, pulling to help him up. As soon as she was sure he was stable on two feet she put the towel round his middle and tucked in the end at his sunken stomach, keeping slightly behind him all the while for decency's sake.

'You'll need to turn and place your hands on my shoulders and step out. I'm afraid

there's nothing else for you to hold on to.'
Mark obeyed, but he underwent more embarrassment when it was necessary for her to stoop and lift each of his feet high enough to clear the side of the bath. Susan pulled the bath stool up close and eased him to sit down on it. She wrapped a second towel about his shoulders and rubbed at his back and arms to get the blood flowing through him.

'Oh God,' he moaned. 'I feel such a fool.'

'There's no need,' she said softly. She dried his feet and helped him into the spare pair of slippers loaned him by Tristan. Then she put his dressing gown over his shivering shoulders. 'Let me help you to your room then you can get dressed.'

He crept along the long landing with her as if he was a bent old man and finally he was sitting on his bed. 'Oh hell to it – sorry, Susan – I was going to ask you not to mention this to anyone, but I've made you all wet.'

'I don't think it would be right for me to keep anything from Faye that goes on under her roof, Mr Fuller. Please don't worry about it.' She brought his clothes to him. 'Try to dress as quickly as you can. You'll soon warm up when you've had something hot to eat and drink.'

'You're a damned fine woman,' Mark said, slipping into the sort of talk he used with the

71

down-to-earth Justine. 'Call me Mark. I feel we are friends. If that's all right with you.'

Susan did not take his compliment as a pass at her, she was thinking she had never met a more genuinely pleasant man, except, of course, for Tristan Harvey, who was the epitome of good manners and gentlemanly conduct. 'That's fine with me. Now, you get dressed. I'll tell Faye she can start your breakfast in a few minutes.'

She was smiling when she went to the kitchen. Faye was stationed at the table, with eggs and bacon and cut bread in front of her. 'Ah, on his way down, is he? Good heavens, Susan! What's happened to you? Has one of the bathroom taps sprung a leak?'

'No.' Susan recounted what had happened. 'The poor soul was so upset, but hopefully I reassured him. I thought I'd dry off and then sort the bathroom out.'

Faye was consumed with jealousy that something significant had happened to Mark and it hadn't been she who had been there to help him. 'You should have called me at once!'

Susan blinked at the snap and drew in her breath. She went rigid, in the same way as when Lance had shouted at her, always over something he'd had no right to be angry about, usually a prelude to prolonged verbal abuse.

Faye was immediately sorry. Susan had

done nothing wrong, and now it looked as if she had brought a shutter down against her. 'Oh, please forgive me, I shouldn't have said that. I was worried about Mark.' Her apology had not impressed Susan. A defensive look was in her eyes and she seemed unsure, perhaps even worried. Faye had to think fast or the slow friendship she was forging with Susan would take irretrievable steps backward. She put the kettle on the hob. 'I'm very annoyed, you see, Susan. Take a seat and have your coffee. I was hoping Mark's things would have arrived this morning. You'd think that after all he'd been through, his wife could at least have arranged something quickly. Uncle Tris is happy to lend Mark whatever he needs, but he's bound to feel more comfortable if he had his own belongings.'

Susan offered no opinion. She was hurt and felt she had been put in her place. She wanted to leave the kitchen and get on with her work, away from the woman who seemed at times eager to make a firm friendship with her, but at other times was haughty and demanding. It was impossible that she and Faye Harvey could have anything except a working relationship, she the cleaner, Faye the employer. They were worlds apart. Faye Harvey was twenty-one, four years younger, but she seemed sophisticated and worldly in comparison. While Susan was wearing a dress and cardigan she'd had for years, faded from the wash, and a print apron and a scarf tied turban-style round her hair, Faye was in her jersey dress, of utility make but stylish, with a cute collar and self-coloured narrow belt and piping. Her ebony hair was in rich waves, pulled up from her temples by antique tortoiseshell combs. Faye exuded the money she had. She owned the village garage and filling station, and from gossip Susan had learned she had inherited a share of a wine business in Truro but had sold it because she didn't approve of her late father's shady partner. She looked like a movie star with her red lipstick and pearl necklace and open-toe slingbacks. Anyone would think she was dressed up for a luncheon engagement. Susan pulled out a chair at the far end of the table and placed stiff folded hands on top of it. She didn't speak. Her happiness at working here had been stamped out, but she should have known it would be short-lived. Her mother had stamped out every bit of childhood hope and ambition in her, and then Lance had taken over in exactly the same way.

Faye was anxious to make amends. She fetched the biscuit barrel and carried it to Susan. She put on her brightest, most eager voice. 'Help yourself. They're delicious, there's real butter in them. You must take some home for Maureen. Oh, here's Uncle

Tris.' Faye's heart hammered in her chest. If Susan continued to look glum, her uncle would have something to say if he found out she'd upset her. He was always singing her praises, and Faye was unsettled by the suspicion he was falling in love with her. And Susan was independent and proud. If she began to hate it here she would leave and rather struggle if she couldn't find employment elsewhere. Suddenly everything had become complicated.

'Hello!' Tristan called out cheerfully, coming in via the back entrance, his boots off after the walk back along the muddy lane. 'I've left Agnes on her own to settle in and get the feel of the place. Ah, Susan.' He had taken the liberty of calling Susan by her first name, hoping she wouldn't mind. 'Has Faye asked you about our little favour yet?'

'Favour?' Susan said warily, keeping her face pointed downward. It had never paid to look Lance in the eye when he was in a bad temper or a brooding mood and it was something she was apt not to do with anyone.

'Yes,' Tristan said uncertainly, glancing at Faye with a question on his face.

Faye made a show of pouring the coffee. 'You're just in time for a drink, Uncle Tris. No, I haven't mentioned it yet. Susan, we're planning to take Agnes out for a retirement dinner at the Red Lion Hotel in Truro, to thank her for all the years she's worked for the family, and of course we'll need someone to look after the children. We were wondering if you'd be kind enough to come and stay the night, you and Maureen. Maureen could share with Pearl, and Uncle Tris would sleep at the farm and you could have his room.' She went on with jolly enthusiasm, 'Actually, I could take his room and you could have mine. We'd pay you, of course.'

Concerned at Susan's dejection, Tristan said, 'Maureen would have a lot of fun with Pearl, I'm sure. If Mr Fuller is still here I'm sure he wouldn't be any bother. He retires early and sleeps the sleep of the dead. What do you say? Would you like time to think about it?'

'No,' Susan said. She wasn't one to sulk or be awkward and she was happy to do anyone a kindness where it was appreciated, in this case for Agnes and Mr Harvey. The extra money would be very useful, and having tidied Faye's room the last two mornings it would be a treat to sleep in such sumptuous surroundings. 'I'd be happy to do it, and Maureen will be excited about sleeping over, she's never done anything like that before.'

'Good! That's settled.' Faye smiled at Susan, and her stomach eased when she was rewarded with a short smile in return.

'When will it be?' Susan asked.

'We thought on Saturday evening. Then we

could all have Sunday lunch together, and if the weather is dry the children could all go riding. I'm sure Maureen would like to learn. I'll supervise her myself,' Tristan said, trying not to admit to himself how delighted he was to have Susan stay and eat at the house. 'Agnes will move into her new home the following Friday.'

'You'll miss her,' Susan observed.

'It's good she won't be far away, just down the lane where we can keep an eye on her now she's getting on a bit, and she'll pop in occasionally for a cuppa.' Tristan sounded casual, but he was thinking how fascinating Susan was. In the last few minutes various expressions had formed on her lovely young face and he'd enjoyed every one of them, even if it was silly and unwise to do so.

Susan drank her coffee quickly, not wanting to linger with the Harveys. They were friendly, well, Faye was most of the time, but it didn't feel right sitting round the kitchen table with them. 'I'd better get on.'

'Of course,' Tristan smiled and stood up as she left the table, always the gentleman.

'I'll make a start on Mark's breakfast. He should be down any minute,' Faye said, putting a frying pan on the hob of the range. Cross with herself over the discomfiture she had caused Susan, she resolved to play things Susan's way from now on by keeping a more formal footing, and never to be sharp with her again.

Tristan took his coffee to the library to get on with business matters. Faye was pleased. Mark ate his breakfast in here, and she would have him all to herself. He came in and bid her 'good morning' as she was lifting the eggs from the pan and placing them beside the bacon on the plate. 'My, that's a generous helping.'

'Food is easier to come by from the farm,' she said lightly. Even so, she had given him her rations for the week. The doorbell rang. She hoped it was no one wanting to see her. 'Uncle Tris will answer that.'

Mark sat down and looked at the food appreciatively. 'Mmm, this look delicious.'

'Good. I'll make the toast. We had a good harvest from the plum trees last year so there's plenty of jam.'

There were voices in the hall. One was loud and chuckling. Mark put his knife and fork down and turned his ear to the door. 'If I didn't know better I'd think that was...'

'Who?'

Mark got up. He grew excited. 'It must be...'

The door was opened. Tristan showed someone in and Mark exclaimed, 'Justine, darling! So it was you. What a lovely surprise.'

The attractive, femininely-built woman ran to him and they joined in an eager embrace, kissing cheeks. Justine Fuller leant back in his arms so she could take a good look at him. 'Well, I had to see for myself just how you were, darling. I'll never forgive myself for letting you give me the slip. I said I'd bring you down in the spring when it was warmer and you'd have been stronger for travelling, remember?' She gently pushed back his hair. 'You are an old duffer, Mark. What am I going to do with you?'

She released herself but took a firm hold of his hands, then turned to Faye. 'You must be Faye. Pleased to meet you. I can't thank you and Tristan enough for taking care of Mark. I hope he's not proving too much trouble.'

'None at all,' Faye got out through almost clenched teeth. 'Mark's very welcome.' *You're not!* The whole situation was ridiculous. Witnessing how close the couple was, it seemed crazy they had even considered going their separate ways. Faye had only known him for three days and had no right to be possessive about him. But she was, and she had already snapped at one innocent woman over him today and was having a hard task not to do it to another. 'Perhaps he should sit down and eat his breakfast.'

'Quite right too.' Justine led Mark to the table as if he was a weakling. 'Go on, tuck in, you're still like a human scarecrow.'

'This is a nice surprise.' Tristan didn't know what else to say, and he was baffled by the frosty reception Faye was giving Justine Fuller. It was a good thing she seemed not to have noticed. 'Justine's brought Mark's things down with her.'

'And a few bits of your own, I hope, darling? You won't have time to travel back today,' Mark said, hopeful she would stay, for Justine was inclined to be elusive, to go her own way. 'We could book a room at a hotel.'

'I've got a week off. I thought I'd come down and keep an eye on you myself for a while. I'd love to meet the Smith kiddies, if that's all right, and your little boy too, Faye. Mark's told me about Simon, said he's quite the sweetest little chap.'

'Did he?' Faye felt as though she could tear the woman's head off, just to stop her annoying animated talk. She'd been like this with certain girls at boarding school and with her younger American half-siblings, impatient with anyone who was over-amusing. Faye knew it was because these people were popular and fitted in easily everywhere they went, while she tended to seek quieter, more serious company, the qualities that she liked in Susan. She realized it was because she had never been the most important one in someone's life, except for Simon. Now she was enduring Justine Fuller's buzzing personality in her own house. She was the sort of person everyone responded to. Her uncle was watching her avidly, carried along by her good nature and sparky energy. 'Simon went down for a morning nap. He should be awake soon.'

As if on cue, Susan was there, carrying Simon, who looked red-eyed from crying and had his thumb in his mouth. Unsure if she'd done the right thing, she said quietly, 'Um, he woke up and was fussing. I knew you were tied up, so I've brought him down.'

'Thanks Susan, that was very kind of you,' Faye gave her the warmest smile before holding her arms out to her son. 'Come to Mummy, darling.' She was furious when Justine stepped in the way and jiggled Simon's chubby hand.

'Hello, little man, aren't you the cutest thing? And you must be Susan. Mark's mentioned you. Thanks for coming to his rescue that day.'

'Not at all.' Like most people meeting Justine Fuller for the first time, Susan immediately warmed to her. 'Did he also tell you that Faye and I were ready to whack him with umbrellas?'

Justine laughed a hearty sound. 'I'm not surprised, the way he went about things.' She put her arms round Mark's shoulders and gave him a tight squeeze, making him drop the last mouthful of food off his fork. 'But you couldn't help it, could you, my old love? Bit fuzzy in the old brainbox.'

It made Faye want to scream at her to leave him alone. How could she refer to Mark's trances in such a manner? It wasn't at all funny. 'I won't hear of you going off to a hotel, Justine,' she said in her most welcoming tone. 'You must stay with us. Mark's room has twin beds. He's quite comfortable here and is looking forward to seeing the countryside. He still needs lots of rest and relaxation.'

'That's very generous of you, Faye,' Mark said, sipping his coffee, happy to let the women make any arrangements they cared to.

'Well, if you're sure another addition won't upset the apple cart, then thanks again,' Justine said.

'Take a seat. I'm sure you could do with a cup of coffee after your journey,' Faye replied in hostess fashion.

'Don't mind if I do.' Justine parked herself beside Mark.

Faye winced, for she was sure the woman was squeezing Mark's thigh. She wasn't sure how long she could endure her tactile and ebullient manner.

'I'll air the bed,' Susan said.

'I'll take the luggage up,' Tristan said, jumping at the chance to be alone with Susan. 'What do you think of her? Justine?' he asked when he'd offloaded the two suitcases and a rucksack in the guestroom.

'It's not my place to think anything,' Susan said, folding back the bed linen.

'Oh, please don't go along with that old class barrier thing,' Tristan urged, not hiding his disappointment.

'It'll be always be there,' she said. It was a matter of fact to her.

'But my family's never felt that it's mattered. Emilia was Ford Farm's dairymaid before she married Alec, my brother, and he was the village squire.'

'But Faye's father thought differently. Everyone called him Mr Harvey or Mr Ben. He could be a...' Susan stopped. Lance had loathed Ben Harvey, calling him a stuck-up bastard. Ben Harvey had been good to her, but he'd always seemed miserable. Apparently there had been a lot of strife between him and the squire, and he'd gone through a bitter divorce.

'Snob,' Tristan finished for her. 'Yes, I concede that. Ben could be arrogant. But I was hoping you'd feel comfortable here, Susan.'

Susan studied him for a moment. He was such a good person, completely harmless and unassuming, the proof of which was she was here alone chatting to him without reservation or worry. 'I do, with you.'

Tristan couldn't have heard better news, although he hoped she didn't view him purely as her employer or in some fatherly way. 'Can I ask if you're finding Faye a bit difficult?'

Susan dropped her eyes. 'Sometimes I'm not sure of her.'

'She is a little mixed up.' Tristan didn't usually air the family bad points, but he wanted Susan to see Faye in a good light. 'Ben treated her quite badly. He rejected her for years. He made things up to her in a letter written prior to his leaving for France. It said he'd realized he loved her. Sadly, his death meant it was too late for them to build up a proper relationship, so as you can imagine, it's left her with some raw emotions. She doesn't mean to be off-putting.'

'No, I don't suppose she does. I suppose I ought to be less guarded ... I find it hard ... Faye wants to be a friend to me, perhaps I should let that happen.'

Realizing she had just opened up to him, Tristan felt he'd progressed with her, but also, if he wanted to get any further he should leave it for now. He shot her another smile. 'That would be nice. Well, I'd better not hang about and get in your way.'

As he headed down the stairs he heard Susan singing.

Six

At the weekend a delivery van rattled over the cobbled yard of Ford Farm. 'That must be for you, Lottie. Nate promised he was sending over something exciting,' Emilia said, craning her graceful neck at the dairy window to get a better view of the crate that was being unloaded.

'Uh,' Lottie muttered, not bothering to look. She and Emilia were carrying pans of cream from the slate-shelved inner dairy for butter making, and she went back to fetch another pan, to make up eight in all.

'Don't you want to rush off and open it?' Emilia was curious about the crate's contents and worried over Lottie's lack of eagerness. Tilda came outside to sign for the crate. The van driver and his mate would be asked to set it down on the kitchen floor. 'I'll finish up here.'

'I'm not interested in Nate's grand gestures. Tins of spam and peaches, jars of coffee and a few luxuries that we can't get over here count for nothing in my book. It's Nate who should be here, not a stupid box of goodies.'

'That's a bit harsh, isn't it? It shows Nate's thinking of you. Go on, go in and open it. There's sure to be lots of things in there for Carl,' Emilia encouraged, wishing she could think of something that would lift her daughter's flagging spirits.

'It isn't harsh at all,' Lottie cried. 'Carl wants his father, not candy, toys and fancy clothes. Nate should put Carl first, not a bunch of ranch hands. I'm getting fed up waiting for him and I'm fed up with having no one to understand how I feel.'

'We do understand you, Lottie, all of us do.' Lottie was so dejected nothing would convince her otherwise. 'Of course you want to get on with your own life, have your own home, and to be thinking about having more children.'

'Not that!' Lottie's cheeks went as red as her hair. 'I don't want any more kids.'

Emilia didn't answer. Lottie had gone through a long difficult labour and birth, made all the more traumatic by Nate not being there. Then Carl had yelled with colic nearly every hour in his first three months, wearing her out, magnifying her misery. With her husband's presence, care and support back then, she might be thinking differently now.

With her head hung, Lottie ignored Tilda as she came hurrying to the dairy. Tilda's eyes above her plump apple cheeks were shining with exhilaration. 'Lottie, my handsome, come quick, there's something for you!'

'I'll come later, Tilda,' Lottie said in a forlorn voice. 'I know the crate's here. It's not a big deal. It should be my neglectful husband instead, if he ever wants to come, that is.'

'Lottie...' Tilda looked worried, glancing behind her.

'Don't try to coax me,' Lottie shrugged, on the verge of tears. She didn't know how much more she could take of Nate's absence. Yesterday when she'd gone down into the village with Carl she'd received remarks that had cut into her.

' 'Bout time the litt'l'un's daddy put in an appearance, isn't it?' the shopkeeper had said. Nosey Gilbert Eathorne had eyed her like a bloodhound on the scent, searching her, as if she was hiding a shameful secret.

A housewife known for her bitter tongue was at her garden gate, arms folded primly. 'Where's your husband got himself to then? Coming over soon is he, or has he better interests? Americans tend to be flighty, in my book.'

'You don't know my husband at all, Mrs Moses, so keep your remarks to yourself.' No doubt she and others must be wondering if Nate had deserted her for good and she found it humiliating. It was crushing her.

She couldn't think ahead and getting through each day was getting harder. She had made the huge decision to give up the home she loved and was now beginning to regret it. She was further bothered over Tom and Jill's excited plans to update the older part of the farmhouse. Tilda was to move into the Victorian wing, and they would have a cosy home within their home all to themselves. Tom and Jill were careful not to show too much affection in front of her now, as were her mother and Perry, and having made the two couples feel awkward simply for being deeply in love made her feel a killjoy, an old crab.

She wasn't sure any more how much she loved Nate. She had been drawn to him at a village dance, as he was to her, and they had declared their love during their second meeting. He had begged her mother to allow them to marry, a somewhat foolish desire on their part, for she, at her own admission, was a spoiled selfish seventeen year old, and he was soon to leave Cornwall's shores for the D Day landings. He was an Army medic and the fear of losing him in battle had been an agony. Of course, she was grateful he'd survived and had come through with just a couple of scars; there had been no need for Tom to fling that at her. She knew love and she knew the emotional pain and turmoil of separation, but the hardest thing to bear was that it seemed Nate did not feel the same way. He couldn't care as much for her and Carl as he professed in his letters and phone calls. It was killing her inside and she felt she would soon explode with misery.

'But 'tis worth it, Lottie, you'll see,' Tilda persisted, beckoning to her.

Lottie glared at her cajoling hand as if she wanted to swipe it off her wrist. Why couldn't people leave her alone? 'I said I'd come when I'm ready. Damn the stupid crate! I don't care what's inside it. Take it outside and burn it for all I care.'

'Oh, Lottie...' Tilda paled, then looked imploringly at Emilia.

Someone eased past Tilda, a tall young man in a rawhide jacket and jeans, with sandy hair, a long scar on his right cheek, and with soft eyes that were usually calm within well-balanced features, but were now troubled and perplexed. 'Lottie, darling, what on earth's the matter?'

Lottie nearly fell over a bussa of potted butter on the red brick floor. 'Nate!' She had dreamed of the moment when he'd come to her. How she would rush into his arms, bubbling over with excitement and deliriously happy. The sound of his soft Texan drawl would be music to her ears, and the sight of him as handsome and magnificent as a wonder of the world. But as the wait had grown and grown and she had felt more and more let down, she had stopped picturing any such magical scene. She burst into tears. She had been letting rip about him and he had heard every word. There would be no romantic, blissful reunion. Instead it was tainted and horrible. It was his fault, but she had the awful feeling she would be made to feel she should take the blame.

'It's good to see you, ma'am,' Nate inclined his head to Emilia. 'I think I should take Lottie outside.'

'Yes, you do that, Nate.' Lottie had frozen on the spot, blubbering like a child, her eyes on Nate with some sort of desperation, and Emilia's heart bled for her. She too wanted an explanation from Nate for his tardiness, but she must take second place. She went to Lottie and led her to Nate. 'It's good to see you too. You and Lottie must spend all the time you need.'

Nate held out a hand to Lottie. 'Come with me, honey. Don't cry.' She put her fingers inside his and his warm hand encompassed them. She felt a reassuring pressure, but she was devastated to have their reunion spoiled.

Once outside in the yard, the blustery wind snatching at their clothes, Nate pulled her gently into a hearty embrace and she latched on to him. Now he was here she didn't want to let go. 'I'm sorry,' she sobbed. 'I wanted this moment to be perfect.'

'And it is.' He kissed her wet eyes, her lips and all over her face. 'You've no need to be sorry, Lottie, but it seems I have. We'll talk it through and I'll put it right, I promise, but let's go inside and see the little fellow.'

They walked hand in hand, Lottie discarding her white dairy hat on the way. 'I love this,' Nate said, running his free hand through her tumbling locks. 'I love you. I hope you haven't doubted that.'

'No, of course not,' she lied. She wanted to pull her head away from his caressing hand. She hated feeling this way, but even in her delight at his sudden appearance, the joy of being in his arms again, she couldn't help resenting his long absence. 'I've been missing you so much, that's all. Did you get passage on an earlier ship?'

'Travel is still a bit haywire, but I managed to get on a few connecting planes. I came as soon as I could, darling. I'll explain later.' Perry had seen them coming and he brought Carl to the door. Nate let go of Lottie's hand and ran to his son. 'Good heavens, you've grown the size of a mountain lion.' Carl gazed at the stranger. 'Hello son. I'm your daddy. Are you coming to me?' Nate offered his hands gently and made cooing noises to the boy. Carl kept on staring at him, one chubby fist clenching Perry's jersey.

Lottie watched. Carl wasn't at all shy; her mother often declared he was just like she had been as a child, outgoing and playful; destined to be just as precocious. 'Come on Carl, son,' Nate stroked his little arm. 'Come to Daddy.' Then Carl delighted Nate by stretching out his arms and leaning towards him. Nate gathered him up and cuddled him in. He put his head on top of the little boy's and wept unashamedly. 'You don't know how long I've waited for this.'

Lottie knew she should throw her arms around them both, but she hesitated for a minute before doing so, wanting to question Nate's emotional statement. Perry retreated inside and left them to it, hoping all the woes, real or imaginary, his stepdaughter had undergone in the last months were at an end. But Lottie and Nate had a lot of adjusting to do. They didn't really know each other. They would have to re-ignite their first passion and find enough common ground and shared interests to make their marriage work.

Susan locked up Little Dell and put the key into her coat pocket. She used the front door during winter, for the back path, despite liberal scatterings of ashes, was always water-logged, due to poor drainage from the wooded slope that reared up behind her little two-up, two-down home. Just in sight above through the bare trees was the long-empty bigger cottage that bore the deceptively sweet name of Rose Dew. Susan never allowed Maureen to play up there. It needed a complete renovation and she worried about the possibility of falling bricks and slates, and it was rumoured to be haunted. She didn't really believe in ghosts, but she had doubts about the sanctity of Rose Dew and was nervous to go outside her cottage after dark. Once, when foraging near the place for firewood, she had sensed a cold bleakness and had got horrid shivers, which had sent her scurrying away. Lance had looked over Rose Dew out of curiosity. He said he had pushed through the broken door and looked in every room, and had sworn he'd seen, in a bedroom, a window latch open as if by an unseen hand and the moth-eaten curtains go crashing to the floor. He had ordered her to keep away from the place but she hadn't needed the warning. Sometimes she felt she was being watched, and like today, each time she left Little Dell she never looked back, in fear she just might see some ominous figure up on the slope and she'd be afraid to return home.

She set off quickly, carrying a large shopping bag with her and Maureen's night-clothes inside for the overnight stay for Agnes's dinner outing. The Smiths had called for Maureen earlier in the afternoon and they were off playing, hopefully inside Tremore House by now. The evenings were drawing out, but heavy black clouds were gaining pace and it would soon darken and there would be rain. The wind was picking up and Susan pulled her headscarf forward to give more protection to her face. Faye had given her an umbrella, but if she didn't beat the rain the powerful gusts of wind would make it useless to put up. Her best bet was to keep her head down and hurry along. The sound of the wind beating through the trees and the dim light as she started down the short, ragged, muddy track to the lane brought the unwelcome thought of the possibility of a neighbouring ghost.

She spied a figure ahead and her every sense was filled with foreboding. Then she sighed in relief. It was a man in a double-breasted camel coat, sturdy shoes and a trilby hat, his clothes too modern and well-cut for him to be the spectre of some former farm labourer. A momentary thought was that it might be Mark Fuller, who now took short restorative walks, but he always ventured out with his wife. Was it Tristan Harvey come to escort her? It was the sort of kindly gesture he'd make. No, the man was shorter and stocky. He didn't move, and after she'd cover a few more yards apprehension and dread burned a furrow up her back. The man's trilby was pulled down across his face, but his manner was horribly familiar. *'Lance...?'*

'I thought he was pushing up daisies on Froggy soil,' the man said with a hard laugh. He pushed his hands inside his flapping coat and stuck his thumbs down the inside of his trouser pockets, a pose she recognized only too well. 'Hello, Susan. Aren't you pleased to see me?'

'Kenny! What on earth are you doing here?' She backed away from him. 'How do you know my husband's name?'

'I've made it my business to find out about you. After all, you're my only kin, Susie, girl. That wasn't much of a greeting to give your long-lost older brother.' He feigned hurt, then put on the leering grin she'd always hated. 'It's been years. Thought you'd have forgiven me by now.'

'For running out and leaving me to put up with Mother's nagging and rotten temper and her drinking, her tight-fisted ways and dirty habits? I don't think so. You stole the money she'd had stashed away. She took it out on me, beat me black and blue, and said I should have stopped you. How, only the Lord knows; you bullied me too. I've got a scar on my back from where you leathered me.' Anger and indignation took over from her fright and she made to march past him. 'Go away, Kenny. I never want to see you again.'

'Where're you off to, Susie? I'll walk along with you. Got half an hour to spare before

95

my lift comes back.' He took her arm and she wrenched away. He didn't seem to care, and matched her fast steps, nonchalantly. 'Shame to find you're the unforgiving sort. You was a sweet little maid.'

'I know better now,' she replied curtly.

'Life treated you badly then? Shame. If you're short of a few bob, I could slip you something.'

She stopped dead still. 'I'll take nothing from you. You've never come by anything legally in your life. Clear off!'

Kenny shook his head, amused. He was blunt-looking with harsh thin lips and piggy eyes, but he had a charmer's tongue and was a master of deception. He was a decade older than Susan, and had a different father; their mother hadn't married either man. He had treated Susan like a slave and a punch bag. 'You was never snappy, you was always too scared to stick up for yourself. You must have something to protect, or someone. Got a little maid of your own, I hear. That your little place back there then?'

Susan's disgust and dread turned to prickles of fear. What did he know about Maureen? He wouldn't be interested in her in the usual way of an uncle; he'd always despised children. 'No, I was calling on someone and they're not at home.'

He leant forward from the waist, and Susan knew he could be more of a threat to her than Lance had ever been. Lance had bawled and shouted at her, demeaned her, criticized her and controlled her. Occasionally he'd thrown things at her, but only weightless things like newspapers and tea towels, not designed to hurt her physically. Kenny had hurt her several times, and he'd enjoyed it, and laughed at her childhood tears. He was capable of anything. 'There's no use in lying to me, sis,' he trilled in a mocking singsong voice. 'I know all about you. Everything. You and your daughter live there, in the little cottage, and your late hubby was as bent as I am and he furnished it out for you with knock-off goods. Your Lance sounded just my sort. We could have gone into partnership together. He should have spivved his way through the war like I did.' He tapped on his leg and laughed. 'He should have had himself a crocked leg. I've spent the last years up in the Smoke. It took me a while to track you down, but this is a nice little village. The shopkeeper is a talkative bloke. I couldn't get him to shut up. He told me about your nice job at the big house not far from here. That you're baby-sitting for your boss's adopted swarm of brats tonight. I'm glad to have found you so well set up, Susie. Your fashion sense is lousy, though. The women I hang about with wouldn't be seen dead in what you've got on. If I was hanging around I'd do something about that for you.'

'You're going back up to London?' She snatched eagerly at the glimmer of hope.

'Oh, God, yes.' He carried on walking, taking her arm and pushing it inside his, and she went along with it to keep him sweet. 'I couldn't stand it down here, not enough fun, not enough action.'

'Why did you come down?' she made her voice light and chatty, hoping this would help ease him out of her life again. You could never be sure with Kenny. He was a born liar.

'Bloke I knew, his old ma snuffed it, and I got curious about my own family. Thought I'd look up the old woman, and you, Susie. Remember Mrs Jago, that stuck-up old cow next door? After I'd been banging on the door for ten minutes she came out and told me Ma had died, in the infirmary, of pneumonia, two years ago. She knew you'd got married, to some good-looking bloke, she said, who was a few years older than you. She wondered if you'd moved up-country, as she hadn't clocked you in years. Didn't you know the old woman was gone, Susie?'

They had come to a crossroads. If Kenny knew all about her, there was no point in heading him in a different direction to Tremore House. Susan pointed left. 'I'm going that way. No, I didn't know Mother had died. I can't say I'm sorry. She hated me.'

Later, when she had time alone she'd absorb the news and see how she felt about her mother's death then.

Kenny put his arm round her waist and hugged her. 'I feel the same way. She hated our fathers, so therefore she hated us. Well, seems we've both risen above it. I can't help noticing you're a pretty piece. Bag yourself a rich husband if you can, live in comfort and without worry. Look around at the older blokes, they're a sucker for a sweet young widow.'

'I'm happy as I am. Are you married, Kenny?'

He roared with glee. 'In name only. I hitched meself up to a rich old dear and moved on when I'd bled her dry. Look Susie, I can see you've got a nice quiet life here and I'm pleased for you, honest I am. I'm off and away tonight and we'll probably never meet up again. You take care of yourself.'

'Thanks, Kenny.' She was relieved he was going, but apart from Maureen, she had no other living relatives, and she took a good look at him. He exuded the same brash confidence of years ago, and although his clothes might be top drawer, he still came across as common. He'd always lived on the wrong side of the law. Perhaps the law or some bigger and more vicious criminal would get the better of him one day. 'You take care too.'

They were closing in on Faye's farm. A big border collie came scampering out, guarding the property, but not aggressively. Susan remembered that the only things Kenny feared were dogs. She stepped in between them. 'Hey Sky, good boy. Lie down.' The dog lay down obediently. 'Don't worry, Kenny, he'll stay until he gets a command.'

Kenny glared at the dog and made a show of straightening his coat cuffs. 'Just as well for the bastard.'

'Sky!' It was Tristan, in the garb of a country gentleman, and Susan was glad he wasn't close enough to hear Kenny swear. Sky bounded off to him. 'Hello, Susan. Oh, you've got company.'

'Um, this is—'

'Susan's older brother,' Kenny said before she could think what to say. He kept his distance until Sky ran away into the farmyard. Then he went forward, all smiles, with his hand outstretched. 'Kenny Locke. Pleased to meet you, um...?'

Tristan's brow rose. He took an instant dislike to the man, and he could see Susan was uncomfortable in his presence. He glanced at her and smiled. 'I didn't know Susan had any family. I'm Tristan Harvey.'

'She only has me and her little girl. Harvey, eh? One of Susan's bosses. I trust you're looking after her properly.' Kenny's small hard eyes flicked from his sister to the man he'd summed up as a soft toff. A toff who admired Susan, going by the warm smile he'd given her.

'Susan is a great asset to the household.' Tristan didn't know how to take Kenny Locke's last remark.

'Look, afraid I've got to scootle off, me mate's due back for me any minute at the crossroads.' Kenny dipped a hand inside his breast pocket and took out a wad of notes inside a gilt clip. Before she could object, he thrust a five pound note into Susan's hand. 'For Maureen, buy her something nice or put it in post office savings for her. Say hello to her from her Uncle Kenny. Well, cheerio, sis. Good luck. Cheerio, Mr Harvey.' He turned on a flamboyant heel and strutted away.

Susan and Tristan stood together and watched him until he'd covered several yards. He didn't look back. Tristan rubbed the back of his neck. 'Well...'

'He's not the sort of relative you want to admit to,' Susan said. She folded the money and dropped it into her coat pocket. She didn't want Kenny's money, but she would put it away for Maureen's future.

'So you weren't pleased to see him?' It gave Tristan the excuse to look into her face as they fell into step to walk the short distance to the house.

'No, Kenny's bad news. He's vindictive.'

'Where was he going? Does he live locally?'

'No, thank goodness. He's going back up to London. Mr Harvey, can I ask you not to mention him to Maureen? Hopefully, he'll never came back and there's no point in her knowing about him.'

'Anything you say, Susan.' They were rounding the bend before the house came into view, and he wanted to enjoy this time of being alone with her. He'd like to ask her out to dinner, but it wasn't appropriate. How on earth was he to proceed with her? She had no idea he was taken with her, and the last thing he wanted was to hurt her. It didn't need a high degree of intelligence or foresight to realize she had suffered already in life. He'd made some discreet probing in the village about the state of her marriage, though all he'd learned was that she and Lance Dowling had 'seemed happy enough.' He should give up all thoughts of a closer attachment with her and simply treat her as an employee. But his heart was ruling his head; he hadn't expected to fall in love again, and he was bewitched and befuddled, and panic-stricken that he'd never win her. At least they now had shared a confidence. 'I heard Faye calling the children into the house a quarter of an hour ago. They were playing cowboys and Indians and making a terrific noise.'

'I hope Maureen won't get too excited

tonight and become a nuisance.' Susan frowned.

'Oh, she'd never be that. With the imagination she's got, she keeps the others continually interested in something, which means they don't grumble they're bored. She's a joy, a real sweetie.' This was true, and praising Maureen was a useful route by which he could make a favourable impression on Susan.

'I was thinking of Mark. He won't want to put up with a lot of giggling and racket.'

Tristan liked her calling Mark by his first name. Perhaps she might not mind if he suggested quite soon that she do the same to him. 'Don't worry about Mark. Justine will keep the children in line if they're bothersome, and they both like the children anyway. They played a game of marbles with the twins in the hall for a short while last evening. She's a lot of fun. She's lifted Mark's spirit no end.'

They had arrived at Tremore House and were strolling up the stone sett drive. 'Do you think they'll reconcile?'

'I hope so. I'd feel relieved about Mark's future, and watching them together I can't see any reason why they should part. Can you?'

'None at all.' In spite of her own unhappiness, Susan was conservative enough to believe that except for violence and persistent adultery, couples should stick to their marriage vows.

They entered by the back entrance. 'Well, here we are,' Tristan said, ushering her inside. 'I hope you enjoy your stay with us, Susan.'

'I'm sure I will.'

She headed off for the kitchen, leaving him in the back corridor, unaware that his good wishes had been so much more than a polite welcome.

Seven

After Sunday lunch at Tremore, Mark excused himself to take a rest. He got into bed in his underwear, tired but for once not exhausted, and he gazed up at the Art Nouveau frosted glass, hanging bells light, thinking he couldn't have come among better people, envying the extended family. He was an only child of uninterested parents, and he'd had no idea until now how natural and comforting a solid home life could be. From the serious talk round the table, he'd gleaned that one of the number from Ford Farm was having marriage difficulties, and the Boswelds and Harveys were all pulling together to form a network of support. The only encouragement he'd got off his parents was to do well at his lessons, to make them proud on the sports field and to marry a suitable girl. They'd approved of all his choices, but if they were still alive they'd be horrified at his and Justine's intention to divorce.

'All right, darling?' Not unexpectedly, Justine was there. She had fussed over him

105

since her arrival and he had enjoyed every moment of it.

'Just a little whacked. You don't need to keep tucking me up, darling.'

'I like to.' She knelt beside the bed and smoothed his brow. 'You mean a lot to me Mark. I'll be leaving here in a couple of days. Are you planning to come with me?'

'How do you mean? To get out of the Harveys' hair?'

'No. I mean what do you hope to do? Have you been able to think about the future yet? You're certainly not in Faye or Tristan's way. They obviously enjoy having you here, and so do all the children.'

Mark pushed back the bedcovers and sat up. 'You want to talk seriously, Justine? Good. I want that too. I'm not really sure where things stand between us now.'

Justine smiled into his eyes. Mark didn't own dreamboat looks, but no one would know, until his face filled out, how arresting and sexy his strong features normally were. She gentled a finger along his temple. 'Are you up to it?'

'Yes. We need to come to some firm decisions. I'll get up.'

'No, no, I'll get in there with you.' She kicked off her shoes, then started on the buttons at the front of her woollen frock. It was a short, plain, utility style. Justine had never bothered with fashions. 'I must get this

106

off, it will crease.'

Mark watched in profound amazement and pleasure as her gorgeous figure became revealed to him. Her magnificent breasts swelled above her brassiere and slip, the silky material of which clung to her generous curves. After their friendship had passed to passion and then marriage, her body, except during the weeks of his release from the convalescent home, had never failed to fill him with desire. Justine was usually of the same mind as he was, but she might not fancy him now he was skeletally thin and smelled offensively – he could not get the fear out of his mind that he stank, despite her reassurances.

With her half-naked before him he was consumed with a terrible lustful need, coupled with a ghastly sense of loss and shame. 'You may not want to come in here with me at this moment.' His voice emerged choked, in anguish, and he wrapped the covers tightly round his middle to hide his arousal.

'Don't be silly, darling,' she said, aware of his predicament. 'I'm pleased to know you're back on form. Let's not waste it.' She pushed a hand tantalizingly through her hair, then in slinky movements she peeled off her slip, her brassiere and French knickers.

Mark had never been more excited. He couldn't move to reach out for her, just stare like some famished beast. Justine pulled the bedcovers out of his grasp and he sat in stunned bliss as she pulled off his singlet. Coming to life all over his starved body, he shook and clumsily wriggled out of his underpants. He was in such a fever of anticipation he could hardly breathe. He could die later this afternoon and he wouldn't care a jot as long as he had Justine. He put his hungry hands on her. Such heaven! She pushed him down and climbed on him, clamped her hands over his and smiled a cat-like smile and licked her bottom lip, always guaranteed to drive him wild.

He went nearly out of his mind. 'Darling, don't be cruel!'

In the past she had sometimes teased him for ages, but she was too kind and wise to torment him now. As she joined them together, she sensed he was going to scream in ecstasy and she put a hand over his mouth. He let himself go with the delights she was giving him, and he used his hands to enchant her. He never closed his eyes when making love with her – she had so much for his eyes to feast on. She was good to him and he could do nothing but go with the exquisite rise and rise and flow and spread of the sensations he thought he'd never experience again.

He had no idea how much time had passed before she lay, hot and perspiring beside him and curled herself around him. He floated on the wonderful aftermath for some time. The daze he was in was not of the kind when his mind involuntarily shut itself off. He was sated. He had gloriously been given a 'good seeing to', an experience, fierce and erotic, emotional and fantastically selfish for him, that he and his fellow officers had dreamed about as they'd languished in capture. Malnutrition had quickly stolen their libido, but they'd taken comfort in fantasy. Many of the men had admitted their wives viewed sex as a duty, a cause for trepidation. How fortunate he was Justine was not like that. Gaining his breath, he kissed her hair. 'Sorry I couldn't do much, darling. Next time...'

She stayed quiet for a while. Holding him. Caring for him. 'Will there be a next time, Mark?'

'Mmm, yes please.'

'I enjoy making love to you so much, darling, but...'

Her hair was splayed on his chest and he twisted a lock of it around his finger, as if he was trying to hold on to her, but he knew that wasn't possible. It was a reality he didn't want to face right now, but he was going to have to be brave about it. 'You're trying to work out where we should go from here. I've thought a lot about us since you joined me. We can romp the life out of each other, and we admire and even love each other, yet we're more like the greatest of friends than husband and wife. You don't want to be settled down, do you, Justine? And I, well, I'd only really wanted the Army, to stay in it until old age or death saw me out of it, and now I've been denied that, I don't know ... I need time to work it out. But us staying married isn't going to work, is it?'

She threaded her fingers through his hand. 'You're so much wiser than I am. Braver too. I feel a bitch to be deserting you, although if you ever need me I'll always come to you, I swear. We probably wouldn't have married if our parents hadn't pushed us in that direction. I've never wanted a partnership and babies, and all that sort of thing. We've never talked about children. Do you want them, Mark?'

'I didn't particularly. You know what it's like for an Army brat – usually it's not much fun for kids. But now after being with the bunch of sweeties in this house, yes, perhaps, if I'm ever up to the responsibility of a family life. The Dowling girl has enormous appeal. Most men dream of having a son, but a little girl just like her would be good.'

'So, we've really no option but to end our marriage, go our different ways,' Justine heaved a long breathy sigh. 'It's the fairest thing to you. No one should be denied children. I don't know if I should feel relieved or tragic. Oh, God, Mark, this is so sad.'

She started to cry and Mark gently wiped

away her tears. 'Don't, darling. We could try to make a go of it. Kids don't matter, not really.' He cradled her, then said, 'But...'

'But what, darling? Don't be afraid to say.'

'I don't want to go back to Surrey. I haven't a clue what I want to do, only that it should be a completely fresh start somewhere else.'

'And I love my home, my job and my network of friends. We have no choice, Mark. It has to be a clean break, but we must remain friends. I couldn't bear it if we didn't.'

'Nor I. We'll stay in touch. You keep the house, of course. I'll sell the shares left to me and divide it up with what I have in the bank. I'll send for the rest of my stuff when I've settled somewhere, if that's all right.'

'Of course, it is, darling. But you keep your money. We've both got enough to live in comfort. And I've got my job.' Justine cried again.

Mark hugged her, forbidding tears of his own and staring up at the ceiling. *'Shikata ga nai koto.'*

Justine pushed the wetness away from her face. 'What's that, Mark?'

'It's a Jap saying. It means, if something is inevitable it's best to bend to it. That's the end of our marriage, Justine.' He gazed at her. 'It's terribly upsetting but we can start a new friendship. I want to see you again,

Justine. For us to be friends for life.'

She nodded. 'You bet. Come on, we must try to buck up. We'll get over this and it will be good, knowing we'll always have the other to turn to. Mark, what will you do immediately?'

'I sure as hell don't want to go far.' The thought panicked him. He wasn't ready yet to face a new place or strangers. 'I don't want to outstay my welcome here; perhaps Faye will rent me a cottage. In Sonkurai and Changi all a chap could do was to live one day at a time, sometimes to only get through the next hour. I'll just let things happen. God must have let me live for a purpose. Hopefully, that will become apparent.' He yawned, suddenly worn out. 'Can't stay awake. Stay with me until I fall asleep, Justine?'

'Of course, Mark,' she whispered soothingly. 'Close your eyes.'

Holding on to her, Mark fell out of consciousness. He wasn't at ease, and twitched and moaned. Justine held him and stayed with him all afternoon. When she surfaced, she would have a word with Faye.

Lottie had cooked a traditional roast for Nate. When ready to serve, she called him in from the garden, where he had slipped outside for a breather with Carl. He came inside, took off his and Carl's outdoor

112

clothes, then sat at the kitchen table with him on his lap. Lottie went to take Carl away.

'He's OK here, honey.' Nate wrapped his arms around his son. Carl, with his curly sandy hair, was a tiny replica of himself, and a joy and fascination to him. He mourned the loss of being here for his birth and so much of his development. He'd had no idea that a child, in his first year, grew from a babe-in-arms to a toddler with a love of exploring everything.

'He needs to go in his high chair. It doesn't do to change a child's routine.' Lottie tried to tug Carl out of his arms but Nate held on to him.

'I could have him here this once.' Nate was emphatic.

'No, you will not.' Lottie was as equally determined. 'Then he'll want to sit on your lap at every meal time and create a fuss when he's not allowed to. If you knew anything at all about bringing up children you'd know it's foolish to break their routine. Give Carl to me. You're not being fair to him.'

Nate handed the boy over with a sigh. He could see the sense in what Lottie said, but he made the sigh one of being hard done by. He wouldn't have minded if Lottie hadn't sounded so impatient with him. He had looked forward to seeing his family so much and had been bewildered and disillusioned on his arrival to overhear Lottie's resentful words. His plan at not saying exactly when he was coming but to surprise her had been a miserable failure, and Lottie operated as if she had unspoken accusations against him. It not only hurt him it was bringing down the atmosphere in the farmhouse, where before, except for the dreadful time when Will Harvey's plane had been shot down by enemy fire, Nate had known only contented chatter, warmth and laughter.

'Have I done something to offend Lottie?' he'd asked Emilia. She'd replied that he must speak to Lottie. But Lottie was reluctant to talk. He would have it out with her today. His in-laws had left them to themselves for this reason, and no matter how difficult Lottie became, he'd not let it go until they'd settled whatever was wrong. He loved Lottie so much, and all he wanted was for their marriage to be strong, to find their own perfect farm, and to raise Carl and a brood of kids.

'Food smells delicious.' He'd make every effort to win her round, and when Carl was taking his nap he'd get her to talk. He would tread carefully. Lottie was headstrong. The first time he'd met her, at a dance in the village, she'd been ripping into some GIs. They had not been bothering her, just trying to be friendly, but she had made up her mind she loathed Americans and showed it by her being rude and superior. She'd been different with him. Remembering how she had looked aghast at her behaviour when encountering him, how innocent and sweet she really was, reminded him why he'd fallen so deeply in love with her.

'It's great having the place to ourselves, isn't it, darling? I'm sorry we've missed out on the farm you wanted us to buy. I should have listened to you. After all, you know best about property round here. We'll have a wonderful time searching for our own place, I promise. We'll find the perfect place for us, Lottie, darling. I want our life to be perfect.'

He gave her a beautiful smile, and Lottie melted inside as she put the platter of pork in front of him to carve. How could she have doubted Nate loved her? Had put her second place to his old life? He was here now and she had him for the rest of her life. She went to him and hugged him tight. It was so good touching him, holding him. 'Thanks, darling. I want that too. I thought I'd open a tin of peaches from the crate, with clotted cream for dessert. Would you like that?'

He slipped an arm round her waist and kissed her shapely cleavage. 'Yes, and then I want to make love to you. We haven't made love yet.' His voice was husky and raw with desire.

Lottie was consumed with heat below her waist. It seemed crazy they had held off in the bedroom – her doing: she knew she had made Nate unsure about approaching her. Which was a crime. Their lovemaking before had been passionate and uninhibited, and physically he had everything that was arousing. A well drawn face, enticing full mouth, muscular vigorous body, and knowing hands. She glanced at Carl. He was becoming drowsy. She had his food pureed and ready to eat. 'Let me feed Carl and put him down to sleep. We can eat later.'

Shortly, with Carl flat out in the nursery, Lottie and Nate were eagerly undressing each other in their room. They didn't get far. Their need was too great and they fell down on the bed, coupled, and cried out in naked rapture and set about making love in almost fanatical motion.

'I love you,' he rasped through the almost excruciating joy of being intimate with her again.

He was holding her so tightly her breath was in danger of being cut off, but she did not feel the crushing. 'I love you,' she got out, her face distorted with pleasure.

Noisy cries heralded the end. They clung on to each other, tighter and tighter, touching, stroking. Rediscovering all the old wonders and delights. Forgetting the pain of their long separation and glorying in this new bliss.

'You're so beautiful,' he crooned. 'My

darling Lottie...'

'So are you.' She admired every part of him. 'Darling Nate...'

'Tell me what I did wrong, darling,' he whispered, kissing her lips, her brow, her eyes. 'Let's get it out of the way then we can get on with the rest of our lives.'

'It all seems so silly now.' In the afterglow of their lovemaking, the wonderful closeness of being a woman with her man, her months of resentment did seem silly. 'I simply thought you were staying in Texas too long. Was I being selfish?'

'A little.'

She didn't like that. He didn't have to say it so fast. Instead, it should have been, 'Of course you weren't being selfish, darling, I'm sorry you thought that.'

'Oh?'

'Well, it took a while for all the legal documents for my emigration to be properly completed. Then I stayed on at the ranch to say goodbye to one of my dearest friends, Jake Olsen, the ranch foreman. I mean to say goodbye to him at the end of his life. He'd been like a second daddy to me and he was dying of cancer.' There was a sob in Nate's voice.

'I'm sorry.' Lottie felt awful about his friend, but she was still crestfallen that he hadn't thought about how his decision might affect her.

'So you see, I couldn't leave him until he'd gone and been buried. It helped me to leave my old life behind, Lottie. To cut the ties which was really hard. It made me look forward more than ever to seeing you and our little boy.'

'I'm glad,' Lottie said. Then she kept silent.

After a bit, Nate asked, 'You do understand, honey?'

'I understand your reasons for staying on until your friend had died, of course I do. But why couldn't you tell me about him? It would have saved me from weeks of feeling rejected, that I wasn't the most important person in your life.' She moved away and picked up her cardigan to cover her nakedness. 'We shouldn't have secrets, Nate. I'm not sure I like being shut out of part of your life.'

He reached and put a hand on her shoulder. 'Oh, God, Lottie, I hadn't thought of it like that. I didn't deliberately shut you out of my life back home. I talked about you all the time, and showed the guys and the folks in town your and Carl's pictures. I've been a fool, haven't I? I've messed up.'

She was quiet for a moment. 'We don't really know each other, do we? We've never had the chance to. I hope you won't regret giving up the ranch and coming over here to be with me.'

'It was my decision when we got engaged,

Lottie. I'd got no folks left while you've got a whole heap of them. I'll never regret it, Lottie. Life without you would be like drifting along on an empty cloud. Now we've got the rest of our lives to get to know each other. I hope there won't be too many rocks in our path.' She was reassured at last and let him gather her into him. 'Let's make plans. Look for our own place and create our own little nest. That OK with you?'

'Absolutely. I've been jealous of Tom and Jill, hearing them decide what they'll do to the old wing, watching Mum and Pappa living their happy lives.'

'We'll go to the land agents first thing tomorrow. Then when we've found the perfect place and settled in, how about we take a honeymoon? We deserve that, but you deserve it most of all.'

'Thanks, Nate, you say the nicest things.' She grinned at him. 'You already know I can be a touchy madam. Will used to say I was insufferable. I hope you don't discover lots of things about me you don't like.'

'And you about me. My momma used to say I could out-stubborn a mule when I had a mind to.'

Lottie clung to him in a moment of panic. Meeting Nate, falling for him and marrying him had all happened under romantic skies. Giving birth to Carl, as harrowing as it had been, had happened in the security of her home. Now at last she was a proper wife, and would soon be responsible for her own home and family. Nate may have moved two thousand miles, but she was also about to give up everything she was familiar with. 'It's a bit scary, isn't it?'

'A little, I guess. We'll be fine if we pull together, treat it as an adventure.'

'You make it sound easy.'

'Yeah, easy.'

'Easy...' She chewed that simple little word over in her mind.

'There's one thing that is very easy,' Nate said. 'Making love to you, darling.' He started familiarizing himself again with her beautiful contours.

On a thought that was terrible to her she heaved him away. 'Wait!'

'What's wrong?' He was disappointed and alarmed.

'We need to be careful. We weren't before. Oh damn! I don't want another baby.' All the women who had spoken to her about labour and childbirth had said you soon forget the pain and discomfort. It might have been like that for them, but they hadn't gone through what she had.

'It'll be all right, honey,' Nate soothed, taking her back into his arms. 'In fact, Carl will be just the right age to have a little brother or sister.' He trailed determined kisses along her chin and throat, aiming for her lips. 'It might be too late anyway.'

She just managed not to scream, 'I'd better not be pregnant!' She leaned her head away from him. 'Gosh, I'm suddenly ravenous. Could we go down for dinner?'

Nate made a wry face. Lottie was worried: would they have another disagreement already? 'OK,' he said. 'Anything you say, honey.'

Anything she said? The future easy? Lottie dressed, hiding her fears that she might just have got pregnant. And if she wasn't, what would Nate say over her determination not to have any more children?

Eight

Faye was hurrying along the lane towards the crossroads. She had a folder, a notebook and a fountain pen in a satchel, her intention being to begin a series of calls on her tenants and make reports of any repairs necessary or damage done to her properties. Her main reason for going this way, however, was to catch up with Mark. She had watched from her bedroom window as he'd left the house to see which direction he'd take. In the last few months he'd taken a walk every day, covering more distance as his recuperation progressed. With nothing stressful thrown at him, which Faye went to every length to avoid, he'd not had a single episode of sliding into a trance in that time, not at Tremore anyway. He kept away from the village. Inevitably, he had met one or two locals on his walks, but he'd said he'd been happy to spend a few minutes chatting to them.

Justine had asked her to look after Mark, but there had been no need, it was a pleasure. With his wife out of the picture, Faye had examined her feelings for Mark. It might be a 'nurse-patient thing', or that she simply felt sorry for him, but she thought not. She had fallen in love with him. She had no idea why it had happened. She accepted it. She wanted it. She wanted him. As he was and how he would be when he was completely well. Or as well as he ever could be. Justine had explained his problem of switching off from reality was caused by the terrible beatings he'd received from labour camp guards while defending the rights of his mates and the men in the ranks. Every opportunity had been taken to humiliate the officers.

Justine had shown her a photo of Mark in his former days. 'Not a good-looker in the usual sense, I'm sure you'll agree,' she'd said, studying his likeness with deep affection, making Faye anxious. 'But alluring with his natural charm, and very sexy. All the girls used to chase him.' Justine had caught him: how on earth could she give him up? It was all very strange to Faye, but she was wholeheartedly glad about it.

Mark wasn't walking fast, even though he could now, and she quickly ate up the distance between them. She could see he was enjoying the first awakenings of spring in the hedgerows and ditches, the bright yellow gorse and celandines. He stooped and sniffed a vivid purple dog violet. As he raised his head he saw her. He pointed to a spot where two moss-covered stones, formed like a step, were flanked by delicate pale-lemon and pink primroses. 'Beautiful, aren't they? And the snowdrops are still about. Are you going my way, Faye?'

Unaware she was doing it, Faye fussed with her military-look doublet jacket. She always took pains to look her best for him. She was wearing a colourful silk scarf, smart dark trousers and her most attractive pair of flat shoes. She'd gone through the agonies of waving her shoulder-long hair with metal combs, and she had carefully applied her make-up. Not too bright a red lipstick or any eyebrow pencil: Mark had mentioned he didn't care for movie star looks.

She told Mark why she was out. 'Uncle Tris has seen to this sort of thing since my father left to train secretly for the war effort. I've been wrapped up in domestic affairs, but I feel it's time I took over. I haven't even met some of the tenants, the frail and the elderly and those who never turn up for village events.'

'Who's first on the list?' Mark said, throwing away the stub of a cigarette and falling in step with her. He was gazing up and all about as if he'd never before seen a lightly-clouded blue sky, or a tiny brown sparrow on the wing, or sheep grazing in a meadow. Faye had no idea how during his captivity he'd dreamed of such simple pleasures.

'If we turn right in a minute, the first place

is just round the corner. A tied cottage where one of the farm workers lives. There are two more cottages side by side as you climb the hill, then further on down the other side of the hill there's Susan's. I thought I'd go to hers first and call on the others on the way back.' She hoped he'd accompany her to Little Dell, to have some time with him alone. At home he rested and was often monopolized by Pearl and the twins, or playing snooker with her uncle. 'I know Susan's working at the house at the moment, and she says all is in order at Little Dell, but she's so modest she might not ask for any improvements. I thought I'd take a look at the outside for myself.'

'It's pretty sound, I'd say. I was there the other afternoon. Susan was home and I had a cup of tea with her. It's very well done up inside, she's got some good pieces of furniture.'

'Oh, you didn't mention it, Mark.' Faye made her voice sound light. Nor had Susan mentioned it. He got on well with her, hopefully not too well.

'Maureen was tearing about in the lane in a cart made from old pram wheels. I thought it looked a bit dangerous, so I took the liberty of taking her home and pointing it out to Susan. She was really grateful. I fixed the wheels tightly and even managed to fit some brakes. Can't say how pleased I was, first time I'd been able to do anything useful in a long time. I guess I forgot until now that I'd been there, the old memory not being too good. Maureen's such a delight. I don't think Susan has a clue what she gets up to with the twins and little Pearl,' he said fondly.

'How do you know what Maureen does?' Faye hid the heaviness in her heart. Mark never mentioned Simon. He played with him occasionally, but not for long.

'She tells me.'

'She does?' Now she had to keep her jealousy in check. 'She's always whispering to Uncle Tris too, and he's very fond of her.' This wasn't a lie. Her uncle often singled Maureen out and she responded to him eagerly. It stood out miles that he adored Susan and was using kindness to her daughter to impress her, although he genuinely doted on Maureen; she was an easy child to get along with, cheerful and bright.

They reached the crossroads. A new white-painted metal signpost had been recently erected. The direction they had come from indicated Hennaford, two miles. Straight across indicated a route that would lead eventually to Redruth, and the left was the short distance to Zelah, then Truro at six miles away. They turned right – it led on to Taldrea, Goonhaven and Perranporth – and they started up the steep Greet Hill. They passed the first tied cottage; the usual white-washed affair, where laundry for a family of five fluttered gaily in the breeze. Watching Mark closely, she went on, 'So Susan invited you inside for tea? I'm a bit surprised. She's usually so reserved. What did you talk about?'

'This and that. You, mostly.'

'Oh?' Faye was cheered. 'Why?'

'We were saying how grateful we are to you. Susan's happy in her job and she's delighted that you and Tristan treat Maureen the same as the other children. We both admire you.' He strode along without bothering to keep his walking boots out of mud or cattle fouling, wiping his hand down his sweater when it got dirty with moss and grit from prodding into a dry stone wall. Faye frowned. He gave Susan a lot of extra laundry, for he cared nothing about smartness. 'Oh, sorry, I'm too used to ... different conditions. It alters your values.'

'It's all right,' she smiled.

'You're too kind,' he smiled back. 'You come from a nice family. Tris has told me about your father, how he was killed while working as a saboteur with the French Resistance. You must be very proud of him.'

'I am. He worked first as an S.O.E. Then he was betrayed by a member of the Vichy, his wireless operator was shot. He could have come home, but he chose to fight on with the maquis. He did a lot of brave things and was shot by the Germans just before D-Day. I think they had respect for him for the daring things he did, although if he'd lived they would have tortured him for information. We didn't really have a good relationship. After my mother left him and took me to America he disowned me.'

'I'm sorry, that must have been rough.'

'It was, very. I came to England before the war, to train for the ballet. I grew too tall, but I wasn't quite good enough anyway. The academy was evacuated to Scotland. I left when I was old enough and worked as a secretary on a large estate.' With her face on fire, she admitted, praying it wouldn't put him off her, but she felt it important he knew the truth, 'I, um, had an affair with the laird. He was a dashing sort. I was infatuated with him. He's Simon's father. He was estranged from his wife but didn't intend to get a divorce. I don't suppose it would have worked out anyway.'

'But you have a wonderful little boy,' Mark said matter-of-factly.

'Yes. Some people think I'm brave for not making up a lie about being widowed; it would have been easy enough with the war on. Sometimes I wish I had; not everyone approves of me, of course, and it makes things difficult.'

'That's a great pity. All new life should be

celebrated. Never regret your decision, Faye.'

'My biggest regret is my father not knowing about Simon. I came down to Cornwall hoping to build up a relationship with him, but he went off for his training and never came back. I should have brought Simon down with me from the start, but I was only nineteen, unsure of myself, and at the time I was afraid my father would shun both of us.' She couldn't prevent tears wetting her eyes over her father's coldness, and then at how during his undercover training he'd realized he loved her. He'd written to tell her so and how he wanted so much to see her and be a proper father to her. With the secrecy of his future mission paramount, she'd been unable to receive the letter until after his death. She filled Mark in on the facts. 'He was a very troubled man. He'd wanted to fight in the Great War, but an accident prevented it and he became bitter. When my mother left him she was pregnant, but the baby was actually my Uncle Alec's, Aunt Emilia's first husband. I loathed my father for denying his son, my brother, but I didn't know the truth then. Oh,' she wiped her tears away with the heel of her hand. 'Yes, I do belong to a nice family, but one with a chequered history. I take comfort in knowing my father died doing something he believed in. And I think he would have accepted Simon and even been proud of him.'

Mark touched her arm. 'Thanks for confiding in me. I'm sure if he'd made it back he would have been a changed man because he'd have had you and Simon to live for.'

'That's what I intend to tell Simon when he's old enough.' Faye was uplifted. She and Mark had consolidated a closer friendship. She would like him to talk about his life. He never mentioned Justine, but she must be on his mind often, for they wrote and phoned each other regularly.

Near the top of the hill were the next two adjoining cottages. Here thick woods towered up on either side of the road. The hedges were high and the trees were bent over them forming a canopy, at times blotting out the sun, making the stretch seem dark and chilly, only allowing the sun to sparkle through here and there. Mark looked up, blinked and shook his head, trying to dislodge disturbing memories. It wasn't unbearably hot and steamy here, but it did remind him of the terrible marches through the jungle. Not looking where he was going, his foot hit a large loose stone and he stumbled. The torment of the thick tangles of Thai overgrowth meant he'd never stayed firmly on his feet for long. He looked down, not seeing dusty tarmac now but treacherous snake-infested jungle floor. He looked up and saw not glimpses of a gentle sun under an English sky above elms and oaks but an unmerciful burning orb peeking spitefully through wild out-of-control trees and creepers. Midges and thousands of other insects were feasting on his skin, leaving bites that stung and itched unmercifully. At all costs he must try to keep his eye on the men as they marched mile after exhausting mile to work on the railway. If any fell behind, Thai bandits would creep out like ghostly shadows and murder would be certain. A tropical storm lashed down out of nowhere, drenching him to the bones, flailing his burning sore flesh, making visibility non-existent and turning the ground knee-deep in mud. Each step took an enormous effort. Each breath in the choking steam had to be fought for.

He slowed down and slowed again. Faye watched him. He was dragging his feet, as if they were too heavy to bear him along, each step a terrible strain that was draining the essence out of him. 'All right, Mark?' His face was tense and knotted with pain, his shoulders drooping. He was like a man suddenly twice his age. She could see he was suffering some dreadful flashback. She took his hand, knowing he couldn't feel the comforting pressure, knowing he couldn't hear her voice. 'It's all right. Don't worry. We'll keep going until we're out in the sunlight again. It's not far.'

They cleared the trees and Faye led him into the middle of the lane, hoping he'd become aware of the light and the sun. She was so absorbed with him she was unaware of a van being driven along the road, albeit slowly and carefully. The driver tooted the horn. She jumped in fright and pushed Mark into the hedge. The driver stopped in a passing place and got out, clearly worried. 'Miss Faye, you didn't see me. Are you all right? Is he hurt?'

'Oh,' she gasped. 'We're both fine, I think. I'm sorry, Jim.'

It was the local builder, Jim Killigrew, who lived in Ford House, just below Ford Farm, where he had formerly worked as a labourer. In his early forties, a well-built, fair-haired individual, he had lost his left arm in the Merchant Navy after the torpedoing of his ship. He managed to drive his old green van and go about his work with the aid of a false limb with a double hook. 'This your guest, former Lieutenant Fuller, then? Poor bugger. Anything I can do?'

'He just needs to be kept quiet. I'd be grateful, Jim, if you stayed for a while, just in case he needs to be driven back to the house.'

'Of course.' Jim peered at Mark from sympathetic blue eyes. 'Must have been pretty bad for him. He's as thin as a yard of pump water; bloody crime, it was. We could put him to sit in the van.'

'Yes, thank you. No! He'd be even more confused to come round in a strange vehicle. He's not been too bad lately. Hopefully, he'll come out of it soon. If we just stay still for a while.'

Five minutes passed. 'How's the family, Jim?' He had married a retired Methodist minister's daughter, and years ago they had adopted two orphans.

'Fine, thanks. Alan's rebuilding a porch in Goonhaven. I've just dropped him off. He'll cycle home. Martha's happy working at the bank in Truro. Elena's the same as always, running about doing good deeds. She's really content, even putting on weight. We're lucky, Miss Faye. I got back nearly intact, nothing wrong in my mind, not like this poor bloke.'

'I'm pleased all is well for you, Jim. And the business? I know you're shortly to start on something for my cousin Tom. I'm about to look over all my tenants' houses. None of them have indoor lavatories or bathrooms. That's not acceptable any more. When I know the requirements, would you be interested in the work?'

'Be more'n happy to, Miss Faye. We can come to an arrangement about a job lot. Ah, look, Mr Fuller's coming round. Shall I go on my way? Don't want to embarrass him.'

'That's very thoughtful of you, Jim. Also,

could you not mention this to anyone except Elena?'

'Will do. Hear from you in due course then.' Jim drove off, whistling 'Kalamazoo'.

'Ohh...' Mark stretched out his arms. 'Did I switch off?'

'Just for a minute or two,' Faye replied. 'Want to go back?'

'No, really. Faye, I'm sorry if you find what happens to me a bit too strange.'

'Not at all, Mark.' Sensitively, she carried on walking and spoke of it no more. 'Look there, through the trees, you can see Rose Dew, it's reputed to be haunted. It gives everyone the heebie-jeebies, even from here it make me feel shivery.'

'There's nothing to be scared of,' Mark said in all confidence.

'You've been there?' She gazed at him as they started down the meandering hill.

'I've looked over it a couple of times. Nothing worried me there.'

'So you don't think it's haunted?'

'I didn't say that.'

Faye shivered, glad she could feel the warm sun on her back. The castle in Scotland where she'd lived and worked had been haunted by a legendary amount of ghosts, of people who all had, apparently, met tragic deaths. She had seen or heard nothing unusual herself, but the atmosphere had occasionally been dark and grim, as if itself a premonition of something brooding in the air waiting to pounce. 'What do you mean? I wonder if Susan finds it creepy living near-by.'

'She does at times, she forbids Maureen to play there.' Again, Faye was narked at his easy references to Susan, and that he knew more about her daily help than she did. 'The first time I approached Rose Dew I saw an old man. He was standing quite still beside the cottage. He could have been anyone, of course, someone out for a stroll. I called to him. He didn't answer. I thought perhaps he was deaf, or some crotchety old local who considered me a trespasser. The more I climbed up towards him the less distinct he became. It was like those dreams you have when the more you try to get close to some-one the further they are away. Then he dis-appeared.'

'What? You mean one moment he was there and the next he was gone?' Faye looked about, fearful she'd see a strange figure.

'Yes. I could have blinked, I suppose, but he couldn't have walked away that quickly. And I'm convinced I didn't look away, be-cause there was something compelling about him.' Mark was totally unconcerned about the possibility of having seen a ghost. He was sure he'd seen the ghosts of his dead friends and other servicemen, and of coolie peasants also forced to work on the Burma-Thailand

135

railway. He had heard stories of ghosts from other men, too, most of whom were now dead themselves. Sometimes it had brought comfort – a mate bringing a goodwill message. Some chaps had thought the visions to be hallucinations brought about from starvation or the variety of dangerous fevers. To Mark it had been a fact – someone had died and had appeared as a ghost, part of them lingering on for some reason.

'And you say he was old?'

'It's the impression I got.'

'What were his clothes like?'

'Just dark.' He thought about it. 'A working man's clothes. The elderly in the village might know of any deaths there. Agnes would probably know. Could simply be some old soul who passed away peacefully in his sleep and likes to come back and take a look at his garden. He wouldn't be too pleased with its current state, though. It's a mess of overgrowth. Needs a few trees cut back from it, too, before the place can be made habitable again.'

Faye was frowning. 'I don't think I'll have anything done to it except pulled down for safety reasons.'

'Oh, you can't do that.' Mark shook his head. 'The cottage is quite sound. The roof needs new slates and it needs up-to-date plumbing, of course. Homes are needed, Faye, there's a chronic housing shortage.'

'I know that,' Faye said, considering his opinion, which had been delivered in a typical officer's tone, direct but not patronizing. She was pleased he was feeling in control of things. 'I suppose you're right. I'll talk to Uncle Tris about it.'

They had arrived at the entrance to Little Dell and followed the stony, rutted track. 'This must prove an awful trek for Susan while coming and going in wet and wintry conditions. I'll see about a proper path being laid up to her door.'

'I observed something while in her kitchen, or rather there was something I didn't see,' Mark said, his eyes on the little planked front door, which was pleading for fresh brown paint.

'Oh, what was that?' Just how much interest was he taking in Susan and her life? Faye then had a thought that was both wrong and selfish but which she did nothing to shake off: she must think of ways to keep him and Susan apart.

'There were no photos of her husband. A widow usually proudly displays photos of her dead warrior husband in uniform, but there's none of Lance Dowling inside, not even a wedding snap. That can only point to one thing. Susan was very unhappily married, to the point that she can't bear having a photo of her husband on display even after his death. Must be why she's so guarded, why she's not interested in men. It's a shame that an attractive young woman as she is seems resigned to a lonely life. Sorry, I'm sounding like a gossip-monger, aren't I?'

'Not at all, I'm interested in Susan's welfare.' And in what might happen between her and the man at her side. With polite and caring friendship from an unpretentious man as Mark, and who showed affection for her daughter, Susan might be led to notice him. But he wasn't the only man in that category, and before she could put a brake on her tongue or consult commonsense, Faye blurted out, 'So is Uncle Tris. He dotes on Maureen and is quite taken with Susan.'

'He is?' Mark made a face. 'You mean in the sense of...? But he's old enough to be her father.'

'That shouldn't matter. Susan is mature, and my uncle is in no way a Don Juan.'

They reached Susan's garden, cultivated with early vegetables. Mark made no more mention of her.

Faye was thinking what to say next when she was suddenly knocked off her feet. She screamed shrilly. A dark shaggy creature ran away from her and shot off towards Rose Dew. Fear clutched her every nerve. She had been attacked, by some fearsome being.

'Faye!' Mark helped her up. 'Are you hurt?'

'I – I don't think so.' Her eyes were rooted in fear up the track to the forsaken cottage, which was just in view. It was surrounded by shadows. 'We should get away from here. I wonder if Susan would prefer to live somewhere else?'

'Why?' Mark was giving her a clean handkerchief. 'Faye, what's the matter? You seem really scared.'

'I was just attacked by a monster. A ghost.' She was incredulous he was taking this so lightly.

'No, you weren't.' He couldn't help smiling. She looked like a sweet, frightened girl. 'It was a stray. I've seen him about a few times. I keep a biscuit in my pocket just in case, and he knows that. He trusts me now. He must have been creeping up to me then ran and skidded in his eagerness to get something to eat that he didn't have to forage for. It's only a dog, Faye. He must be more scared than you are.'

This was the worst moment of her life. She had made a complete fool of herself. She rubbed at her dirty jacket and trousers. 'I must look a mess.'

'You look lovely. You always do.' He turned and headed off up the track, taking a biscuit out of his pocket. 'Hey, here boy! I've got something for you.'

Faye was still a little shocked, but full of joy that he'd paid her a compliment. So he had noticed her. Brilliant! She was bubbling over inside like a young girl out on a secret tryst.

She loved Mark even more. She had to have him and she'd do anything to get him. She stopped wiping herself down and went after him.

The stray dog ambled shamefacedly back down the track towards Mark, who kept encouraging it while crouching low. Faye stood back a few inches and watched, believing, as the dog took the biscuit from Mark's hand and allowed him to pat its filthy back, that it was the most charming scene she'd ever seen. Faye wasn't fond of dogs, she allowed none in the house despite the Smiths' pleas for a pet, pointing out there was a collie and two gun dogs on the farm they could romp with, but now she had found a way to impress Mark. 'Oh, the poor thing. No wonder he's wary, lots of pets have been killed because people aren't prepared to stretch their rations. It looks like a Labrador-cross. You can hardly tell with his coat so terribly matted. He needs a bath and a good feed.'

'You mean it's all right to take him back and clean him up? I thought it too much of an imposition to ask before. I've tried washing him down in the stream, but he was too hungry to want to hang about.'

'Well, we can't just leave him here. He's quite young and has survived so far, but it's only a matter of time before someone shoots him, perhaps even someone from the farm. You've gained his trust, Mark, he deserves to be taken care of.' Cautiously she reached a hand out to the dog. It edged away.

Mark held on to him. 'Are you sure? He could sleep in the ancillary room. I'll find something to make him a bed. I'm handy at knocking things together. I'll pay for his food and veterinary treatment, of course. Thanks a million, Faye! You're one of the best.' He looked at Faye with sparkling eyes. He was so different to when weariness was weighing him down and when his mind shut itself off. 'I think he'll follow me. Come on, Addi.'

Faye went first so the dog wouldn't feel threatened by her. She would abandon her task for the day. She couldn't call on her tenants in her messed-up state anyway. Mark took a few steps away from the dog and called to him. It followed, halted, then padded along as Mark kept up the friendly encouragement. 'You already have a name for him, Mark?' she looked over her shoulder.

'I've been calling Addi for a while. It's after one of my closest friends, Lieutenant Clive Addison. He didn't make it back from Changi. He'd be thrilled about this. We used to talk about getting home and keeping dogs.' Instead of eating the scraggy mutts they'd felt lucky to lay their desperate hands on, or cats and any other remotely edible creature, living or dead.

'Well, Addi's on his way to his new home now.'

'You're so kind, Faye. Don't worry, we won't impose on you forever. We'll get our own little place, and I've an idea about that.'

'You're not ready for that yet, Mark,' Faye asserted, her heart plummeting. 'Have you thought where you'd like to settle – one day?'

'Not until a few minutes ago. Not too far away, perhaps.'

She was pleased at this. Her greatest fear was that he'd return to Surrey or decide on somewhere else far away. Next instant she was in for a sharp drop in her hopes when he said, 'Come on, Addi. Let's see if Susan's got some tasty leftovers. Maureen's going to love you.'

Tristan had spent the early part of the morning in the garden, sowing marrow, salad beets and rows of carrots. Tremore was self-sufficient in food and there was too much work for the elderly, part-time gardener to cope with alone. Knowing Faye had left the house shortly after Mark, and with the children at school, and Simon in with Agnes, he could hardly wait to go in for his morning coffee and spend time alone with Susan. He shrugged off the old cricket jumper he kept for outdoor work, changed his boots for shoes, and whistled merrily as he washed his hands in the scullery. He studied his reflection in the bottom of a gleaming copper saucepan. Did he look his fifty-four years?

Older? Perhaps he could allow himself three or four years younger. Agnes often said he 'did himself proud' and 'was 'in fine fettle', but he didn't know what she'd meant in terms of his age, and he hadn't cared about it until now. True, he had a slim waistline and held himself straight. He didn't have many frown lines or crow's feet, and the silver in his black hair gave him a touch of dash, so he hoped. Perhaps he should lose the moustache. It might make him look a little more youthful.

'Are you out of your head?' he whispered to his suddenly nerve-stricken image. 'You've finished with that sort of thing, love and romance. And Susan wouldn't possibly want someone so much older. If you want female company, pick someone your own age. A matronly type who wants nothing more than companionship.' But he wasn't ready to be put into that category yet.

He chastised himself further, putting every obstacle in the way of forming something close and meaningful with Susan. He did this a hundred times a day, and into the small hours each night, for his brain was in a constant whirl about her and he couldn't sleep. Did he have bags and dark circles under his eyes? He thrust his face forward to consult the saucepan. 'You really are mad. You've never been vain before.' But it wasn't vanity, he was just anxious to know if he looked a suitable prospect for Susan. He didn't want her horrified at the prospect that a haggard, middle-aged man was trying to impose himself on her. Or worse still, that he wanted to get her into bed. Susan seemed to like and trust him. He couldn't bear to lose their polite and informal relationship.

He'd go back to the garden, then. Or to the farm and get a drink there. He went to the door, opened it, looked down at his earthy boots lined up beside the iron scraper. A token gesture. How could it be otherwise? He wasn't going anywhere, except to the kitchen, where Susan was probably putting the kettle on for her own morning break. He'd allow her to pour his coffee and then he'd take it outside. Like hell, he would. He came up with all the possibilities and hopes. That Susan might, *just might*, somehow, some day, if he went about it the right way, and if the gods were kind to him, and if fate played some magnificent hand, that she might see him differently than as one of her employers. Was it such a strange thing to hope that she might even fall in love with him? He had a lot to offer her and Maureen, security, a better home, status. He'd happily settle for Susan seeing him as the provider of these things and hope she'd view him with affection. These were the other thoughts that kept him awake at night and filled him with daytime fancies. But he wasn't going to win her by dithering on the doorstep.

He tried to ignore the horrible squirming feeling in the pit of his stomach. Susan was on the other side of the kitchen door. 'Right then. Through the door and into battle, so to speak.' He straightened his collar-less, open-neck shirt, grinning to himself. Then he collapsed inside. 'Oh God,' he looked up in agony, spreading imploring hands. 'Do I have to go on behaving in these idiotic over-jolly terms?'

Susan wasn't in the kitchen. His heart crashed down to the shiny tiles beneath his feet. Had she gone shopping? He touched the kettle on the range. It was cold. She hadn't had her break. She could be somewhere in the house. Right, he'd look about for her, on the pretext he'd forgotten his cigarettes.

He listened for her singing. There was silence. What day was it? What was her routine? He was so flustered he couldn't remember. The library door was open. There she was, her ash-blonde hair shining like a sheet gold where the sun beamed down on her, a picture of youth and loveliness. She could have been wearing a floating evening gown with jewels in her hair, for he did not see her plain dress, apron and boring shoes. She was gazing down at the long library table, her caddy of cleaning things on a chair.

He stole up beside her. 'Hello.' He used the softest voice.

She looked up. 'Mr Tristan. I'm sorry, I was looking at these.' She indicated a mass of photographs spread across the table. 'You'll be wanting your coffee.'

'In a minute,' he said. He wasn't going to waste the opportunity of holding her interest in something. 'I've been sorting them out to put into separate albums for my children. They tell my family story.' He pointed out his parents and brothers.

'It must be sad for you, losing all your brothers,' Susan said with sympathy.

'Yes. I miss them a lot. Don't know what I'd have done if Faye and Simon hadn't turned up.'

'You've had a lot of tragedy, but you've got the Smith children here now.'

You and Maureen too, if you're willing, one day.

She picked up a studio portrait of Winifred Harvey, which showed her patrician grace. 'I saw your wife about a week before she was knocked down, while you were both here on a visit. I was walking to the shop and she was taking a stroll in the lane. We chatted about how the war was going and she kindly asked me if I was coping all right.'

'That was Winnie,' Tristan said, sad again at his loss. 'Kind to a fault. I was very lucky to have had her.' He showed Susan other

146

photos. 'This is our daughter Adele in her Wrens uniform. She married a naval captain last year and they're currently in Hong Kong, where's he serving. And this is Winnie's daughter, my stepdaughter, Vera Rose. She lives in London. And this handsome chap,' he went on proudly, 'is my son Jonny, by my first wife.'

Susan took the photo of a strikingly good-looking RAF officer. 'Oh, I've met him too.'

'He didn't bother you, I hope. He's a bit of a one for the ladies.' Tristan smiled down fondly at the picture that displayed his son's thick coal-black hair and gleaming white teeth.

'I gathered that. He was charm itself. The sort to make you feel you're the only woman in the world. Maureen was with me, she said she's going to marry him when she grows up.' Susan laughed. 'How's his hand now? I know he got shot down just after D-Day and suffered some burns.'

'It allows him to instruct the younger pilots, but he gets frustrated he can no longer zoom along looping the loop.'

Susan pointed to a lady in an ankle-length suit, a high-neck lace blouse, and a wide-brimmed hat over a cottage-loaf hairstyle. 'Who's this, may I ask? She's so beautiful.'

Tristan took a moment to answer. Herein lay some of his saddest memories. 'That was Jonny's mother, Ursula. She died when he

147

was five years old, from childbirth ... it wasn't my baby.'

'I'm sorry. I didn't mean to upset you.'

Tristan loved her for the compassion in her eyes. 'It's a long story. I was on injury leave from the Front, and Ursula was about to leave me for her lover and take Jonny away. I took it very badly, and when the fellow abandoned her I left Ursula to die alone. I'm ashamed of what I did.'

'I can't imagine you doing anything to hurt anyone. You mustn't blame yourself.' Susan took a searching look at him.

'Thank you.' Her declarations heartened him, and the fact she was allowing him to entrust her with these most personal of memories. 'But it's all rather complicated. Jonny's half-sister was adopted and brought up in Truro without either of them knowing about it. It was my decision to keep it a secret – I was too hard. Thankfully, it was all resolved in the end and Jonny was united with Louisa.'

'You had your reasons for what you did. You suffered. People don't always know what goes on ... well, it's good that you've got a lot of family members.'

He plunged in with a personal question. 'Have you anyone else apart from Maureen and your brother Kenny?'

She shook her head. 'No one, but please don't think that makes me unhappy.' She looked over the photographs again.

'I'm glad to hear that. Was there anything else you'd like to know about?'

She pointed. 'I was wondering about the fine house there. It looks as if it's by the sea.'

'Ah, that's Roskerne. It is by the sea, at Watergate Bay, near Newquay. It's where I lived with Winnie. It was her house, and after she died I felt it only right it should pass on to Vera Rose. She kindly allows the family to use it for holidays. Faye and I took the children there for three weeks last summer and we're planning to do so again this year. Agnes came with us. She doesn't want to come this year. You and Maureen must come instead.'

Susan's lovely blue eyes lit up as if the sun was shining straight out of them. 'Really? You mean it? We've never been to the seaside before. Maureen would love it.'

'It would be a holiday for you too, just as it was for Agnes last year. She deserved it and so do you. I insist.' Tristan smiled down on her, while longing to tell her how important she was to him. He felt certain she'd never been told that before by anyone except Maureen. 'Vera Rose employs a local man and his wife to look after the house and see to the garden, and Mrs Loze is happy to cook and make up picnics for us. I've got an antique and curio shop in Newquay. You must pay a visit there.' He would take her there personally.

'What about Mr Fuller?'

'If he's still with us he'll be welcome too, of course. Some sea air will do him a power of good.'

The long case clock in the room suddenly chimed eleven o'clock. 'I'd better get on,' Susan flushed guiltily. 'I'll make your coffee first.'

'You mustn't miss your break, Susan. It's I who's kept you talking.'

They went to the kitchen together, both looking forward to the summer at Watergate Bay, but for different reasons. 'Someone's coming in,' Susan said, going to the scullery door.

'Drat,' Tristan muttered under his breath. More time alone with her was being denied.

'Oh, you've got the stray!' she exclaimed, as Mark and Faye entered in unkempt states, they and the dog dirtying her spotlessly scrubbed floor. 'Maureen begged me to let her have him but I couldn't really afford to feed him. I've given him what I could spare.'

'Susan, would you mind if I gave him a bath in here?' Mark said. 'And have you got any scraps? He's ravenous.'

'Do what you want for him, Mark. Poor thing, I'll see what I can find him to eat. Have you brought him back for the children, Faye?'

'No, he's going to be Mark's, but they'll love having him here,' Faye replied. 'There's an old tin bath in a shed at the farm. One of the farm hands is bringing it over for us.' Faye stressed the 'us'.

'Meet Addi,' Mark said, crouching beside the nervous dog. 'You're not going to be too much trouble for Susan, are you, old boy?'

'I'll fetch some soapy water and rags to clean him up,' Susan said. 'After your tummy's full, eh, Addi?' She put a hand out to Addi and he licked it, trusting her from seeing her before.

'He's going to need to have his fleas combed out,' Mark said to Susan.

'He's going to need a lot of attention,' she replied. She had forgotten all about the coffee.

Tristan and Faye stood back and watched. Forgotten too.

Nine

The school grounds were laid out with desks and trestle tables borrowed from the Methodist social rooms. Emilia and Elena Killigrew, who together headed all the village committees, had arranged an end of summer term Bring and Buy sale to raise funds for a new heating system for the school. They expected a good turnout. The locals didn't want the children to shiver through another winter.

Faye arrived with Simon. For a long time after her return to Hennaford, she had been wary about getting involved in village events, but with her aunt in charge, no one yet had dared make direct remarks about her lack of marital status, although she often got the sense some were itching to. She was proud to show Simon off. He was well behaved and appealing, a handsome child. It was time the villagers saw more of him. Time he took his place in Hennaford. After all, no matter what people thought of her, her precious son had done nothing wrong.

She found herself manning the toy stall, its

wares mainly knitted or sewn from old garments, or made from scraps of wood and metal. There were tired and well-loved old toys sacrificed for the good cause. The stall was down the far wall of the girls' concrete playground. On the other side was a long field of Ford Farm's, alive with breeze swaying maturing corn. Away across the fields she could see her cousin Tom driving a tractor, haymaking, and cattle grazing in another.

She was joined by Lottie, who settled Carl next to Simon, the boys in their pushchairs, content for the moment to gaze at the busy scene of nearly all women getting ready for the opening. 'Hello. It's a lovely day for this. Just think, in a couple of years Simon will be going here. I feel quite sad to think Carl won't be attending my old school.'

'Any prospects of a farm of your own yet?' Faye unpacked the box she had brought with her.

'Nothing yet.' Lottie picked up a tiny rag doll Faye put on the table and spread out its crinoline dress, made from oddments of silk and lace. 'Nate and I can't seem to agree on exactly what we want. Yesterday we looked over a smallholding at Allet. Too small, of course, but I thought we could see about buying the land around it. Nate wasn't interested. There was a place down at Land's End, but I said it was too far away. Nate says he's used to distance, that Land's End at just over forty miles away is just a stroll to him, and he's now decided to look out of the county. I've told him I've no intention of settling far away from Hennaford. Why should I? Family ties are important to me. He's not taking me seriously.'

Nate had unsettled her last night when he'd said firmly, 'It's a man's place to provide a home for his wife and family, honey, and that's what I intend to do. I'll get you your own car. When the gas rationing is over you'll be able to see your mom as often as you like. Don't frown, Lottie, you were an adventurous girl when I met you. Can't see what your problem is.'

Even if she told him, he wouldn't understand, so she said nothing and hoped her dream of a farm nearby would materialize soon. 'You'll all be off to Roskerne in a few days. Is Mark Fuller going with you?'

'Yes. He says he's looking forward to roaming the beach with Addi.'

'I hear Susan and her little girl are joining you this time. It will be nice for them. Can't recall them leaving the village, even for a Sunday School tea treat.'

Faye got an unwelcome picture of Mark inviting Susan and Maureen for a walk along the little beach below the cliffs at Roskerne. 'Pretty, isn't it?' she indicated the doll Lottie was admiring. 'Susan made the body from a hanky and stuffed it with duck down. She's clever like that. You're not likely to find what you're looking for close to home, Lottie. When you think about the size of a local farm, well, Nate's used to vast prairie land. For even a small acreage the size of his ranch, you'll have to look up country.'

'There's no question of that,' Lottie said stiffly.

Faye looked at her. 'Is everything all right?'

'Of course,' Lottie forced a smile. She was making every effort to show she was as happily married as the other two couples at the farm. 'I've got a bit of a headache. Susan must be a great asset to you. Every time you want a new outfit you can turn to her for her seamstress skills. I'll get her to run up the curtains for my new home. Is she here, or coming along when the children are let out of their classes and the sale begins?'

'Aunt Em's put her on tea duty with Mrs Frayne.'

Lottie put some Hershey bars on the stall, taken from Nate's delivery. 'Mark won't be showing his face, I don't suppose? How is he these days?'

'Getting stronger every day,' Faye said proudly. Mark spent so much time outside his skin was a healthy tan, and some of the people who had seen him had complimented her for nursing him towards fitness. 'Renovating Rose Dew is doing him a power of good. Jim drops supplies off to him. He'd be there from dawn to dusk if I didn't insist he work for only five to six hours a day. He and Addi are inseparable,' Faye wittered on. She loved talking about Mark. It made her feel closer to him, that he was hers. 'I got a terrible fright the day after we brought Addi home. I went into the ancillary room and found Mark lying on the floor beside him. I screamed thinking he had collapsed. Turned out he was worried that Addi would fret in a strange place so he'd crept downstairs during the night to keep him company and had fallen asleep.'

Lottie was gazing at her.

'What?'

'You sound very taken with him.'

'Don't be silly.' Faye blushed but couldn't help smiling coyly. 'He's just a nice man. He's not good-looking or anything.'

'Well, you're obviously smitten with him. He's getting divorced, he's free to cast his eye round.' Lottie patted her cousin's arm. 'And you're hoping it will fall on you. I hope it does. It's time you found someone, Faye.'

'Mark doesn't show me any interest in that way,' Faye admitted sadly

'He will, he must still have a lot of adjusting to do, but when he's ready he's bound to look no further than you,' Lottie said confidently.

'How can you be sure?' Faye burned with

hope. Being in love for the first time was a painful, almost annoying experience, watching jealously in case Mark was drawn to Susan. It wasn't at all like the wonderful event she'd hoped it would be in her girlhood years. It was an agony fearing the man of her choice would never feel the same way.

'Easy, you've got so much going for you. You're beautiful, you have a great figure, you're kind and caring. Mark must find Simon adorable. He doesn't venture far, so there's no one else around for him to take a fancy to.' Lottie sensed Faye growing taut and saw that her eyes were on someone coming round with a tray of teas. Ah, Susan Dowling, the attractive young widow. Susan didn't have money, flair in clothes, or the sophistication that was natural in Faye. She was quiet, restrained and rather boring, but she had an unconscious beguiling way about her, an innocence that must charm men.

Susan reached the other side of the stall. 'Here you are, ladies. Mrs Frayne thought the helpers deserved a cuppa.'

'Thanks.' Lottie took two white cups and saucers off the tray. She tested the waters. 'Faye's been telling me about Mr Fuller's efforts at Rose Dew. You must be pleased to have someone sorting out that creepy old place, Mrs Dowling.'

'It is a relief, Mrs Harmon,' Susan replied. 'He's convinced, though, that the place isn't

157

creepy.'

'You'll be pleased when someone's living there, I daresay. Won't be so lonely for you then,' Lottie went on.

'I suppose not. If you'll excuse me, I must take round the rest of these before they get cold,' Susan said.

'Oh, there's Uncle Tris,' Faye suddenly blurted out. 'Could you offer him a cup, Susan, please? I don't expect he'd have had time for a drink before coming here.'

'Of course,' Susan replied, withdrawing.

As Lottie had expected, Susan didn't seem attracted to Mark Fuller. She was surprised by something else. 'Uncle Tris doesn't usually come to an event held in the afternoon. It'll be mothers and old people mostly.' She received a tin jack-in-the-box from a pupil's mother for the stall, who gave Faye a stiff look before going away. Lottie glared at the woman, hating it when someone was obviously making a moral judgment on Faye.

Faye hadn't noticed. She kept her eyes on Susan and her uncle. Good, they were engaged in friendly conversation. 'Well, this is more important than most occasions. He's concerned about the children's welfare. A new boiler and radiators doesn't come cheaply.'

'Good old Uncle Tris. You'll be looking for a tenant when Mark's finished with Rose Dew. You never know, he might like to live in it himself.'

'What?' This was a good and a bad idea to Faye. If Mark lived in Rose Dew it would mean him staying in Hennaford, but he'd be in close proximity to Susan every day. 'I think I'll have a word with him. Lottie, do you really think I stand a chance with Mark?'

'Of course you do. If you want him go after him, Faye. Use all the resources you can.'

'I'm already doing that,' Faye said, grateful to have the encouragement. She would continue to do what she could to push Susan and her uncle together. She had suggested to him that he take the children to the pictures, something he did regularly, and that Maureen shouldn't be left out. That if he felt four children rather a lot of responsibility, then perhaps Susan might consider going along too, to enjoy the treat. He'd replied immediately it was a good idea. The more she thought about it the more she considered an alliance between them not to be a bad thing. It would be doing Susan a favour, a secure future for her and her daughter with one of the kindest men on earth, and her uncle would not sink into an undeserved lonely old age. How everyone would fit into Tremore House was another matter, and one not to worry about for now.

Harriet Frayne, the headmaster's wife, and Elena Killigrew came to them with the float. 'Well, isn't this nice?' Harriet Frayne, thick of body, neck and ankles, cooed to the boys. 'We only need Mrs Jill Harvey to produce and we'll have the full compliment. I'm sorry you're planning to leave us, Lottie. Mr Frayne will be retiring soon but he'd like to have thought there would be little Harmons running in and out of the school gates. I'm so pleased you're reunited with your husband.'

Faye was aware the woman's interest wasn't quite so approving when she viewed Simon. There was an edge of sanctimony about it, as if Simon didn't quite qualify for the same consideration. She had not attended the village school but had started off her education privately in Truro, but she had known Mrs Frayne to be a rosy-hearted woman who cared in a motherly way for her husband's pupils. It was a shame that this didn't extend to children like Simon, but Faye supposed she must understand old-fashioned ideals. It still hurt, though. Faye felt something new and it filled her with an aching guilt. She was letting Simon down. She should have lied and said she was a widow for his sake. He was likely to be ostracized wherever he went because of what she had thought to be a brave decision.

Harriet Frayne noticed her hard frown and had the grace to look embarrassed. 'Um, I hear your guest is doing very well, Miss Faye. Little Pearl and the twins talk about

160

him a lot. You and your uncle must be so pleased.'

'We are,' Faye replied as if in challenge, daring her to ask personal questions about Mark. There was tittle-tattle going round the village about his impending divorce. No one blamed him – as usual, it was the woman's fault for domestic failures, and Justine had been called some insulting names. Faye had explained to one or two people that he and Justine had just drifted apart but that had not altered anyone's opinion. Marriage was for life as far as the majority of the inhabitants of Hennaford were concerned, to work at, to make compromises, and if that failed to endure until death.

Lottie sighed impatiently. There were loose women in the world, home wreckers and the like, but Faye wasn't like that. She had made a mistake, or rather the older man whose charms she had fallen under had. The Scottish laird should have behaved more responsibly. And Justine Fuller was bravely facing the fact that it was better to end her marriage than to hang on to something that would only give her and Mark years of futile unhappiness, bringing them both down.

There was a prickly silence. Elena Killigrew, eternally good-natured and always the peacemaker, coughed to politely intrude, and was about to say something to make the conversation commonplace but suddenly

161

she groaned and put a hand to her head. Her hands shot out to grab the stall. 'Oh, dear...'

'What is it, Mrs Killigrew?' Faye came round the table to her. 'Do you feel ill?'

'Actually, I do a little,' Elena said breathlessly. She always understated a dilemma of her own. Her head was whirling and she thought the playground was coming up to meet her.

'You need a chair.' Lottie signalled to her mother and Emilia hastened to them with one that was of canvas and iron-framed. Elena sat down gratefully, lily-pale and trembling, and Emilia took charge. 'Could someone fetch some water?'

'I'll bring some from the house.' Mrs Frayne hurried off.

Emilia did the usual things like feeling Elena's brow and rubbing her wrists, while shielding her from view of curious onlookers. 'You've been overdoing it, Elena,' she said gently. 'Always dashing about, running yourself ragged for good causes.'

'It isn't that.' Elena's cheeks were blazing. She whispered for Emilia's ear only, 'I think I'm having the ... I mean to say, I must be on "the change".' I haven't had a monthly for ages. Jim's noticed I'm often queasy and hot and a bit bothered. I don't feel weak or anything. I'm eating well. In fact, as you can see, I'm putting on weight.'

Emilia gazed into Elena's flushed face for

162

some moments then down at her body. 'There could be another reason for your symptoms.'

'What do you mean?' Elena was panicked, her mind going off to cancer or some other deadly disease. She was a deeply religious woman and sure of an afterlife in heaven, but she didn't want to leave the husband she loved so much and their two adopted teen-aged children. She was only forty-six. She had years yet of serving the Lord, if He allowed it.

'Would you mind...?' Emilia placed a hand over Elena's expanding tummy. A tense moment passed for Elena. 'I thought as much. Put your hand where mine is.'

After a nervous glance up at Emilia, and receiving a persuasive nod, she did so reluctantly.

'Feel it? That little movement?' Elena smiled.

'Yes, it's wind.'

'I don't think it is. Elena, I've been wondering about it and now I'm absolutely sure. You're having a baby. Congratulations.'

'What?' It was some moments before the news sank in, then Elena's modest, dear features broke into a magnificent smile 'After all these years? Fifteen years!' For the first time ever she was shouting in excitement, while being consumed with raptures. 'I can't believe it. Oh ... we never thought it would happen. I must see Jim at once. He'll be so delighted. After all our hopes and prayers. He's at your house with Alan working on Tom's refurbishments. You will excuse me, won't you?' Elena was up on her feet, hands clasped, hopping about like an excited child, all feelings of sickness gone. People came running to hear what was her joy. There was an outbreak of applause.

'Of course you must go to Jim.' Emilia gave her friend a swift hug. 'And you mustn't bother coming back. Make sure you spend the afternoon with him.'

Harriet Frayne flapped back into the playground on her heavy feet, a glass of water held importantly in her hand. Elena faced the crowd, aglow, on air, unaccustomedly vivacious and demonstrative. She flung her hands out wide. 'I don't need that, Mrs Frayne. Did you hear? I'm having a baby!'

The rest of the setting-up was done in good spirits and noisy chatter. Faye saw that one person wasn't joining in. Lottie was totally uninterested in Elena's sudden good news, and even seemed edgy. 'Aren't you glad for her? She's got Alan and Martha but it must have been awful hoping for a child of her own and failing over the years.'

'Of course, I am. I was thinking that a baby at her age isn't a good idea. It might be slow or have a condition.'

'I can't see Elena and Jim minding that too

much. They'd still see it as a blessing.' She leaned away from the stall and dropped a kiss on Simon's dark head. He beamed a chubby happy smile up at her, their love for each other shining through. 'Every child is.'

Lottie sighed, and Faye probed no more. Her cousin was hard to understand at times. Now that Nate had joined her she had everything a young woman could want. Her son had not been produced 'under the blanket' as Simon was. Soon, she would have her own lovely, prospering home. She had no idea that Lottie was scared.

Again, Lottie counted up the weeks. She was four months late and there could be no doubt that she was pregnant. Throughout her life she had been strong and bold, had laughed at warnings to do things carefully, to avoid risks, but now she was frightened to the point of panic at the thought of giving birth again. Why? It was silly. She'd pushed Carl out of her body and although it had been quite dreadful, she had survived with no ill effects. Her mother and the midwife had said the first labour and birth was the worst. That it would be easier next time. So in a few months she should deliver this new baby like shelling peas. It was how she must think about it. And she ought to tell Nate. He'd be as thrilled as Jim Killigrew was going to be about his child.

She felt a cold shivery clamminess, like

walking into a thousand spider webs, like sensing there was a ghost beside her. She must ignore it. Remember she wasn't the type to be easily frightened. Think of first things first. Find her new home and forget this baby for a while. Concentrate on moving into the perfect place with Nate and relish all the new experiences it would bring, delight in her own kitchen and sitting room, her own curtains and linen, her own dairy and hens. She'd be bigger in the pregnancy then and it wouldn't be so bad. When the birth was closer she wouldn't be so scared. When she got huge and cumbersome, and if her ankles swelled up and she could hardly walk she'd be glad when the birth pangs started and it would soon be over. Then she'd go secretly to another doctor and get herself fixed up so she'd never have to go through this hell again. She'd have it all, Nate, a home, and two children. Life would be perfect then.

The children filed out of the three classes an hour before the usual time they went home. The Smiths were delighted to see their Uncle Tristan, calculating how many pennies they could wheedle out of him to spend at the stalls. The twins shot off with sixpence each – it would do for now, leaving Pearl to tag along holding their uncle's hand, and to Tristan's pleasure, Maureen stayed with them too. He suggested a tea for himself and lemonade for the girls. Susan would serve them, hopefully.

Faye was happy about the little group too. The afternoon went well, but there were comments about it not being the same without Elena Killigrew buzzing about to ensure everyone was content and all was in line. It gave her an idea. She approached Mr Frayne. The headmaster was a little man in a three-piece tweed suit, a heavy watch chain, and thinning grey hair. With his hands behind his back, he was hovering about as if the central figure. For the richer parents of his pupils he wore an ingratiating smile. 'Good of you to help out, Miss Harvey,' he said, bobbing up and down in his brogues.

Faye got the impression he wanted to edge away from her. 'I'm delighted to, Mr Frayne. I was about to confer with my aunt about an idea I've had to raise more funds for the heating, but I thought I'd consult you first. It's occurred to me that Mrs Killigrew's expected happy event is going to mean, at least for a while, that she won't have as much free time to organize such things. I thought I could hold a coffee morning at Tremore House. Anything left unsold today could go towards another Bring and Buy at the same time.'

Mr Frayne dragged down his lower lip with a ponderous hand. 'Well, it's very kind of you, but I think we've got enough events

167

coming up, actually.'

'But one more wouldn't hurt, even if it only raised a pound or two.' There would be no shortage of people attending. They would come out of curiosity to see inside her house – her father had never held anything there but dinners for family or business associates. They would come hoping to see Mark. There could be only one reason the headmaster was raising an objection. The fact she wasn't married. She was considered unsuitable. She would set a bad example.

'Well, you see...' Mr Frayne's terrier-dog face deepened a burning red, but there was a chilliness about him too. It was obvious he was uncomfortable, and displeased to feel he had been put in an awkward situation.

'I see, Mr Frayne.' Faye's voice was grim but did not give away that she was blazing mad. 'I see very well. Excuse me.'

She walked away with her head held high to show he couldn't put her down, her mind a mill of recriminations against all those who had humiliated or hurt her. Her father might have come to realize he'd loved her, but at the start of her life he had not wanted her. He'd wanted a son. His selfish conduct had led to her mother leaving him. Understandable, but Brooke Harvey had not accounted for the tremendous wrench it had been to Faye to be taken away from all she knew to the other side of the world. Brooke had accused Faye of being a difficult child – was it any wonder? When Faye had begged to be allowed to train for the ballet in London, Brooke had let her go, too blind to see it as a ruse to get Brooke to beg her to stay.

Then during the war she'd fallen under the spell of Fergus Blair, and Simon had been the result. Another result was she'd come away from Scotland not trusting men. Fergus had disregarded her hopes of a settled life by refusing to divorce his errant wife, he'd put his position first; a divorce would have made him unacceptable in society. Although he'd seen she was well cared for during her confinement and had settled a very generous amount on her and Simon, he had left her afterward to go out into the world and cope alone. Fergus had pressed her to take the easy way out and have the baby secretly adopted, but she'd wanted to keep it, to have someone to love who would love her back.

And Simon did love her. He was everything to her and deserved to be protected in every way, whatever it took. He deserved the best, and the best she could do for him was to get him away from this village where small-minded people would always seek to put him down. He might be heir to her estate and the garage, but there was sure to be someone who'd try to make him feel inferior, less of a gentleman. The worst thing from such an existence was that he might never be able to love someone properly. He might, like she had herself recently, allow himself to become infatuated with the wrong person, to be plagued with hopes for the wrong reasons. She saw now why she had been drawn to Mark. She had met him while he was weak and needy, unable to be a threat to her. He was a good man, but he too had hurt her. While he willingly heaped attention on Pearl and the twins, and even affection on Maureen Dowling, he more or less ignored her own dear Simon. She knew what she had to do.

She marched back to Lottie and looked her full in the face. 'I'm about to solve your biggest problem.'

'What are you talking about?' Lottie was troubled by her dark incensed expression. 'What's wrong? I could see Mr Frayne said something to upset you. What was it?'

'Never mind him. You want a large farm and property near to home. Well, you can have one. Mine!'

Ten

He could see the old man again. He was often here at Rose Dew. Watching him. He had not come so close before. Addi always fretted but this time he stood stiffly, ruff up, ears pinned back, sniffing and wailing. 'It's all right, boy,' Mark said, putting down the slate roof tiles he was about to carry up the ladder. 'It's only Jude.'

Mark knew the name of the ghost. He had called on Agnes in Back Lane and she had told him all about the Tremore farm labourer who had lived here a century ago.

After declaring it was good to see Mark looking so well, Agnes had invited him into her gleaming little front room. She looked settled in her new home as if she had lived there all her life. 'I'm delighted to be the first you've called on, Mr Fuller. I hope we see more of you out and about in the village.' She poured tea and then poured out the tragic tale. 'People don't like to talk much about Jude Keast. They think it's unlucky, that some of what that poor soul went through might rub off on them, but I'm a religious woman and therefore not particularly superstitious. The Tremore estate stretched much wider in them days, and gentry lived in the old manor house, long gone now, just beyond the crossroads. You obviously aren't afraid of him haunting Rose Dew.'

'It doesn't bother me at all, Agnes. Jude doesn't like me being there, but I don't get the sense he means me any harm.' Mark ate a shortbread biscuit with a hand hardened by work with stone and wood, hammer and saw. He was pleased with his labours on Rose Dew and pleased with the health and vigour and the sense of purpose it gave him.

'There's not many who's had a sadder life than poor Jude. He was the second son and the second best. When his elder brother died of consumption, his parents were heartbroken. They never got over it and Jude could never please them. His mother quickly pined herself to death and his father died from a heart attack not long afterward.'

'So Rose Dew has seen plenty of sorrow.' Mark nodded. There was a sense of melancholy surrounding the place.

'I haven't got started yet. Jude tried to make a life for himself. He married a girl from Perranporth, met her during a beach outing there. It was no love match, but they rubbed along together. She had a baby and Jude was thrilled. But one day Jude went home from work and she and the baby had disappeared. There was no sign of her taking a thing out of the house. Seemed she just went out and vanished off the face of the earth. Drove poor Jude nearly out of his mind. He searched for them every spare minute he got. Each time he came back with no clue to their whereabouts and he got lower and lower in spirits. He became a recluse. Never went to chapel or down to the village, grew what he could to feed himself, and kept a few chickens. No one ever saw him except about the farm. After a while no one called on him anymore, all too afraid he'd gone soft in the head. The years passed. Then one day he didn't turn up for work and the steward went over to Rose Dew to find out why. Found Jude in bed with a high fever from blood poisoning. He'd cut his leg on a rulling hook and it had gone anguished. He died two days later. All alone he was, poor soul. After that some strange happenings were reported there and people got too scared to go near it. I must say, I always pitied young Susan, living so close. Now, does that settle your curiosity, Mr Fuller?'

'Yes. Thank you, Agnes. It's a terrible thing not to know what has happened to a loved one.' He knew that from fellow POWs. It had been hard enough when a man got a Dear John letter and had been left to endure captivity under the rejection, but sometimes letters would dry up from home, leading to anxiety, bewilderment, or anger and resentment. Jude Keast must have suffered all this. 'I suppose Jude is buried in the churchyard.'

'He is, but not next to his parents and brother. Lonely in life, and lonely in death. As I said, it's a sad story. But I'm glad to see renovating the place is doing you good. That you've got colour in your face and that you've put on a bit of weight. Miss Faye is looking after you very well indeed.'

'I owe her a large debt of gratitude. One day I hope to repay her.'

He had smiled while speaking and gazed into space. Agnes hoped he was picturing Faye. Eyeing him, she said meaningfully, 'She's a fine lady, and her Simon's a dear little boy.'

'Yes. I confess I haven't taken a lot of notice of him. Infants scare me.'

'But you feel comfortable with older children?'

'Well, they don't dribble all over you, and you can talk to them properly. I never had brothers or sisters, so I enjoy playing games with Pearl, Maureen and the twins.'

'You'll find Simon will do more each day,' Agnes said pointedly, issuing him a second cup of tea.

Mark didn't miss the edge of chiding in her tone. 'Oh. Faye might be thinking I don't care all that much for Simon. I'll rectify that this evening. Offer to read him a bedtime story.'

'Miss Faye would appreciate that.' Agnes smiled with satisfaction. She had seen Faye's efforts to cosset and please him and her hope that he'd notice her. She considered herself a good judge of character, and had liked Mark from the start. Agnes thought he would make an excellent husband for Faye. If only he would see it.

On the walk from Agnes's home to Rose Dew, Mark had thought about Faye at the Bring and Buy with Simon. How brave, to take Simon with her. As the only unmarried mother in the village, she must inevitably have to ward off a certain amount of disapproval. She was a lot like Justine, able to make strong decisions and stand her ground. She was hospitable and caring. He'd done little to show his appreciation. Working for nothing on a scrap of her property was not nearly enough, and as he was hoping to rent Rose Dew, it was for his own benefit too.

'I'd never be this fit if it wasn't for Faye,' he told Addi, as he set about replacing missing and broken roof tiles. 'And there's something else about her. She's wonderful. She's a damned beautiful woman.'

He talked to Addi constantly. The dog was his faithful companion and trusted confidant. He could tell Addi things he could never bring himself to tell a person. And now he was talking to Jude Keast. A slightly indistinct figure, in dark serviceable clothing, a neckerchief and tattered flat cap, hovering just inside the broken-down garden wall. 'Hello. I'm Mark and this is Addi. We don't mean to intrude. We don't want to take the place away from you. I don't think you like seeing Rose Dew falling down and the garden left to grow wild. We could all exist here together, going quietly about our own business.'

Mark heard a tapping noise. He glanced away for a second, and when he looked back, Jude had gone. Addi relaxed and stretched out comfortably under the front windowsill to doze. 'I think Jude's getting used to us, boy.'

He climbed the ladder to begin inserting tiles. He had nearly finished repairing the roof and was down to the guttering, which the Cornish called laundering.

'Afternoon.'

'Jude?' Mark swung round. At the same instant Addi was up on his feet and rushing towards the wall.

'That ain't me. Here, that dog going to stay on your side or what?'

Mark stared at the stranger, summing up, that although he was nervous of Addi, and despite his slick appearance, he was an undesirable and a show-off. 'Can I help you?'

'Only if you can tell me where I can find

Susan Dowling.' The man employed a friendly tone, but with a touch of sharpness. He obviously felt a mutual dislike of Mark. 'Thought she'd be home at this time of day.'

Mark climbed down off the ladder. 'What business have you got with her?'

'No need to come over all defensive, mate. Susan's my sister and her little girl Maureen is my niece. I've the ruddy right to know where they are. The name's Kenny Locke. And who are you when you're at home?' While casting anxious glances at Addi, Kenny Locke was leaning forward as if ready for trouble, or to hand it out.

'I had no idea Mrs Dowling had a brother.' Mark was at his most formal, while searching Kenny's hard face. 'My name is Mark Fuller. I live in Hennaford. There's a fund-raising occasion at the school. Mrs Dowling and Maureen will have stayed on for it.'

'I see.' With narrowed eyes, Kenny glanced at the cottage. 'Last time I was here I saw a glimpse of this place. Ruddy creepy. Just bought it and doing it up, are you?'

'No. Do you live locally?'

'No.' Kenny was not to be any more forthcoming than Mark was. 'I'll go wait for Susan.' Giving Addi one last glare, he strode away, lighting a cigarette, puffing the smoke back over his shoulder as if to convey an aggressive snub to Mark.

Mark got the message. He knelt beside the

dog and hugged its broad soft, sandy-coloured neck. 'There were a few chaps like him in the camp, Addi. Only out for themselves. They'd steal the last sweaty rag off a man's back or his last grain of rice. I saw men give up and die because their only scrap of hope had been cruelly snatched away from them. We're going to have to keep a close eye on Susan and Maureen.'

That evening in the sitting room at Ford Farm, Lottie moved in front of the fireplace to centre stage. She was a confident figure amid the plush Victorian furnishings, the huge moulded, scrolled and beaded mantelpiece lending her an important backdrop. 'I've got an announcement to make.'

'Honey, you've been looking excited for hours. Have you got good news for me?' Nate left Edwin, Tom and Jill at the card table and joined her. Emilia turned off the wireless play she and Perry were listening to. Tilda put her knitting down. Everyone was gazing at Lottie's tummy, making assumptions, exchanging knowing glances.

Lottie had more important news than her pregnancy. 'Yes, darling. I was offered the perfect place for us today!' She gave a little hop and clapped her hands.

'Great. We'll look over it first thing tomorrow.' Nate smiled. He was pleased to see her happy, bubbly and vital, as she'd been when they'd first met, rather than the touchy, angry stranger she had become.

'We won't have to go very far.' Lottie's eyes were aglow over her wonderful news, which had been hard to keep secret until the right moment.

'What are you talking about, sweetheart?' Nate was puzzled, but he had captured a little of her excitement.

'Oh, it's just the best thing to have ever happened! It's Tremore! Faye offered it to me today. She's selling up. She wants to move away. And I've accepted! We'll only have to move across to the other side of the village. Isn't it wonderful, Nate? Can you believe it, everyone?'

The whoops of glee Lottie was expecting didn't happen. All were stunned. Nate was cool. 'You shouldn't have made such a big decision, even about your cousin's property, without talking to me first and alone. I don't mean anyone here any disrespect, but I'm sure they'd all agree that important issues between a man and his wife should be first discussed just between the two of them.'

A lot of troubled glances were passed around the room, followed by lowering of eyes and a tense hush. It was clear everyone agreed with Nate.

Lottie felt as if she had been struck by a giant wave of freezing water. The rapid change from elation to a dark sense of

179

rejection and resentment made her feel faint. She put out a hand to a winged armchair to stay on her feet. 'But—'

'But nothing, Lottie,' Nate growled. 'When are you going to consider me as the other half of our marriage?'

'Why on earth is Faye thinking of selling up anyway? It's all too sudden,' Emilia whispered to Perry. She felt sorry for Lottie, it was awful to see her suddenly deflated, but she wouldn't dream of interfering. It was understandable that Nate should be aggrieved. The telephone rang. Perry excused himself to answer it. Tilda, hating what was obviously to be more confrontation, took the opportunity to slip away to the kitchen.

'I'm sorry,' Lottie whined at Nate. 'Maybe I should have talked to you first, but don't you think it's the best thing?'

'Maybe doesn't come into it, Lottie.' Nate was angry that she couldn't see his hurt. He wasn't being bloody-minded or stubborn. He came from a long line of hardy pioneering folk, who had fought cattle barons to gain and hold on to their land. The women had been tough, but the men had always headed the family. He felt that Lottie treated him with contempt and made him feel an outsider.

'Why can't you be happy about it?' Lottie hurled at him in accusation. She may have been thoughtless, but it was hardly the crime

180

of the century. He was making her feel small in front of her family.

'I'd be more than happy to look over a place with you, but not to be told it's a finished deal. I thought you were going to say you were pregnant.' Nate threw up his hands in exasperation.

'Actually, I am!' she snapped back. 'Does that make you happy?'

With a scrape of her chair, Jill suddenly got up and left the room. Tom shot a glare at Lottie, one of discontent at Nate, and went after her.

'Whatever's the matter with her is not my fault.' Lottie crossed her arms and turned her back on Nate.

'You can't blame anyone for feeling uncomfortable. It's not the first time you've caused discontent in the house,' Nate fumed. Why couldn't Lottie see how selfish she was?

'OK, so I'm not perfect, but neither are you.' Lottie turned and pointed at him. 'But Tremore is. Can you get off your high horse for just one moment and see that?'

Emilia was on her feet. 'Will you please both calm down?'

Perry put his head round the door and beckoned to Emilia. They spoke outside the room for a few moments – while Lottie and Nate carried on their quarrel – then they both returned. Emilia put up her hands for

181

silence. 'Right, the pair of you, before you say anything else or come to any decisions there's something you must listen to.'

'What?' Lottie said moodily.

'I think you'd better sit down, Lottie.' Emilia was worried about her daughter's high colour and gasping breaths.

Lottie ignored her. Nate sighed in frustration at Lottie. 'I'm sorry, ma'am. Go ahead.'

'Perry's told me that it was Tris on the phone. It seems he's just received the same news.'

'And? Trying to change Faye's mind, is he?' Lottie demanded.

'Not trying, Lottie. He has.'

'What? He can't! She can't! It's not fair!'

Emilia tried to coax Lottie to sit in the armchair. 'Sit down and listen, please, my love. You'll understand then.' Lottie refused to budge. Emilia's look of appeal to Nate failed; he was too angry with Lottie to care about her comfort. Emilia went on. 'Tris was as shocked as we all were by Faye's sudden decision to sell up and move away, to start a new life. It wasn't as if it was something she'd been considering for a while. It seems Mr Frayne upset her this afternoon. He made her feel unworthy to take part in village life because she's not married, and now she's worried that any prejudice and deadly whispers will have a bad effect on Simon. She's determined to move away and pretend she's a widow so Simon won't be shunned.'

'If she's moving away, and who can blame her if people like that old fool keep picking on her, then what's stopping her selling Tremore to me?' Lottie interrupted. 'To us,' she quickly aimed the last words at Nate, with an impatient twist of her mouth. Nate stared back stonily.

'I'm afraid when Faye spoke to you, Lottie, she hadn't given herself time to think it all through,' Emilia said. 'Tremore is Uncle Tris's and the Smiths' home. He and Faye took the children in together. I'm so sorry about your disappointment, darling, but I think you'll agree that it's only right and fair that Faye should have offered Uncle Tris first refusal on Tremore. And of course, if she really does go ahead to start again elsewhere, he will buy it. She sends her apologies to you.'

'No! I won't accept them. She offered Tremore to me first. She and Uncle Tris can't override that,' Lottie fumed.

'I'm afraid that is what will happen. He doesn't want Faye to go away. He's talked her into going to Roskerne to think things over for a couple of weeks. She's leaving with Simon in the morning. No one must mention this outside these four walls. There's no need for Pearl and the twins to know about this if she decides to stay.'

Lottie understood the position of all those at Tremore House, but she was also angry with them. To have everything she had wanted handed to her, to have spent a few wonderful hours planning and revelling in what she'd thought was to be her future, then to have it all taken away, was too much to bear. She was shaking. Her fists were clenched. Tears streamed down her face. 'It's not fair.' She meant to say it as a whisper, but the cry of despair came out as a twisted snarl.

'Not fair?' Nate exploded. 'Don't be so bloody childish. Your cousin's going through hell. She's desperate about her son's future. She's thinking she's got no option but to give up her home and family and to face a lonely life. That's what's called sacrifice, Lottie! Haven't you any notion of that? You only think about yourself. This should be the happiest and most promising time of my life. Sharing my future with my wife, my son and a new baby. Damn it, if I'd have known...' He glanced at Emilia, Perry and Edwin with utter frustration. 'I'm sorry.' He left the room.

The sitting room stayed in stunned silence except for Lottie's uncontrollable sobs. Nate could be heard stamping out of the farm-house. Lottie had lost all sensation in her body, and was not conscious of her mother and stepfather sitting her down.

'Poor maid,' Edwin said. Usually he was a fount of wisdom and common sense, but all this had left him flustered and he was wringing his old flat cap round and round in his hands. 'I'll get Tilda to bring her some tea.'

'Thanks, Dad,' Emilia said. 'But it's going to take more than that to put things right.'

Edwin trudged along the passage to the kitchen. Lottie's thoughtless actions were threatening her marriage. She had her family to turn to, but Nate had no one.

Tom and Jill were in sitting in a field, on the other side of the hedge where the ford passed across the lane. There was only a trickle of water in the narrow stream, for there had been little recent rain, but here, in one of their favourite spots, was always a wealth of wild growth. Common valerian, water avens and forget-me-nots and, more rarely, pink marsh orchids. Tom was chewing on peppery watercress leaves. 'Want to go for a drink, darling?'

She gazed at the grass blade she was twisting round her little finger. 'I'd rather stay here. I shouldn't have rushed out like that, adding to the drama.'

'You mustn't feel sorry. You've the right to expect peace in your own home. The way Lottie treats you is out of order. When you came to work at the farm, she made a close friend of you. Now she seems to resent you. You do nothing to get in her way. I can't stand you being treated unfairly. Are you hurt?'

'Not really. I think understand Lottie. She envies me. I've seen you every day since we first met. I've not had to endure long separations like she had. I have your undivided attention, which, in the light of Nate not coming to her straight after his demob, can't really be said for him. I have a settled home. The refurbishments are going ahead, and Lottie's had to listen to me and your mother talking about new curtains and stuff. Lottie's never lived away from home. She's always been spoiled. She's strong-willed, but she's still young in her mind. She had a great excitement to share, but sadly for her she didn't go about it the right way. She must be feeling humiliated. And now she's pregnant she's bound to be emotional. She's a bit of a powder keg waiting to go off. She's terribly unhappy, Tom. It's easy to see that.'

Tom kissed her and held her close. 'You're so kind-hearted and sensitive. Always ready to forgive. Just some of the reasons I love you so much. Makes me wonder if Lottie really fell in love with Nate. She saw him, she wanted him and she got him. But she didn't get the chance to get to know him. All they had were a few hours together when he got leave. It's an awful thought that he might have given up everything for her, that she's put all her hopes in him, only to find they aren't at all suited. And we can't do a thing to help them.' Tom snuggled Jill into him even closer. 'Darling, apart from the unpleasant atmosphere, was there any other reason why you ran out?'

Jill took a moment to luxuriate in his devotion. 'It was the way that Lottie admitted she was pregnant. The way she was so blasé about it made me angry. And it upset me. With the good news about Elena Killigrew, it made two announcements of a baby on the way in one day. I've started to really long to have a baby. I was going to tell you tonight that I'm getting a bit worried about it.'

'Oh, Jill.' He squeezed her gently. 'We probably don't have to worry yet. Do we? I mean, it took years for Elena to be having this baby. And don't forget about Mum. She was married to Perry for years before Paul was born.'

'Put like that, it is early days for us yet, I suppose.' Trying to forget how quickly Lottie, and many other women she knew, had conceived, Jill kissed him hungrily on the mouth. 'We've got all the fun of trying.'

Roused instantly to passion, Tom pushed up her blouse and put his hand inside her brassiere. Jill hauled up her skirt then started on his belt. Sometimes they indulged in love play, teasing and tantalizing each other, making it last for hours, sending out secret signals, to finally delight themselves with lengthy, do-everything intimacy. This was to be quick and delicious.

Sensing something, they both stopped, pulling their clothes together. Someone was marching down the hill from the farm on heavy feet. 'Who is it?' Jill whispered.

From the other side of the hedge came an angry exclamation.

'It's Nate. He's in one hell of a temper, probably on the way to the pub. Couldn't blame him if he gets blotto.'

'Perhaps you should go with him, Tom.'

'I don't know. Might be better if he was left on his own. Everywhere the poor bugger turns there's a Harvey. He needs space to work out what's happening between him and Lottie.'

'What do you mean, exactly?'

'Pretty obvious, isn't it? They're in danger of breaking up. I hope their marriage can be saved, of course, but I can't see how unless one or both of them give way. Lottie's stubborn, and right now she's hysterical. Now I've seen more of Nate, he's a stubborn so-and-so too. They're both always ready to dig in their heels, and neither of them might emerge the winner.'

Eleven

Nate woke flat on his back, a thundering headache making it unwise to open his eyes. Where the hell was he? He was on a firm surface, but not in bed, that was for sure. He felt about with his hands. Grass. He was outside somewhere. His hands were stung – nettles. Twigs. Leaves. His clothes were damp, his skin clammy. Birds were singing the joyful wake-up call of early dawn. He'd had too much to drink in the Ploughshare and stayed out all night. Lottie must have been worried about him. No, she'd be absolutely furious, thinking him thoughtless and irresponsible, a selfish swine. He couldn't argue with that.

He preferred sleeping under the stars. Had spent weeks at a time back home camping out on the prairie with his herds, free and alive. With nature and in nature: cattle, eagles, buzzards and wild cats; distant mountains and vast rolling treeless land. He and the hands had sung to guitars and harmonicas, played cards, talked of their dreams. Most of all they had enjoyed the solid friendship, the trust of men totally relying on each in case of a stampede or wild critter attack, or rattler bite. He had given it all up for Lottie, who didn't love him.

'Hello. How long are you going to stay down there?' It was Jill's soft voice.

He had not heard her approach. Groaning, he stretched his stiff limbs and eased himself up on to his elbows. Jill was gazing down on him, holding a basket with both hands. 'Oh, Jill. I guess I've disgraced myself. Does Lottie know I didn't get in last night? She'll be madder than hell.'

'I haven't seen her yet. I got up early to go mushrooming. I expect she'll have thought you slept in one of the spare rooms.' Jill was full of sympathy for him. He was going to get it in the neck when Lottie surfaced. 'Want a hand getting up?'

'I think I'll be obliged to.' He stretched up a hand, she put the basket down, and after a lot of hauling he was on his feet, gripping the back of his head. 'Thanks.' He sighed out the tension.

'You're welcome.'

'I don't suppose Tom's ever gone AWOL on you like this. Can't see you ever driving him to drink.' Nate liked Jill. She was modest and good-hearted. None of the Harvey touch of arrogance and quick temper had rubbed off on her. She was a pretty sight, with her long wavy ash-blonde hair, in a light sweater, trousers and Wellington boots. In a long white frock she'd look like an angel. 'I've slept out many a night with my unit during training and the Liberation. French countryside is a lot like it is here. I used to pretend I was still at Feock, getting ready for the landings, with Lottie just a few miles away. I saw so much pain and suffering, but as crazy as it sounds, life seemed so much simpler then. Lottie resents me and I don't know what I can do about it.'

'Nate.' Jill was about to ask the question on the lips of all the family. 'Do you regret leaving Texas?'

He raked a despairing hand through his hair. 'Hell, Jill, I don't know. I'm pleased to be with my boy. But the way Lottie was yesterday, well, I just couldn't stand it anymore. I feel an outsider here. Redundant. I hate hanging about doing nothing. All I get to do is to exercise the horses. When I ask to help out on the farm, everyone encourages me to spend the time with Lottie and Carl. They keep reminding me how long we've spent apart. How am I supposed to learn the difference between running an English farm and ranching? Why does no one ever see my point of view?'

'We do, Nate, but I can see we need to do more for you.' Jill kept her voice gentle and soothing. 'I suppose the thing is Lottie's full of energy and likes to go her own way. We're all too used to letting her have it. Tom picks her up, but he often drops an argument just for the sake of peace.'

'What can I do? I hope you don't mind me asking, seems to me you're the best person to go to for advice. You've successfully blended in with the family.'

'Since you've asked me that, Nate, do you want me to be totally honest?'

'Fire away.' He braced himself, sure his honest sister-in-law would tell him stuff he would find hard to accept. He needed to know. He couldn't put things right if he didn't know all that was wrong, and what decisions, perhaps some painful, that he'd have to make.

Jill took a deep breath. She never sought to tell home truths. This wasn't going to be easy for her and probably not for him, although Nate didn't possess the sort of pride that was selfishly blinkered. 'I think you're right about Lottie resenting you, for two reasons. Nate, we all feel you left it rather too long to join her, and you should have at least told her why. Lottie was hurt. As your wife she should have come first, even above a dying friend. It's how Tom would have treated me. Perhaps your experiences during the fighting desensitized you to the usual feelings, but Lottie didn't go through the same things. All it seemed to her was that she was kept waiting and waiting and not really knowing why.'

'Well,' he puffed, rubbing at his neck, 'that hit straight home. I guess I haven't really taken her feelings into account. And the other reason? What else have I done wrong?'

'I might be way off the mark, and it might sound a bit strange, and I hasten to add it's only what has occurred to me, is that you're the one who is going to take Lottie away from her home. She's eager to go, to have her own home, and I'm sure she'd happily go anywhere with you, but again you are missing how much it will mean to her to give up all she's ever known. Since she was a little girl Lottie had been expecting to inherit part of the farm, but she handed her share over to Tom so she could have a totally new start with you. Lottie doesn't want to compare her sacrifice with the one you've made, but it's important to her that you see what she's done.'

Nate leaned against a beehive, using his thumbnail to pick off a bit of the white-painted ridged wood. 'So what you're saying is that I'm blunt and my finer feelings have been dulled. And that I've swept aside all that really matters to Lottie. I guess you're right. I've spent nearly all my life roughing it with men. Goodness knows I didn't know how to behave with Lottie when I first met her at the village dance. I'd been with women before, but I fell instantly in love with Lottie, it spooked me and I ran out on her that night. Now I've got to get to know her, all about her, and figure out how to make our marriage work.' He went quiet.

Jill lifted the basket and turned over a few of the plump white mushrooms, their undersides showing brown. 'I'll leave you to think, Nate. I hope you and Lottie put things right soon. You've got Carl and a new baby to look forward to. Then come in for breakfast. Tilda will be frying these in butter, I know you like them.'

He nodded, grateful for her advice and company. He was unable to speak, for tears were blinding him.

He went into the house shortly afterward, hoping not to have to face Lottie in front of his in-laws. He was in luck, and he slipped upstairs to their bedroom. Lottie was dressed but half-sitting, half-lying on the bed.

'You look a mess.' There was no accusation in her husky tone, and he guessed right that she had cried through most of the night. She seemed defeated and lacking all her usual spark.

He went up her. 'I'm sorry, I mean it, Lottie. I had too much to drink. I think the locals put it down to my not being used to English beer, so there shouldn't be the wrong sort of gossip. Do you want to talk?'

'If you do,' she mumbled, looking straight ahead, her fingers picking at a hanky.

He sat on the bed and leaned across her,

194

putting his hands down either side of her. Lottie returned his solemn gaze. 'I don't really know where to begin, but I think, and I hope you'll agree, that we need to be on our own. I mean away from the farm. It isn't right anyway that we upset the rest of the household. Lottie, would you consider us renting a house somewhere until things are settled?'

'Settled? Do you mean if we decide to stay together or find our own farm?' She looked directly into his eyes.

He met her stony gaze. There was no question of them parting; there was no way he was giving up his son and expected child. 'It won't be Tremore, but I'll get you a farm that's just right for you, I promise.' He had an idea to save his marriage, and he would use any means to accomplish it.

Susan was alone in Tremore House, going mechanically through her household duties. Once a place of joy to work in, the house now felt bleak and empty. Faye had left with Simon this morning for Roskerne, saying she wanted to spend a few days alone before the migration of the whole household went ahead. Susan had seen that Faye was tired, but she had been tight-lipped and frosty, had seemed hurt and angry, and after hugging Tristan and the Smiths goodbye, she had given her and Mark only a curt farewell. It was as if she'd had something against them both.

Tristan had made a lot of cheery noises, but Susan and Mark had communicated anxious looks. 'Has Faye been overdoing it? I hope I haven't been a burden to her.' Mark had chewed a fingernail. 'Perhaps it's time I moved out. I was intending to ask about renting Rose Dew anyway. It won't be long before it's habitable. Do you think it would be all right?'

'Faye just needs a little time to herself,' Tristan had replied, keeping up the bright and breezy manner. 'She's left all the decisions to me. I'd be delighted to have you rent Rose Dew, to have you stay among us, and I'm sure Faye would be too, but please don't feel you should move out until the cottage is ready and you feel ready yourself.'

Susan was left feeling bad for not making a closer friend of Faye. Faye might have confided what the problem was, and she might have been able to comfort or advise her. She felt her position at Tremore would never be the same. It certainly wouldn't be if she acted on an unscrupulous suggestion of her brother's from the day before.

Taking ironed laundry into Pearl's front bedroom, she relived the horror of seeing Kenny waiting on her doorstep. He'd made a jolly fuss of Maureen, and the inquisitive, friendly girl was quickly won over by the large box of chocolates he'd brought for her, and the porcelain doll he'd proudly announced came all the way from Paris, France. In another box was a sumptuous dinner gown for Susan, and there had been perfume and make-up. No doubt, black market goods. There had been no choice but to invite him inside to share their tea.

'Mum bought a cake from the cake stall.' Maureen had chattered about the Bring and Buy. 'I've got this. It's a nightie case, made from real satin and lace. Mr Tris bought it for me.'

'The gent from Tremore House? He must dote on you, and no wonder, you're a bobby-dazzler.' Kenny had tweaked her nose. 'Now you've got your Uncle Kenny to dote on you too. I should have kept in touch with your mum. I was naughty. Got lots of birthdays and Christmases to make up for. We've got lots of fun ahead, Mo, just see if we don't.'

'Really?' Maureen eyed her uncle as if her brain was ticking away.

Susan shook her head. She could see her daughter was working out what she might get out of her 'long-lost' uncle; Maureen had inherited some of her father's calculating nature. She would put a stop to Kenny shortening Maureen's name. Silently, she had set the table. 'I'm afraid there's not many sandwiches. Bread rationing has just got tighter and I haven't had time to bake my own.'

'Never mind, Susie girl. It's the company that matters,' Kenny had grinned at her. It had been a friendly grin, but it didn't lessen Susan's distrust of him.

Maureen had giggled at her uncle's reference to her mother. 'Shall I go up and ask Mr Fuller if he wants to join us, Mum?'

Mark had been heard tapping in roof tiles, and Addi had appeared at the top of the track and stayed still, as if on guard. Usually he came bounding down to greet them. It could only be Kenny's presence that had caused the change.

'So that bloke Fuller's been here for a meal before?' Kenny gave Susan a meaningful wink, which made her colour up in anger. Kenny saw everything in an unsavoury light. He pulled the blue ribbon off the box of chocolates. 'Here, princess, you can put this in your hair. I spoke to Mr Fuller earlier. I reckon he just wants to get on with his work today. Tell me all about yourself. I don't like kids, but you're my flesh and blood. That makes you different, special.'

While fiddling with the ribbon, and gazing longingly at the chocolates, which she wasn't allowed to eat until after tea and then only four each day, Maureen told him how well she was doing at school and how much fun she had playing with the Smiths. 'And now we've broken up for the summer holiday I'll do a few jobs on the farm every day with them to earn some pocket money.' Kenny had listened while devouring all the food Susan put in front of him, then he followed it by bragging about his high connections in London, and how many famous film stars and singers he knew. Susan didn't like the starry-eyed look it gave Maureen, and she ordered her upstairs to change out of her school clothes.

'What's brought you back here, Kenny?' she asked bluntly. She started to stack the dishes on a tray, hoping Kenny would take the message and leave.

'Come on, girl, don't be like that.' He leaned back in his chair and swept his hands through his Brylcreemed hair. 'I've decided to leave the Smoke. I've made a stash, but not enough to run with the big boys. I like to wheel and deal, and I admit I'm a hard sod, but I ain't as ruthless as them up there. So I've come back to Truro, back to my roots. I'd rather be a big fish in a small pond then a small fish in a big one. I've already put out feelers for a business or two,' he added proudly, then crossed his fingers, smirking. 'Strictly legit, of course.'

Susan was horrified. 'You're not staying here with us!'

'Relax. I'm staying at the Red Lion. I'll be getting meself a nice big house and you and Maureen will be welcome there any time. In fact, with me around, you'll always have someone to turn to.' Kenny casually lit a cigarette. 'You're on to a winner round here, Susie. Got toffs eating out of your hand. Didn't take to that snobby bugger up at the cottage above you. What's his game then?'

Susan fetched him an ashtray from the dresser cupboard. 'You're the sort of man who provokes that sort of question, not Mark.'

'Mark is it? First names, eh? What's he labouring for?'

'He isn't, not really.' She gave him a few brief facts about Mark.

'Well, if he's getting divorced there's a chance for you then. But the Harvey bloke's your best bet. Plain as day to me it was that he thinks the sun shines out of your backside. Get anything you'd want out of him, I reckon. You could live like a lady, never have to worry about money or to skivvy again.'

'Don't be ridiculous!'

'Why're you offended?' Kenny made a wry face. He'd spent years taking advantage of any situation by any means his crafty mind came up with. 'You've not got something against the grand Mr Tristan Harvey, have you?'

'Of course I haven't. He's the kindest man I know.' Susan had squirmed in discomfort. It felt horribly intrusive and disloyal to be discussing Tristan Harvey in this mercenary manner.

'There you are, then. Think what he could do for Maureen. You owe her the best. The bloke you married was bringing you down.'

'You don't know anything about Lance.'

'Oh, but I do. I've made some of the same contacts he had. Did you know he was keeping knock-off goods in the cottage up there? The locals' belief that it's haunted was a great help to him. Just think, Sis, if the Krauts hadn't finished him off he might be in the nick by now. Lance didn't only receive and pass on to fences, he went out on the jobs.'

Susan had shuddered. Instinct had told her Lance had been dodgy, but she'd had no idea by how much. 'Keep your voice down,' she'd hissed. 'I don't want Maureen hearing this. She believes her daddy died a war hero and I don't want that shattered for her.'

'That can never be shattered, Susie. He died for his country. And I'd never do anything to upset the girl. She's a sweetie. So are you. You're lovely.'

'Oh, suddenly developed a soft spot, have you, Kenny?' Susan said sarcastically. 'Well, I'm not falling for it.'

'I wouldn't take that from anyone but you.' Kenny pointed at her with his cigarette. 'But you and Maureen are family, you're all I've got. And I've heard all about Lance Dowling's controlling ways and his nasty moods. You must have had a hard time with him. So what's wrong with you looking for a bit of pleasure and security? Love, even? A chap like Harvey could give you all that. Don't you want Maureen to look up? Do better in life? Seems to me you've got a God-sent opportunity just along the lanes but you're refusing to see it. Maureen won't thank you for it. Takes just one glance to see she's bright and'll want to go places. Your attitude's holding her back. Can't you see it? There's more than one way to be a good mother.'

'By behaving like a tart trying to snare a rich man! I'm not like that.' Susan was appalled. She could almost cry at the suggestion, the interference in her life, the anxiety Kenny was bringing to her snug little world.

'I know you're not. I've seen many gold-diggers in my time, and if I'd have found you was one I'd smack you in the gob. I admire you, Susie. You've kept your dignity. You're a lovely, decent young woman, and that's what Tristan Harvey's fallen for. I'm only pointing out that life could be different for you, that's all. I can see the thought's scared you, but why not have a quiet think about it, eh?'

Kenny had wittered on, 'And I can offer you and Maureen another future. When I'm all set up, you could come and live with me. You and Maureen would have everything you want, with no hard graft ever again. I'll pay for her to have a private education. She could end up as a doctor, a scientist, any-thing. I've met and admired women like that. It's in a woman's grasp nowadays if she wants it. I'd like to see Maureen do well, one way or another. You can't deny her a better future, can you? She'd end up hating you. Think about it, Susie. Think about it.'

Apart from her surprise at Kenny's change of view from pure chauvinism, she had thought about nothing else between his unwelcome arrival and Faye's dismal depar-ture. It seemed her world was being splinter-ed, and she'd had ideas thrust upon her that were unnerving. It had been hard to act naturally with Tristan during the few min-utes they'd spent alone in the house before he'd left for the farm office. He'd said, 'I'm taking the children to the pictures tomorrow, the afternoon matinee. There's a re-billing of *National Velvet*. It's about a girl and a horse. Maureen likes horses. She's a steady rider now. And there will probably be a Tom and Jerry cartoon too. Perhaps she'd like to come and keep Pearl company.'

Susan was sorting out the linen basket for ironing so she wouldn't have to look at him. She had been pleased before to have her daughter included in the Smith children's treats. But now after all that Kenny had said, she realized that Tristan had gone out of his way to spoil Maureen. Did he really have hopes for her in the romantic sense?

Glancing at him and receiving back a look of shining hope, she saw that Kenny had been right. Now what? If she refused his kind offer, she'd have to come up with a feasible excuse. And when Maureen discovered she had been denied this outing she'd kick up a tremendous fuss and demand to know why. How could she answer?

There was only one way she could answer. Her eyes on the pillowcase she was folding, she said, 'Yes, yes, she would. Thank you. It's very kind of you.'

She heard him expel a deep breath. 'Splendid. Um, the thing is, well, I'm not sure if I can cope with four children on my own. The girls will need a lady to um ... take them to the um ... perhaps you'd like to come along yourself?' Without looking at him, she knew he was blushing, and probably not because he was referring to the ladies convenience. 'We always finish with a fish and chip supper. Make a good day of it. What do you say? Would you like to think about it?'

Yes. Think about how she could get out of it! Oh, why was everything suddenly so complicated? She said, 'Yes, I'll think about it,' for there was nothing else she could say.

'Good. You can tell me what you decide later.'

She had until lunch, when everyone would crowd in for a summer salad, to come up with a valid reason for her and Maureen not to go to the pictures. Moments later Maureen provided her with one, and because it was a serious matter, she left the house and went straight to the farm.

Within the thick, whitewashed walls of the little office in the ancient Tremore farmhouse, Tristan was trying to wade through Ministry papers and fill in account books. 'Damn and blast it!' He threw down his fountain pen. Ink splashed on an important document and his shirt cuff, and while blotting it up, he resorted to some choice soldier's language. He felt useless at being unable to soothe Faye in her distress. She'd phoned to say she'd arrived safely at Roskerne, that she hadn't changed her mind about selling up, and that she'd appreciate it if she were not disturbed. Then he'd made a mess of things with Susan. He'd tried to be casual, but had come across like a bashful youth. And there had been something different about her today. She had been distant, ill at ease. He broke into a panic. Had she been on to his motives? He was hoping she would notice the extent of his interest in her at some point, but after ... when ... oh, he didn't know when. Twice he had married, but romancing a woman had not been this difficult before.

His wrist was stained with ink. His shirt should be soaked in cold water. He was hardly going to endear himself to Susan if he gave her extra laundry. Well, he'd just throw the damned shirt away. It was ruined anyway. She'd never know. Now he asked himself why was he being pessimistic. She hadn't appeared horrified at him asking her to join him and the children at the pictures. She might like to go, to see the film herself. She might not have read anything into his invitation except a kind gesture. If Susan enjoyed the film, enjoyed being with all the children, and him, well ... the next step might be easier. But had he put her in a spot? Well, even if he had, she still might enjoy the outing. And then...

Susan knocked on the low office door, which was slightly ajar, an item in her hand digging into her palm for she was holding it so tightly.

'Cyril?' Tristan assumed it was Cyril Trewin, manager of the farm from Ben's arrival at Tremore. 'Come in.'

Susan pushed the door open a couple of inches. 'No, it's me.'

Tristan shot to his feet, his heart shocked into a fierce pounding as if he was suddenly thrown into a military charge. He was consumed with a crazed mix of hope and expectation. He was sure his face had gone as red as a turkey's wattle. Coming round the desk he hid his arm behind his back to hide the soiled cuff. 'Susan, come in. Is everything all right?'

'I need to talk to you, Mr Tristan.' Now she was here, on an errand of shame actually, rather than with a reason to decline his offer of a trip to the pictures, she reddened with equal brightness. A man as honest and full of integrity as he was might now see Maureen and herself in a different light.

'Do have a seat.' He pointed to a ragged armchair beside the little hearth. The scraps of furniture in the room were all charmingly abused by decades of farm workers. It lent a cozy, old-fashioned ambiance and here was one of Tristan's favourite places, where he lingered over a cigar and a glass of single malt from Ben's secret hoard. 'You look very serious. Has Faye telephoned? Told you anything?'

She ignored the chair. She should remain standing for this. 'No. Should there be something?'

'Um, no.' Tristan couldn't reveal why Faye had left early for Roskerne, but it seemed wrong not to tell Susan, or Mark, the truth. 'You go ahead.'

'I'm very sorry—'

'For what?' he interrupted. 'You're not giving in your notice?' Had his invitation offended her? Frightened her into taking flight?

'No. But you might want me to after I show you this.' She held out her hand and unwrapped a child's hanky, to reveal inside a small round metal case and two pieces of broken glass.

Tristan took the broken article. 'It's from my collection of stop watches. Did you break it while cleaning? Well, you mustn't worry. It was an accident.'

'I'm afraid it wasn't.' Susan wrung her hands together. 'It was taken. By Maureen. I found it wrapped up in a cardigan of hers and left in Pearl's room. She must have taken the stop watch to time a game and then broken it. I'm so sorry. I'm so ashamed that she would do something like that and then try to hide it. Can it be repaired? I'll pay for it, of course.'

'That won't be necessary.' Tristan examined the stop watch. 'There's no damage to anything except the glass. There's a chap I use for repairs for items like this for my antique shop. He'll easily find a new glass to fit the watch.' She seemed so vulnerable and forlorn. He smiled at her, wanting to enfold her in his arms and tell her she need never worry about a thing. 'I'm sure you'll enjoy a visit to the shop while we're at Roskerne. I've an excellent manager and assistant there. I sell a little furniture, it's collectables mostly, from figurines to war memorabilia. Maureen will be fascinated, I'm sure, by some clockwork animal toys I've recently acquired.' His most enjoyable work involved scouring for treasures for his shop, but these days he begrudged the time if it was during Susan's working hours.

Susan bypassed his enthusiasm. She didn't want to think about how understanding he was. And he had other attractions. He was more than presentable. Handsome in the striking way he smiled. 'It's a relief to know the watch can be mended. The real crime is Maureen borrowing something that doesn't belong to her and keeping the breakage a secret. I shall punish her, of course. I won't allow her to go to the pictures tomorrow.'

'Oh, please don't do that!' The disappointment made Tristan beg. 'I mean, Pearl would be so disappointed. It would be letting her down. May I suggest you think of something else?'

She had found a way out of a tricky situation. If she insisted on Maureen being punished her way, he wouldn't continue to persuade her otherwise, he being such a reasonable man. And so kind, he wasn't the least bit cross about Maureen's misdemeanour. All she could think of was how kind he was. A thought shot into her mind. Would it be too awful to consider Kenny's suggestion that she should consider him as a way to provide all her and Maureen's needs? Did she owe Maureen a better way of life? Opportunities she'd otherwise be denied?

She couldn't look Tristan in the eye while giving place to such thoughts, and she stared down at the threadbare mat. Could she bear all the duties of a wife again, the bedroom duties in particular? She had to stop this. She was embarrassed and breathing raggedly. He would notice and wonder what was the matter. 'Most people would be furious over what Maureen had done.'

'All children get up to mischief. If it makes you feel any better, I could give Maureen a dressing down.'

How could she refuse such consideration? 'Yes, I'd be glad if you did that. She must be taught what's right and wrong. My brother gave her chocolates and a doll yesterday. I'll confiscate them for a while.'

'He's back, Susan?' Tristan was jubilant the outing was going ahead. They would be seen all trooping on to the bus to Truro tomorrow. It was as good as announcing that he and Susan were stepping out together. 'Another short visit?'

'No such luck.' She told him about Kenny's intentions.

'Are you worried about it?'

'He seems to have softened a little, but he's a con man, never to be trusted. He's heartless. Maureen took to him immediately. In fact she was cross with me for not telling her she had an uncle. Kenny could be a bad influence on her.' *You can't always protect her by yourself.* It was as if a subconscious worry had spoken inside her head. If Tristan became Maureen's stepfather, he would protect her. Susan couldn't stand these self-seeking thoughts. She would not bring Maureen up believing money and position were all-important, that any action you took, even to be able to live to your full potential, could be justified. She had accepted her life, and she would teach Maureen to do the same. 'I suppose I'd better get back. Oh, your shirt!'

'Sorry, I was careless.' He held out the offending sleeve.

'That's not like you.'

There was a moment of silence. One of delight for him, for she had acknowledged that she knew his ways. She was comfortable in that moment, for it had felt natural to make such a remark. She had been alone here with him for some time, and suddenly she was in no hurry to scamper away. 'You can't stay like that.'

'No, I'd better go home and change. Perhaps I could have my morning coffee at the house instead of here.'

'Yes, of course.'

Chatting with ease, they walked side by side to the house. A man met them at the gates. He lifted his tweed hat to Susan, revealing thick dark hair. He was in his mid-forties, hardy and distinguished-looking, with the air of a country gentleman. 'Good morning.'

'Good morning. Can I help you?' Tristan said.

'I'm looking for Miss Faye Harvey. This is where she lives?'

'I'm her uncle, Tristan Harvey.' Tristan peered at him closely. 'May I know what business you have with her?'

'I'm Fergus Blair. Laird of Glenladen. Does that explain who I am?'

Tristan nodded and sighed heavily. Blair's timing couldn't be worse. He saw no reason not to reveal his identity to Susan. 'Susan, this is Simon's father.'

Twelve

Faye was shaking so badly she had trouble clipping on her pearl earrings. She smoothed her hair, which she'd pinned back in a chignon, then smoothed her linen, square-shouldered, panelled dress over her hips, her hands trembling like an old woman's. Make-up. How on earth was she going to put it on? Why bother anyway? It wasn't as if her expected visitor meant anything to her.

'Why did you have to come now?' She aimed the question at the last image of Fergus Blair in her mind. Outside his highland castle, Glenladen, with the tranquil waters of the loch below. Handsome, dark and powerful, concerned and sorry for what he had done. 'I shouldn't have been so irresponsible,' he'd said. 'I hate it that you have to go away. Mrs McPherson will look after you. She and her husband have farmed on this land all their lives. I don't want you to go without anything. I've paid two thousand into your account, and I shall add three hundred each year on the child's birthday. Mrs McPherson will keep me informed. I wish you well, Faye. I'll never forget you, I swear.'

Was that why he had turned up at Tremore this morning? Had she been imprinted on his mind these last four years, and in the end he'd had to come to her? Fergus would probably know from Mrs McPherson that she had not met anyone else – she kept in touch with the woman who had been so kind and motherly during her confinement. Although she had been hurt and rejected by Fergus's refusal to divorce his wife, a part of her, in quiet, contented moments, had thought it would be nice to see him again one day. They had enjoyed an impassioned, happy relationship, and despite the terrible let-down, she couldn't hate him. His timing to come here could not have been worse. While her emotions were in turmoil, while she was considering whether to go ahead with the decision she had made in Hennaford's school playground. While she was feeling guilty for deserting Mark before he was completely well, and for shunning him and Susan. Then there was the hurt she had caused Lottie. Lottie was considered the most selfish one of the family, but she had done nothing as terrible as she had, throwing her a magnificent gesture only to destroy it hours later, leaving Lottie bereft and humiliated. She wouldn't blame Lottie if she never forgave her.

Since the phone call from her uncle telling

her of Fergus's arrival in Cornwall, she'd forced away all thought that he might still mean something to her. No doubt, Fergus only wanted to see Simon, and as she was accepting his financial support for their son, it gave Fergus the right to see him. From the start she had made up her mind to never refuse him access. The time she had spent with Fergus had been wonderful, and she realized she had not fully left him behind. Now she was determined to. His arrival might just be the catalyst she needed to tidy up all the loose ends in her heart and go forward in the right direction, to move on successfully with her life, for her own and Simon's sake.

While getting ready to see him, memories had filtered into her mind, so real and alive some of them seemed to have happened only yesterday. From the start there had been a reciprocal liking. Fergus was strong and fun, with an old-world charm that was enticing. He knew he held a potent appeal to women and he'd used it and laughed at it. Faye had found it hard to understand why his wife, the mother of his three children, all away on war service, had forsaken him years before, running off to Florence – with a younger, brittle lover, according to accounts from the staff. Fergus had explained that she had become restless, wanting to travel and socialize, but the estate and his duty to it and love for it, and the slow, traditional, sometimes hard way of life it demanded, was all he wanted.

They had spent many hours alone, sharing their deepest thoughts on long walks through the glens, fishing on the loch and over his ancient banqueting table. They had slipped into taking a nightcap together, climbing the vast worn stairs at the same time, and one cold winter's night, instead of separating on the wide draughty landing, he had slipped an arm round her waist.

He had drawn her to him and she had gone into his arms, seeking his lips as instantly as he had sought hers. 'That wasn't a mistake, Faye,' he had said, letting her go. 'You're so lovely. So perfect.' She had thought him perfect.

The next night, in the same place, after exchanging lingering glances and warm touches all day, they had kissed for ages. When he had finally drawn away, Faye was sure that it must already be morning, and she had spent the long hours of the night with him in blissful contact. Then the clocks had chimed midnight, the magical hour of a fairy tale. But she had not wanted the night to end. Fergus had taken her hand. 'Will you come with me?'

She had squeezed his hand and nodded.

It was cold in his room with the wartime restrictions on fuel, but she had not felt herself shivering as he'd quickly undressed her. Fergus had nearly scalded his bare legs on the old porcelain hot water bottle the housekeeper had put in the large ancestral bed. How they had laughed. And loved. And it had been like that every day for months until the horror of the moment she had realized she was pregnant.

The fairy tale had come to an end. She had known it would. Fergus had never said he loved her, he had never promised her anything. It had not occurred to Faye a baby would part them, as Fergus had said he'd 'take care of that sort of thing'. He had slipped up, and it had been a terrible wrench for her to leave Glenladen, a place of inestimable beauty. Of pine forests, wild deer, shaggy-coated cattle and clean air, where she had felt valued and cherished. After her initial fear and regret, she was glad to be having a child, someone she could share a lasting love with. Simon mattered more to her than anyone in the world. He loved her without question, and she would always put him first. It would be hard for her to face Fergus, but it was right that he had come for Simon's sake. She didn't want her beloved son to feel rejected by his father, like she had by hers. She saw Fergus's timing now as a sign. It would soon be revealed why he had come, and she would put up a shield and stay wary of his intentions.

★ ★ ★

217

The attractive young woman with Tristan Harvey had gone on into Tremore House, and he had put himself in Fergus's way, frosty and determined. 'Faye's not here. She has gone away for a while. I suggest you write to her and ask if she'll consider seeing you. I'll pass on your letter when she gets back.'

'Has she gone far?' Fergus was just as determined. He would not be put off easily.

'That's really none of your business.'

'I take it that she hasn't. Look, Mr Harvey, I'm pleased you feel you should protect Faye, but let me assure you that I'm not here to upset her in any way. I'd very much like to see her and our son. I know Faye. She won't thank you for treating her like a child. I think she would like the opportunity to speak for herself.'

Reluctantly, Tristan Harvey had invited him inside Tremore, keeping him in the hall, and agreed to ring her. He had returned from the library, grim and sighing. 'She's agreed you may go to her, Blair. I wanted to go too, but she feels strong enough to face you alone. Let her down or hurt her and I'll come after you. The last thing she needs is more complications.'

Fergus wasn't given to nervousness, but he was anxious about the reception Faye would give him. He should have got in touch from Glenladen, but he was afraid the distance would make it easy for her to feel it unwise to see him. He heard her coming down the stairs, then her light steps heading his way. He felt as goosey as a boy braving his very first date.

'Hello Fergus.' She was there in the doorway, as gorgeous as ever but presenting herself with pride and sophistication. He had thought about her every lonely day since she had left his castle. He had been drawn to her from the first instant, and that sweet attraction had grown into something beautiful, which he'd kept in his heart. Seeing her now, so lovely, so wonderful, part of her back to the melancholy girl she had first been, that beauty inside him burst into life and nearly overwhelmed him. He knew he had loved her in all the years since their parting, and he so wanted to tell her this, but he must be careful and sensitive with her. To his shame, he was responsible, partly as least, for the reason why she wasn't happy and content as she deserved to be. He cursed himself for being a weak fool in letting her go.

As if they had a will of their own his hands stretched out to her. 'Hello Faye. It's so good to see you. You look beautiful, just as I expected. I hope you don't mind me coming down unannounced. I was afraid you might put me off.'

With him actually here in front of her, Faye wasn't sure what her reaction would have been if he had got in contact first. He had not changed a bit. He exuded the same enticing masculinity and he searched her face as he talked, letting nothing distract him, focused totally on her, just as before. An easy smile lit up his gorgeous dark features and his vivid green eyes hinted of mysterious depths, as deep and as exciting as the loch on his home shores. He had the same powerful persona, looking much younger than his years. He seemed less comfortable not being on his own ground, but she didn't put that down to anything to do with her. She clasped her hands together formally. 'I presume you at last want to see your son?'

'And you too, Faye,' he said, hoping he was conveying his sincerity. 'It was a devil of a job to wear your uncle down and get him to agree to ask you to see me. He warned me very thoroughly not to upset you. As if I would, Faye. I suppose he's a really decent sort.'

'Uncle Tris is one of the best.'

'Um, I hope you don't mind, I've managed to get a room at the local hotel even though the holiday season's in full swing. I must say I enjoyed the journey through the maze of lanes and little villages. And when I got my first glimpse of the ocean, why, I was completely bowled over. It's astonishing, magnificent. I hope to see lots more of it, and to see more of you, Faye. How are you? I got the feeling from your uncle that you're not too good. And how's Simon? Can I see him?'

She felt no threat from what Fergus said. He was hesitant and seemed not to have come sweeping back into her life with arrogance. But she wasn't about to give away anything personal. 'Simon's fine. He's taking a nap. He should wake soon.' She indicated they should sit down. She perched on the end of a sofa.

He took a seat across the spacious room, not wanting to crowd her. 'It's all rather simple, Faye. My wife Sheila is dead. She and her lover were drowned three weeks ago in a boating accident on the canals. The instant I heard, when I knew I was free, my thoughts went straight to you. What you had meant to me. What we had was so much more than an affair to me, I hope you always knew that. I've thought of you a lot since you left Glenladen. There's been times I became quite determined to seek you out, but I felt it wouldn't have been fair to you, so I always talked myself out of it. I arranged for Sheila's body to be flown back for burial, as her will requested, in her family kirk at Fort William. The next day, Donald, Isabel and Jamie came to me in force and urged me to make a life of my own, to find someone. Isabel, in particular, stressed that I'd been married to the estate for far too long. Did I really want to be a lonely old man? Then she mentioned you. She took to you that one time you met. She realized we were closer than boss and secretary, and she'd told her brothers about us at their mother's wake. Then I found myself telling them about the real reason why you'd left and about Simon. Isabel suggested, as you were, apparently, on your own too, that I look you up. Faye, my three children would really like to meet their little brother. I dithered for a while, concerned how you would take all this, then I got on the next train. So, here I am, to see you and our son. I'm hoping that I can persuade you to come to Glenladen at some time. Faye, I want Simon to know me as his father, to know his brothers and sisters, and his little niece. Donald's married now, and has just presented me with my first grandchild. Please think about it.'

Faced with her best hopes for Simon, to be fully accepted by the man who had fathered him, to get to know the other branch of his family, Faye felt some relief, but there were still concerns. 'What about the people on the estate? I wouldn't countenance pretending Simon was another man's.'

'No need for that, Faye. It's got around, everyone knows. I think Isabel told Mrs McIntyre, the housekeeper, and after that human nature took its course. There will be little or no prejudice, no moralizing. Now

I'm free, people are expecting me to do the right thing by you. I've been told to by many in no uncertain terms, including the minister. I should have done that over three years ago. I was a coward. I've been told that too.'

Faye's jaw was sagging. 'Fergus, what exactly are you saying?' She feared she was about to be placed in an impossible situation.

'I've not come to play games with you, Faye, so I'll be straight with you. You know it's my way. There seems to be no one else in your life, so,' he took a mighty breath, 'if you'd have me, I'd so very much like for us to marry. Please don't feel you have to say anything. I don't want you to feel under any pressure. If you want me to go away I will, but I'm hoping you'll see if anything could be recovered between us.'

She had to force herself to take it in. Was this really happening? The offer of what she had once longed to receive. It would solve everything. She wouldn't have to go to some strange place and pretend to be married. She could live in the wild beauty of a place where she had known some of the happiest moments of her life, fully accepted, married to Simon's father, making Simon legitimate. 'This is all such a surprise. I've no idea what to say.'

She got up and paced about the room, knowing his eyes were on her every move.

Her feelings for Mark were still strong, but even if he changed his view of her, Simon must come first. There couldn't be anyone better for him than Fergus. He had been honest with her, admitting his faults, the mark of a good man, but allowing him to stay on in the bay could be a terrible mistake, and she had made so many of them in her life.

Fergus was sinking by fathoms. Her expression was grave. Was she angry, offended? 'I hope you won't send me away.'

'Mummy.' A little voice was heard outside in the passage. In the intensity of their discussion, they hadn't heard Simon padding down the stairs. He appeared in cotton dungarees, bare-foot and pink-faced and rubbing his eye. Trailing a large teddy bear from one hand.

'Oh, my word,' Fergus gasped. 'He's just ... he's beautiful. And he's mine.' Gulping back his emotion he got up and fell down on his knees in front of the little black-haired boy. 'How could I have missed all this until now?'

Simon took his fingers from his eye, saw the man, blinked, and gazed at Faye for reassurance.

Faye went to them, and Fergus gazed up at her with desperate appeal. She couldn't send him away, it wouldn't be right. She caressed Simon's tousled hair. 'It's all right, darling. This is your daddy.'

Thirteen

Mark was out riding. It was years since he had straddled a horse, but allowing for his aching legs and seat, he was enjoying the experience, with Addi jogging at his side in between shooting off to sniff new territory. He recalled Maureen's pleas at the stables to go with him.

With the other three children, she had watched him saddle up. 'I can sit up in front of you, Mr Fuller.' She had clung to the bridle while he'd mounted the dark bay hunter. 'I won't be any trouble, I promise. Please can I go?'

He had looked down on the scrap of a girl in a grubby cotton frock, with wayward socks and unruly hair. 'I'd rather go alone, Maureen.'

'I won't make a fuss, promise. Mr Tris is teaching me to ride, and I've ridden the ponies in the paddock bareback.'

'You shouldn't mess about with the ponies or horses, Maureen,' he'd frowned. 'You mustn't annoy them. You could get hurt.'

'I won't.' She had tried charm, putting her

hands together prayer fashion. 'I want to go with you now. Please, please, please.'

'Sorry, Maureen. I've said no.'

'Stop it, Maureen, or I'll tell your mum you're playing up again,' Bob had muttered darkly. Len had nodded agreement. Maureen was undermining their leadership, as boys and the elders of their gang – the Fearless Four – and they were increasingly turning to Susan or Tristan to settle matters. While Pearl didn't mind, impressed by Maureen's devil-may-care ways, the twins were jealous of the attention she drew, especially from their Uncle Tristan, and they had made attempts for her to fall out of his favour. Her punishment for taking and breaking the stop watch had had no effect on her. The twins had complained to Mark that she'd been naughty in the fish and chip shop after the pictures, showing them up by singing 'The Good Ship Lollipop' loudly and tapping out the tune with her knife and fork. She had fidgeted and cracked jokes that had included bad words – learned, to her mother's anger, from her Uncle Kenny. Other diners had tutted. Then she had gone up to the counter and demanded more bread and butter. The proprietor had pointed at her crossly, 'Sit down young lady and be a good girl for your mummy and daddy.' The twins said it had made Mrs Dowling turn a funny colour, but that their Uncle Tristan had 'for some strange reason' actually seemed pleased. It was all very puzzling to the boys.

'Do you think Uncle Tris and Mrs Dowling are stepping out?' Bob had asked him. 'It's what people in the village are hinting at. Pearl went with her and Maureen to the shop yesterday and when Mrs Eathorne was weighing out our sweet ration, she said to Mrs Dowling, "I hear things are getting cosy for you at Tremore now Miss Faye's away. You couldn't do better, if I may say so."

' "I don't know what you're talking about," Mrs Dowling had said back, and Pearl said her face went as red as a beetroot.'

Len took up the tale. 'And when we called on Agnes we overheard her talking to her neighbour about them. She said, "All we got to do is just wait and watch nature take its course. There's an age difference, of course, but it's better to be an old man's darling than a young man's slave." '

'Alice wouldn't tell us what she meant, Mr Fuller,' Bob had whispered, bringing his ear close as if he was hoping to learn some great secret of the universe. 'Ladies say some strange things. Who's a slave? Mrs Dowling? What will happen when nature takes its course?'

Mark was used to speaking frankly to troops, but he'd been lost at what to say to a pair of sharp boys. He didn't want them to work it out for themselves and cause Susan further embarrassment. He would hate to see her frightened away from something that would be totally right for her, and for Maureen. Tristan showered devotion on Susan from afar, and although Susan acted as if she might be aware of it and was often distant with Tristan, she sometimes forgot to be careful and unconsciously responded to him. 'I've never really understood ladies. Chaps don't. I'm sure if we did it would spoil things.'

'What things?' the twins, wide-eyed and heads forward, had asked together.

'That's a subject for another day,' he had answered firmly. The boys had been satisfied with that, not inclined to pester and delve and pick away, like Maureen would.

He smiled as he rode along Back Lane. His refusal to allow Maureen to join him meant she'd give the twins a hard time today. From his vantage position he waved to Faye's labourers in the fields. As he neared the end of the lane, he reined in to chat to a pensioner and his wife over their garden wall. So broad was their accent he grasped little of what the white-haired and dark-clad couple said, but he gathered their sapper grandson had been killed by a German booby trap at Tobruk. He felt it was important to them that they tell him this, him being a former officer, and he had offered them his sympathy. He accepted their good wishes for his continuing health. It had been nice talking to them. He could have made his way anywhere along the network of lanes and avoided people, but he now felt able to show his face in Hennaford. He had heard a lot about the villagers. No doubt he'd soon meet some of its strongest characters.

He headed in the direction of the pub, and after a few yards was a row of cottages; in between them was the butcher's shop, and at the end, the general stores. He dismounted outside the stores, tying the hunter's reins to the wooden gate at the side of the long cream-painted building. He ignored the discomfort in his lower limbs that would make it hard to get started the following morning. 'Addi, stay. I won't be long.'

Before he climbed the four wide mismatched granite steps, a ruddy-faced man opened the door, making the shop bell tinkle merrily. 'You can be no other than Mr Mark Fuller, guest of the Harveys at Tremore, sir.' The man thrust out a thick paw. 'Proud to make your acquaintance, to have you call on my humble little establishment. I'm Gilbert Eathorne; shopkeeper and sub-postmaster in this here tiny spot of the world these past forty-odd years. Come inside and meet my good lady wife, Mrs Eathorne, Myra. The horse will be fine there. No one'll touch her.'

Once inside one of the central meeting

places of the village, Mark shook hands with the Eathornes. He knew it was from this bespectacled pair, in their early seventies and still sprightly, where a lot of the gossip was gleaned and passed on. Mark glanced about. Before the war he had enjoyed these sort of old-fashioned places, but he was finding it a bit claustrophobic here. The shelves were close together and packed with a diversity of goods. The Eathornes were able to order just about anything anyone wanted, from linoleum for floors to make-up, from walking sticks to baking soda. There were written apologies for scarce and unattainable goods, with references to the rationing and polite pleas for patience. Inviting smells of boiled ham, toffee and tobacco mingled with those of paraffin and coal tar soap.

There were two hoop-backed chairs for customer use, and taking the weight off her podgy, veined legs on one, was a beady-eyed housewife, in a wraparound print apron, droopy cardigan and severely tied paisley headscarf. She had a well-used, checked leather shopping bag on her lap. It bulged here and there, so she had been served and was lingering. Mark was introduced to Mrs Moses. He could see she was a stalwart villager. The downward turn of her grim mouth pointed to her being intolerant and prudish. She did no more than nod when he said, 'Pleased to meet you,' but he got the uneasy sensation she was trying to look into his soul. Here was someone who was bitter and spiteful. Who was probably feared by her family and didn't have one single friend, nor deserved one.

Myra Eathorne, doughty, a natural giver of smiles, with stone-grey permed hair and starched white apron, examined his face every bit as finely as a doctor would. 'Glad to see you're up to getting about at last, Mr Fuller. You're still far too thin, but I'm sure Miss Faye will sort that out. How is she, by the way? Will Mr Harvey and the little ones be joining her soon? And you also?'

'Tomorrow, actually, Mrs Eathorne.' Mark wished she and her husband wouldn't stand so close. He felt pressed in on all sides.

Mrs Moses snorted. Mark had no doubt she was one of the locals who had made Faye feel unaccepted. Tristan had filled him in on Faye's troubles to avoid him saying something unfortunate when they joined her. This particular gossip had better not say a word against Faye. He wouldn't have her maligned. Faye didn't deserve any sort of pain. She was a wonderful woman, and he missed her. He was glad for her and for Simon that the boy's father had made contact, but he had no wish to meet Fergus Blair, who was staying on at Watergate Bay.

The shop door was swung open and the bell protested with a clatter. 'Ah-ah!' The

231

owner of the bellow and a hearty chuckle came rushing inside. His white coat, striped apron and boater pointed to him being the butcher. Mark's insides jumped at the commotion. There was nowhere he could go to get away from the butcher, who leapt on him and pumped his hand up and down. 'I said to my boy, I believe that there's the stranger from Tremore. I'm Sidney Eathorne, brother of Gilbert. It's an honour, Mr Fuller, to meet one of our brave fighting men. Got the kettle on then, Myra?'

'No tea for me.' Mark had to draw a deep breath to stop his head turning muzzy.

Gilbert went round the serving side of the heavy wooden counter. His ruddy face broke into a toothy grin. 'What can I get you, Mr Fuller? You're welcome t'look round and browse as long as you like.'

Mark felt surrounded by avid faces. He stepped away from Sidney and his beaming curiosity, but the butcher relentlessly closed up each gap. 'Just cigarettes, please. Have you any State Express 555?'

'As it happens I do. I'm proud to say we keep in a few of the finer things for our more discerning customers.' Gilbert turned round, took a packet off a shelf and put it down with a friendly flourish. He raised his bushy brows. 'Matches?'

'No, thank you. I have a lighter.' Mark sensed hard stares coming from Mrs Moses.

He wished only to pay for the cigarettes and leave. He produced a ten shilling note and hoped Gilbert wouldn't take his time with the change.

'Hear you've been doing up Rose Dew? See anything of poor old Jude who haunts it?' Sidney asked. 'You must be some brave or mazed to work there for so long. Nearly finished it, is it?'

Mark saw Jude from time to time, and Jude didn't seem to mind him being there. He was determined to protect the former farm worker's privacy. 'I've found nothing creepy there,' he said. 'Working on the cottage has been therapeutic.'

'Well, I'm glad to hear it. What do you think Miss Faye will do with the place, Mr Fuller?' Myra ventured. 'You might not find anything scary there, but I can't see no one local choosing to live there.'

'I'm thinking of asking for the tenancy myself, actually.' Mark thought he might as well admit it. If he stayed on in Hennaford, these people would be his neighbours.

'Not thinking of going back to your wife then? As you very well should,' Mrs Moses said, with a noisy sniff.

Mark saw all three Eathorne faces burn with embarrassment on his behalf. No doubt they'd all like to learn the private details of his marriage breakup, but it was good to know this was not the sort of gossip they went in for. He turned to face his accuser. Mrs Moses put her nose in the air and aimed back a gaze direct. He guessed rightly that she rarely looked away from a confrontation. As she tightened her hard features, her skin wrinkled to walnut likeness and she seemed like a witch. People must be more frightened of her than of Jude. 'It's none of your business.'

'Don't believe in divorce,' Mrs Moses remained sitting, like a highborn lady pronouncing on the lives of serfs under her jurisdiction. 'You should get back up to her and work things out. She should make the effort too. This war hasn't done any of us any favours.'

'Specially not the dead and maimed and bereaved, Mrs Moses.' Mark took his change from Gilbert. He knew he should excuse himself and leave, but there was something despicable about the Moses woman and he wanted to slap her down.

'My cousin lost her two boys in the fighting, and my brother was killed in the Great War. I know about bereavement.' Acid dripped off her every word, and Mark wondered if she actually mourned her family loss. 'Bad examples are being set everywhere. Your hostess being the main culprit in the village. She'll encourage the young maids to flaunt themselves. And Mr Harvey's no better, preying on that young widow.'

'There was no need for that, Mrs Moses!' Myrna gasped. 'Perhaps it's time you left.' She turned her shocked face to Mark in apology.

'Perhaps it's time you shopped elsewhere,' Sidney said, opening the door for the caustic woman. 'You won't be welcome in our shops if you go on saying things like that.'

Mrs Moses rose slowly, lips puckered primly. 'You Eathornes are bound to jump to their defence, you're too eager for Harvey custom. But I've only said what others have been saying, including you lot.' She marched out on her heavy feet.

Mark was furious. The Moses woman had insulted the two most important women in his life. He missed Justine at that moment. And again he missed Faye, so much.

A blustering Gilbert said, 'We all like a bit of tittle-tattle, Mr Fuller, but please don't think we share that woman's views. We allow for human nature and people's mistakes, none of us are lily-white, after all. Mrs Moses's husband left her for another woman years ago and she's never forgiven him. She never was a pleasant person, and now she's bitter and twisted. Can't understand how she dares show her face in chapel.'

'I'm afraid there's little one can do against people like her,' Mark said, wishing the Moses woman would one day know what real suffering was like. 'They have no feelings, they're rotten. Good day to you.'

When he reached the door, Sidney blurted out, 'P'raps you'll do the honour of accepting a drink from me and my brother in the Ploughshare one night, Mr Fuller.'

'Yes, perhaps,' Mark said. It would be a while before that was likely to happen.

Needing a smoke, he lit up and rode on, taking the turning beside the pub. Setting the horse at a brisk pace down Church Lane, he looked over the fields of Emilia Bosweld, hoping the hot sun and fresh air would quickly dissipate the bleak mood thrust on him. He cantered through fallow fields, jumping over the occasional low hedge, working up a sweat, growing thirsty. Wondering how Faye was. Her decision to leave Hennaford was understandable, but it was terrible that she felt she must go because of a few poisonous tongues. Justine had mentioned over the phone that she'd had a few unkind remarks over the divorce but she had laughed them off. She didn't have the vulnerability of being an unmarried mother.

He bypassed Ford Farm – he'd call in there on the way back – and wandered the fields and lanes for another hour. Stopping at the church, he read the names on the war memorial. William Harvey, Lottie's brother, had been added in neat black lettering, with eight others of those lost between 1939 and 1945. How close his name had been to being laid on a Surrey stone. He saluted the dead comrades-in-arms and left.

He took another long canter, then turned back, eventually coming to a meandering sloping meadow, the lower reaches stubbly from cut hay. A gently curving stream ran along at the bottom and red clover, meadow clary and comfrey figured among the pretty wild flowers. He jumped down and led the hunter along an oft-used path beside the cooling lazy stream. Addi raced off excitedly, and he saw why. A young woman was sitting near the bank under a towering oak tree. After receiving a welcome and a patting from her, Addi lay down at her feet. Mark reached Lottie moments later. 'Hello. Hope we're not intruding.'

'Not at all. You're welcome to join me.' Lottie gazed up, shielding her eyes from the sun. 'I've got some lemonade, if you're thirsty.'

'Thank you.' Mark eased himself down beside her, rubbed at his sore limbs, and gratefully soothed his dry throat with a drink. He gazed into the stream, which chinkled along over a stony bed. 'This is a very peaceful place.'

She gazed up at the old heavy branches high above, thick with summer growth. 'It was my father's favourite spot. He used to come here to find peace, and it's where, one early morning, he came to die. He had a tendency to brood, but I like to think he found the peace he was looking for in the end. I'm here now trying to find some peace for myself.'

'I'm sorry about your father, and sorry that you're troubled,' Mark said quietly. He had only seen her once, the day she had come to Tremore House with her mother and their infants, and Lottie Harmon had been vivacious and purposeful then. Now she was almost lifeless. Her eyes were dull and her skin was grey. Unless weighed down with burdens, expectant mothers were usually radiant.

'I suppose you've been told my circumstances.'

'Yes. I feel for you.'

'Do you really?' Her words were flat. 'I can easily sympathize with you. You've endured some of the worst things a person ever could. You hardly know me, but you must have heard what a selfish cow I can be. I should feel that I've got everything I want, don't you think? I've brought my troubles on myself.'

'I'm sure others have contributed to them, Lottie. I know what it's like to think everything you've been longing for is within your grasp, only to be snatched away. It's a feeling that wipes out everything you have in you. It's hell to deal with. Would you like to talk? You might find it helpful to talk to a stranger, and you have my word it won't go any further.'

Pulling in her face to forbid the tears lurking behind her eyelids, she nodded. 'Thanks. The thing is, I'm a mess. I shouldn't be, of course. I've never gone without anything and I've always had the security of a large family. But there was one important person I never really knew. He ignored me most of the time. He didn't even seem to like me. My father. He died when I was five, and all through those years he became more and more remote and sometimes behaved strangely. No one knew, not even he did until the end, that he had a brain tumour, the reason why he couldn't stand a noisy, rebellious little girl around him. And he'd wanted me to be sweet and dainty, he didn't approve of me being a tomboy. My mother explained it was because of the baby girl they had lost. Jenna had been soft and delicate. He never got over the loss. Sadly for me, I felt rejected by him, although not in the way Faye suffered because of her father's attitude. The Harvey men tend to be a brooding lot. My brother Will was a bit like that too. Thank goodness the trait can't be found in Uncle Tris and my brother Tom.

'Anyway, to try to understand the person I am, I've come here to somehow try to get to know my father. This place was special to him. He chose it as his last place on earth, and even though he loved my mother desperately, he chose to die alone. He didn't tell anyone he had a terminal illness. I don't know if that's terribly sad or wonderfully poignant. My poor father, he was only forty-two when he died. Before you arrived I sat for a whole hour hoping to sense something of him still lingering here, to see if I could form a link with him, and he'd comfort me and tell me what to do.' Her tears could no longer be denied. 'I'm sorry.'

'Cry as much as you like, Lottie.' Mark put a firm touch on her arm. 'And did you feel anything?'

'I'm not sure,' she said between sobs. 'I thought I heard him whispering my name. It might have been just the breeze, but I'm sure it was he calling to me. Is that crazy?'

'I don't think so. I believe the dead come back to comfort and direct us. Did you sense anything from the call?'

'No advice or anything like that, but I felt he wanted me to know he loved me. That he understood that I'm in turmoil. It meant a lot.' She wept with her head bowed over her knees for some moments. 'I don't believe that my father deliberately tried to hurt me by making me feel rejected, but it's a horrible feeling, isn't it? Then I felt betrayed and misunderstood by Nate, my husband. He didn't mean to hurt me either. But I took what I saw as his neglect very badly. His homecoming was ruined, and nothing has been right between us since. I've been beastly to just about everyone. I've been jealous of my thoroughly pleasant sister-in-law, Jill. I thought she had everything, you see, until I heard her crying the other day. I asked her what was wrong. She said she was thinking of something sad. Then I overheard her saying to Tom, "No luck again." Then I realized they'd been trying for a baby and were unsuccessful again. Here I am, soon to be a mother of two, and I don't really want this second baby, I didn't want another child yet anyway. Strange, isn't it? So many of us don't appreciate that we have exactly what would make someone else blissfully happy. Jill and Tom will in all likelihood have a family. I hope they do. They deserve every happiness. They're so much in love. But things aren't going to easily be put right between Nate and me.'

It was a statement of her belief. Mark offered no platitudes. 'I'm sorry.'

'If you and your wife had children, I suppose things would be different.'

'Yes. A family might have given our marriage a purpose. Justine and I should have stayed simply as friends. I'm thankful we'll always have that.'

'I thought I'd married for the right reason – love. Now I'm not sure how much I love Nate. People say the war, the uncertainty of everything, heightened our emotions, making us do foolish and spontaneous things. Perhaps it was like that for Nate and me. While GI brides and babies have been shipped off to the States to start a new life with their husbands, Nate did it in reverse, for my sake, and I'm terrified he'll hate settling here and end up hating me for it.'

'Do you think there's a chance you might rediscover what you had with Nate?'

'I don't know. I'm scared I made a terrible mistake when I married him. And now Faye's in a quandary about her marriage proposal.'

Mark's brows shot up. 'The Scottish laird has offered her marriage?'

'I shouldn't have disclosed that. I phoned Faye to reassure her I had no hard feelings over her changing her mind about selling Tremore to Nate and me, and she told me Fergus Blair had proposed the same afternoon he went to Roskerne. She confided in me because we're the same age, I suppose, and both facing an uncertain future. She doesn't want everyone to know yet, to be pressurized one way or the other. You won't mention it, will you?' She studied Mark. What were his feelings about this? It seemed he had no inkling Faye was in love with him. He was frowning in thought, but otherwise his thin face was expressionless. But why should he be thinking about love? He had not long given up on his futile marriage and was still coming to terms with his POW experiences. It was too early for him to be considering a new romance.

'I see. Did she say how long this chap is staying around?'

'He has to go back for a business meeting at the end of the week. Faye's planning a dinner at the Watergate Bay Hotel for you and Uncle Tris, and Susan, to meet him.'

'I'll have to think about that.' Mark suddenly felt weary. The ride had drained nearly all his energy. 'It's really a family thing. Are you going home soon? I think I ought to return and take a rest. Tell your mother I'll call on her another day, if you would.'

'I must get back to Carl.' He helped Lottie up. 'And I've got packing to finish off. We're moving out tomorrow into a house on the outskirts of Truro, in a tiny hamlet called Highertown. It belongs to a friend of my stepfather's. He's a doctor and travels about a lot doing research and he's happy to let the family use it. I shall find it very strange living away from home. Nate's looking forward to us being on our own. He's quite overwhelmed by my family. He's at Highertown now getting things ready.' At last she dredged up a smile. 'He's been quite excited by it. He's promised we'll have a farm of our own before the baby's born. I should consider myself lucky, shouldn't I? There's so many people going through far worse difficulties.'

'Yes, there are,' he said, as they walked along with the horse and Addi. 'But it doesn't mean we must feel guilty just because our own problems are less. Suffering is suffering. I'll drop in to see you when you've settled in, if I may, Lottie.'

'I'd like that. Thanks Mark. It's been good talking to you.'

Fourteen

Nate was not in the house at Highertown. He was in Taldrea, one of the neighbouring hamlets to Hennaford, at Coose-Craze Farm, the farm that Lottie had set her heart on buying while he was still in Texas, before it was bought from under them. The farm rested roughly in the middle of a densely wooded area and was a world of difference from the vast open spaces he had been used to on the ranch. But he could see enough sky and nature to ease his soul, and he unexpectedly liked the cosy feel of it. The sheep and cattle in the fields seemed healthy, and the wheat, barley and other crops appeared not to be attacked by blight or disease. When he bought the property off the retired major – and he would do so by fair means or otherwise, for he was utterly determined to get it for Lottie – Coose-Craze would be just right for them to make a fresh start.

The track leading to it was more rutted and potholed than was usual for an undressed approach to a local farm, and although Nate was wearing walking boots, he had purposely come dressed smartly, in new English-bought tweeds. He had made some casual inquiries about the new owner of Coose-Craze, and he had gleaned that Major Randolph Gittens was close on to being a septuagarian and was irascible and unapproachable. And also, 'He's a bit mazed in the head. Thinks he's back in the days of the British Raj, he does.' His workforce tolerated him because he didn't interfere with anyone. Nate had come prepared, spruced up like a prosperous American gentleman to talk to an old-fashioned English gentleman, and bringing a gift. Clamping a bottle of gin under his armpit, he hoisted his trousers up at the knees, and it took a while to avoid the deepest mud heaps. When he owned this farm he'd order the track gravelled.

The farmstead had the usual barn with a loft above the cowhouse, stable and hay store. There was a cart-house and a long, low piggery. These and other outhouses circled the yard. Beside the goathouse were wrecks of a dog cart and a trap, much infiltrated with weeds and nettles. A surly billygoat, tied on a long rope to an ash tree, stared at Nate while chewing on what seemed like a white shirt. Nate thought he'd best mind his own business about that. There was a lot of rusted old farm equipment lying about, as if past owners had been content to keep relics of the past. Nate would order it all to be scrapped properly and safely, or it would be dangerous for Carl to toddle about here. He wended his way through a clucking, quacking and gobbling medley of hens, ducks and turkeys. He was wary of the geese, plump and white and hard beaked. Ford Farm's geese could see off a stranger more ruthlessly than the Jack Russells.

A young, long-haired border collie with a dirty coat nipped into the yard with the intention of taking a drink from the granite horse trough under the plain, cast-iron pump. It veered off course at spying Nate and raced up to him. With a timely raised hand and a firm command, Nate managed to get it to lie down. 'I like you, boy. I wonder what you're called.' As he moved on, the collie lapped up some water then chased off to roam the fields. The farmhouse was run down and only about the size of two average cottages. Its whitewashed walls were coated in decades of dirt and climbing moss. Nate made a mental note of the work and extensions he'd be asking Jim Killigrew to do on it. Some of the outhouses needed rebuilding. He was looking forward to the challenge, which he'd include Lottie in every step of the way.

He rapped on the solid door, causing some of its peeling brown paint to fall and scatter over his boots like rust. He used his handkerchief to dust them clean. A dog barked somewhere, but not the young collie, he was sure. This one sounded bigger or heavier, and he looked about cautiously. A minute or two ticked by. He hoped he wouldn't have to go round the house and through the cattle yard at the back to see if anyone was about. He would collect mud nearly up to his knees. He rapped on the door again.

'Wait a minute, will you?' A hurried female voice. Nate heard a key being turned in the lock. The latch was lifted and the door juddered as it was opened a crack. 'Whoever you are, you'll have to push on it. Door's stuck. And be quiet. You'll wake him up.'

Who was 'he'? As far as Nate knew, there were no children in the house. He pushed on the door. It jarred and creaked and finally yawned open with a shuddering groan. A young woman faced him. She was of average build, had flowing dark brown hair and was wearing a man's shirt rolled up to her elbows, corduroy trousers, and a folded down apron round her trim waist. She had dark, probing eyes. In one hand she held a paring knife and a potato she had been peeling. 'People don't never come to the front door. What can I do for you?'

It was a simple question, not delivered in a blunt or rude way. Nate saw she was dauntless, yet ordinary and uncomplicated. 'Pardon me, miss. Is Major Gibbons at home? I'd like to see him.'

Her mouth gaped at Nate's Texan accent. She looked him over. 'He's dozing in the front room. There will be merry hell to pay if he's woken up. He's a mighty fierce old boy. Are you a film star?'

Nate thought he might pass for that in his expensive three-piece suit and shiny silk tie. He had let his sandy hair grow since the days it had seen Army butchery, and it was curling about his neck and temples. Not feeling tense today, because he had a sense of purpose, he had slipped back into his normal free and easy manner. 'My name's Nate Harmon, miss. I haven't come far. I've been living in Hennaford until recently. Perhaps you know my wife's family, the Harveys. Perhaps I could come in and wait for the major to wake up?'

'Yes, I know them. Of course! You must be Lottie's GI husband. My name's Violet Treloar. Everyone calls me Vi, except the major, he's a stickler for correctness. I don't mind you waiting for him if you don't mind coming into the kitchen. Don't expect a welcome from him, though. Hospitality's not on the top of his list, not by a long chalk.'

'Thanks, Vi.' The instant Nate stepped into the slate-paved passage, he liked the feel of the place. It was dark but not gloomy, small and low-ceilinged but not claustrophobic. It smelled of dogs, fresh baking and dried lavender. Violet seemed chatty. He was

249

pleased to have the opportunity to find out something more about the major. In view of the major's terse reputation, he probably had a tough time ahead.

'Who the bally hell is at the door?' a loud gruff voice suddenly bellowed, not as if from within the house but at a distance.

'Here we go.' Violet rolled her eyes. 'He's pushed the window up and is bawling out of it. He does it all over the house. He thinks me and the men and the dairymaid are always on parade. It'll be easier to talk to him outside, Mr Harmon, not that it'll be much use to you.'

Nate went back out through the porch with Violet following. He saw a man's head, wearing a deerstalker's hat, sticking out of a small sash window. 'Violet! Who is it, for God's sake? Who's this chap?'

Violet made a wry face at Nate. In the full daylight, he could see she had a healthy complexion. A few early wrinkles were gathered at her eyes from outdoor work. 'It's a Mr Nate Harmon, Major. He'd like to see you.'

'What about?' Major Randolph Gibbons had a voice like a dinner gong.

'What shall I say?' Violet asked Nate.

'It's a matter of business,' Nate told her.

'A matter of business, Major.'

'Tell him to bugger off! You shouldn't have answered the door to him. Get on with your work, Violet. And next time you're in the house, wear a frock! You're a woman, for damn sake!'

'I'd better go back in,' Violet said to Nate, totally unruffled by her employer's coarseness and umbrage. ''Fraid he was woke up. You won't get nowhere with him today. Bye.'

'Goodbye, Violet. For now.' Nate shot her a friendly smile and made for the open window, skirting some wayward shrubs. 'Please hear me out, Major.'

The major snorted like a cantankerous horse and made to slam the window down, but it was stuck fast. Caught out for the moment, he shook himself bolt upright, glared out through the glass and looked prepared to do battle. Nate could see he would stubbornly fight to the last shot. 'Harmon? Nate? What kind of a bloody name is that?'

Nate was to learn that the major swore in almost every sentence. 'Forgive me for calling without first asking for an appointment, Major.'

'A Yank!' the major roared, throwing up his arms as if insulted. 'What possible business could a British gentleman have to do with a bloody Yank? Clear off or I'll set the dog on you. Interrupting a chap's tiffin. Damned cheek!' The major spoke in quick clips making his bristling grey eyebrows jerk above his hooded eyes and his waxed moustache jerk above his twitchy upper lip. Nate could smell tobacco and gin on him. In his angry passion spittle fell in blobs on his tweed front.

'If you allow me the honour of speaking to you for a few minutes, sir, I think you'll interested in what I have to say,' Nate said diplomatically. Here was an argumentative man, much out of his time, who liked to keep the colonials in their place. To placate the blustering old fool, Nate bowed his head. 'I've brought this. Perhaps it would help your tiffin along nicely?'

Randolph Gibbons stared at the large bottle of Booth's gin Nate held up to his eye level. He slowly ducked under the window and thrust out a hairy paw for the bottle. 'Why didn't you say so in the first place, blithering idiot? Climb in through. Won't have that useless young female disturbed from her work again.'

It was a struggle for Nate to get his broad frame through the space and he scraped his stomach on the latch, hurt his legs, banged his head and nearly lost a shoe, but he would have ripped the window frame out if necessary. The cramped front room was stuffed with paintings of famous battle scenes, cane furniture, breakfront bookcases, paperweights, ornaments of dogs, and, curiously, a collection of dolls, many in foreign costume. Amid the clutter, Nate was on parade in front of the simmering little person. In gaiters and brogues, a gold watch chain as big as a town mayor's regalia hanging outside his checked waistcoat, the major was stock still, taking in every inch of him. Then he brought the gin up in front of his chest and screwed up an interrogatory eye. 'Want a drink yourself?'

'I take mine in a tumbler. Can't bear a man who can't take his liquor. There's plenty more where that came from.'

'Right answer!' Major Gibbons boomed. Leaning against the drink trolley – the opened shape of the world globe – he splashed out two large gins. From the stains on the threadbare carpet, obviously laid well before his time here, he was often careless this way. 'Well, what do you want? Don't think to waste my time, Harmon. Serve over here, did you?'

The major flopped down in a club chair, bringing a walking stick into handy reach. Nate took the liberty of seating himself on the buttoned day bed. While his host lit up a fat cigar, he told him about his war history and its consequences. 'So I ended up marrying a Cornish girl.'

The major tossed back an enormous gulp of gin. 'Well, you're a bloody damn fool! A woman should follow her husband, not the other way round. No wonder she's got no respect for you.'

Nate hated that remark. 'What makes you

say that?'

'You've got a certain look about you. Seen it in the officer's mess and in the ranks. Brow-beaten under a petticoat government. You should be ashamed of yourself. Just one step away from a nancy boy.'

'I can assure you, Major, my wife is a wonderful woman.' Nate was ruffled and had to fight to keep a steely composure. He saw all too clearly the truth of the offensive little man's sneers. Lottie really did have no respect for him. How did that happen?

'So you gave everything up for love? Your funeral. Never saw the point in saddling myself with a memsahib. I've met the family you're wed into. The Harveys. Well known in farming circles. Dined at a table next to 'em in the Red Lion one market day. If your wife is anything like her mother you've done well in the looks department. Emilia Harvey, or Bosweld, I should say, is the most striking woman I've ever seen. A fine filly. As proud as a Grand National winner. Now, Harmon, let's get to the reason you're here.'

Resolute once more, Nate put his finger-tips together to show he was in control. He was utterly determined about this. 'I want to buy this farm from you, Major.'

Gibbons sprang forward on his chair. 'Straight to the point. I'll give you that. Can't stand a chap prevaricating. Got no intention of selling up. Drink up and bugger off.'

Nate stared coolly at the old man. 'I shall make you an offer you can't refuse.'

'Is that so?' Gibbons maneuvered his narrow shoulders as if preparing for battle.

'I'll give you double what you paid for it, Major.' Nate leaned forward to show he wouldn't back off.

'If you think I'm going to hand over a piece of England's green and pleasant land to a jumped-up Yank you can think again. Stuff your dollars up your jacksie. Don't think you could have been much of a military man, Harmon, otherwise you'd know when to withdraw. Jolly decent of you to bring the gin, but off you go before I take a trip to my gun cabinet. See yourself out the way you came in.'

Nate knew he must leave things where they were today. Major Gibbons was going to be a hard nut to crack, but he had found his weakness. Gin. Next time he would bring cigars. 'I won't be leaving the matter like this, Major. Thank you for seeing me. I'll bring a crate of the clear water with me next time. I've found a good supplier.' On the black market.

Gibbons helped himself to another tumbler of gin. 'You'll risk life and limb.'

'My wife wants this farm. She's worth any risk.' As he said it, he meant it. He loved Lottie more than ever. He'd get her this farm, build her a house as big as a mansion, and somehow, whatever it would take, he'd regain her respect and make her fall back in love with him.

He entered a second fight to haul himself out through the window. This time he ripped the seat of his trousers. He put a hand there to cover his shorts. 'Damn, how will I explain this to Lottie?' He heard chuckling at the window. The major was there, a little unsteady and swinging his empty glass. He grinned maliciously and bawled at the top of his voice. 'Lofty! Lofty! Where are you, damn it! Intruder! Get him boy!'

Nate heard loud fierce barking. Forgetting his indignity, he made a dash for it as from round the side of the house a white bull terrier came bounding into view. It wasn't a breed that lent itself to this dog's given name, but any dog protecting its master's territory could be fierce.

'Are we really going to Roskerne tomorrow?' Maureen was heading for Tremore Farm's washhouse swinging a basket full of eggs. Pearl and the twins were with her. She had collected the afternoon laying, one of the jobs Tristan had given her to pay her dues for breaking his stop watch. Now she must wash them carefully and count them. Bob or Len would write down the number of eggs on the chart.

'Yes, we are,' Bob said, eyeing her with

disapproval. 'And you'd better behave yourself. We don't want you ruining it for the rest of us.'

'Maureen wouldn't do that.' Pearl skipped along merrily.

'She might. She's too naughty at times,' Bob said darkly. He was jealous that Maureen was more daring and outspoken than he was. She was cheeky to grownups, and even to the teachers at school. It sometimes brought gasps from the other children. He was jealous he couldn't deliver shock and horror or invoke admiration from his peers in the same way. 'Maureen, stop swinging the basket. You'll lose the lot and get us all into trouble.'

The words were hardly out of his mouth before all the eggs came tumbling out as Maureen gave the basket an extra wide swing. Every one cracked, and a yellow and gooey mess splattered and spread on the hard ground. All the children got sticky splashes on their legs, socks and sandals. 'Oh heck.' Maureen stared down at the mess.

'Oh heck! Is that all you can say?' Bob pushed on her hard, wrenching the basket out of her hand. 'People are going without enough to eat because food is short and you've just wasted all that good protein. You're a useless little sod.' He pushed her again and Maureen slipped on the eggs and fell on to her bottom, her skirt becoming horribly wet.

'You beast!' she screamed, scrabbling to her feet. 'I'll get you for that.' She launched herself at Bob and hit him in the face.

He yelled and hit her back. She shrieked in fury and balled a fist and thumped him in the chest. Next instant they were scrapping in a full fight.

Len tried to pull them apart. 'Back off, both of you!'

Pearl shouted at them to stop. 'I'll get Uncle Tris!

Bob yanked on strands of Maureen's hair until he'd pulled it out. She screamed with pain and swore at him, a very bad word. 'I'll kill you! You dare to hurt me like that.'

Pearl was frightened by the fierce fighting and was crying. She tore off to the farmhouse. 'Uncle Tris! Uncle Tris!' He was in the office with Cyril Trewin, the farm foreman.

Tristan had heard the shouts, but as the children were always noisy he'd taken no notice. Hearing Pearl crying and screaming, he came out to see what the commotion was about. Cyril, stocky and swarthy, followed him, and the longest-serving farm worker, Eliza Shore, came out of the dairy. 'What's going on, sweetheart?' Tristan stooped to Pearl. 'What's the matter?'

'You've got to stop them, Uncle Tris!' Pearl pointed towards the washhouse. 'Bob and

Maureen are fighting. They're killing each other.'

'Take care of her, Eliza,' Tristan ordered the old, mannish woman. 'And fetch Mrs Dowling.'

Moments later he reached the sparring children. They had ended their fight, but he was shocked to find them both crying and nursing bruises and scratches that were bleeding. They had been slipping and sliding over the broken eggs and their clothes and hair were coated with the thick mess and farmyard dirt. Len was gawping at them, bewildered, and like Pearl, he was scared. He wasn't wrong in assuming there was going to be big trouble over this.

'Little Pearl weren't wrong about it, Mr Tristan,' Cyril gasped. 'They must have been behaving like a pair of hell cats.'

'She started it!' Bob sobbed, pointing an indignant finger at Maureen. The evidence showed he had come off worse in the fight and he was furious and embarrassed. 'She's nothing but trouble. I hate her! I don't want her playing with us no more.'

'Snivelling cowardy-cat,' Maureen mocked, despite the pain where he had kicked her in the shin. She leapt towards him, eyes ablaze, fists up like a prize fighter. 'Want some more?'

Tristan grabbed her, and it was necessary for Cyril to take hold of Bob to prevent him executing a counter launch. 'Now that's enough, the pair of you!' Tristan used the harshest tone. 'There will be a loss of pocket money and treats for a very long time over this. I'm angry with you, Maureen. Your poor mother is going to be most upset that you have behaved like a little savage. Bob, I'm ashamed of you for fighting with a girl and one who's four years younger. Go to the house, get cleaned up and go to your room. I shall speak to you again later.'

Before Bob could react, Maureen struggled within Tristan's grasp. 'Let me go! I only dropped the eggs, it was an accident, and he went for me, called me names. I won't have it!' She started to scream and scream.

'Stop it, Maureen!' Tristan pleaded.

'Here! What the bleeding hell's going on? Get your hands off my niece or I swear I'll rip your guts out!' Caught unsuspecting, as everyone else was by the newcomer, Tristan didn't see Kenny Locke hurtling towards him. Kenny punched him on the jaw. Tristan was sent crashing to the egg-slimed ground. He wasn't given the chance to scrabble to his feet. Kenny kicked him in the ribs, once, twice, three times. Tristan groaned in pain, and as he put his hands up to ward off further blows, Kenny kicked him again and again on the forearms. 'Think you got the right to bully my niece, do you? Just because you're some bloody toff? Go near her again and I'll finish you off.'

'Stand back!' The strident command came from Mark, who had just returned from his ride and had thrown himself off the hunter. He didn't stop to bandy words with Kenny Locke, but he landed a hefty punch in the softest part of the man's belly. Kenny doubled over on to his knees, yelling in agony.

Susan arrived on swift feet with Eliza and Pearl, who had filled her in about Maureen's latest misdemeanour. She had witnessed Kenny laying into Tristan and Mark thumping Kenny. She could hardly believe her eyes. Bob was hurt and distressed. Her daughter was the same, and white with shock as she stared down at the two fallen men. Blood was trickling from a gash on Tristan's chin. 'Oh, my God, what's this all about? Don't just stand there,' she shouted at Mark and Cyril. 'Get Mr Tristan up. Kenny, why on earth did you hurt him?'

Kenny got up with a struggle. 'Your swine of a boss was pulling Maureen around and shouting at her, making her scream with fright. You and the maid are coming with me to my new house. I came here to tell you all about it. You're coming with me now to get your things packed. If you're owed any wages I'll make sure you get 'em.'

'He's lying,' Len cried indignantly. 'Uncle Tris was only trying to get Maureen to calm down. She'd made trouble again. She's always causing trouble.'

'I don't need anyone to explain, Kenny,' Susan advanced on him. 'Mr Harvey would never hurt Maureen. He wouldn't hurt anyone at all.'

'Whatever the truth of it is, you're not staying here, that's for sure,' Kenny snapped. He glanced from Susan to Tristan, who was now on his feet, supported either side by the two other men, then back to Susan. 'Just because he's sweet on you doesn't give him the right to send your daughter into hysterics. I encouraged you before to win him over, to get yourself hitched to him so you could live like a lady. Not any more. You wouldn't have much of a life with him. He's a sissy, didn't put up any sort of a fight. We're leaving, me, you and the girl, now.'

Susan was mortified, but she faced her brother in fury. 'We're going nowhere with you. What gives you the right to come here and throw your weight about, to hurt the kindest, most decent man anyone could ever possibly know? He didn't deserve what you did to him. You're a brute, Kenny. You used to beat me. Remember? You're trouble and you always will be. Get away from here! I never want to see you again.'

'Turn me away, Susan, and I swear that even if you were to end up in the gutter I'd never lift a finger to help you or the girl.'

Kenny's features were a hard twisted mask of intimidation and warning.

Susan wasn't moved. Neither was she afraid. She was disgusted by him and appalled. 'I've never needed you before. I never will. Now go!'

'You heard her, Locke,' Mark said sternly. 'Leave this instant or you'll be escorted off the property. By my dog.'

Kenny saw Addi, standing rigid and alert near his master, mouth open and showing his teeth. 'You might regret this one day,' he snarled at Susan. Then at the rest of the company, 'You all might!' Picking up his fallen trilby, he banged on it to dislodge dirt and stalked off, head up, muttering under his breath.

Susan went forward to Tristan. She wished she could speak to him without an audience. 'I'm so sorry. This is all Maureen's and my brother's fault.'

The pain in his ribs was making Tristan sag between Mark and Cyril. His emotional pain was a thousand times worse. The truth of how he loved Susan was out. Everything was ruined, brought down to a squalid level. He nodded at her. Then, unable to face her any more, he turned away.

Susan went to Maureen and took her hand. 'We'd better go home.'

Later, Mark called at Little Dell to see if she and Maureen were all right. He found them in a state of gloom. For once Maureen was quiet, scrunched up on a stool at the kitchen hearth. 'We're only concerned about Mr Tristan,' Susan said. 'How he is?'

'I managed to get him to agree to allow the doctor to call,' Mark replied. 'He's strapped up Tristan's cracked ribs. Eliza and Cyril are keeping the children at the farm until bedtime to give him some time to himself.'

'Everything's gone wrong,' Susan wrung her hands. 'Things were said ... Mark, would you stay with Maureen while I go to the house?'

'Of course. Take as much time as you need.'

She hurried off, still wearing the pinny she had been working in when Eliza and Pearl had roused her. She had to speak to Tristan. Not least, she had to find out what her position at the house was now. He had probably telephoned Faye. They might consider that Maureen was a bad influence on the Smith children and wouldn't tolerate her presence again. Kenny had added complications. He had made Tristan look a fool. He had belittled the hope Tristan had been carrying for her. It was going to be doubly difficult for her to face Tristan because of it. Their relationship had grown a little closer lately. They had been at ease with each other. She had actually found herself thinking about him in unexpected moments, and occasionally deliberately so. And she had enjoyed these thoughts. Tristan was much more than a kind person. He had a smile that dazzled, and he was fun. His tall lean physique and dark grey eyes made him attractive. Lurking not far under his careful gentlemanly exterior, she felt there was an earthy passion. Now, if she ever wanted to show a personal interest in him, thanks to Kenny's spitefulness, it would be impossible.

She crept into the house, through the ominously empty kitchen, into the corridor, and listened for Tristan. He might be lying down in his room. She heard the click of a cigarette lighter from the direction of the library. The door was open. He was in the room where they had shared their first cosy conversation and become friendly. She tiptoed there. Tristan was behind the desk, smoking, the chair swivelled round and facing the window.

She went as close to him as she dared. He seemed to be staring into space. He had clean clothes on and his chest was bulkier because of the bandages. He sighed deeply, brought a hand up to an eye and sniffed. He might be crying. She hoped he wasn't as devastated as that. Her insides, already a mass of knots, jarred and squirmed. Her face and neck grew hot with anxiety. If he was crying, and if he knew that she was there and saw him, it would escalate his humiliation. She should have knocked on the door and alerted him to her presence. It would have been the correct thing to do.

Wearily exhaling smoke, Tristan suddenly got the eerie feeling someone was watching him. He shot his head round. His eyes widened to see the woman who was never out of his mind. He stood up and stubbed out his cigarette.

Susan leapt back in guilt, blinking. Her heart went out to him. His eyes were red-rimmed as if he had been weeping. 'H – Hello. Sorry, I should have ... I had to see you ... we should talk.'

'You don't have to say anything,' he murmured, dropping his gaze. He couldn't look at her. He had never backed down from facing anyone before, but he couldn't look the lovely young woman he loved so much in the eye. She was speaking softly, but she was probably horrified at having thrust at her the fact that he, a man so much older than her, had designs on her. She likely saw him as an old fool, or worse, a lecher who had been playing clever and biding his time to snare her. True, she had stressed some nice things about him to her brother, but that might have been to save face. To give her a reason to rid herself of Kenny Locke, whom she loathed. 'I think you should go.'

'Go? You're sacking me?' It took an effort for her not to wail.

'Not exactly.' Her sudden presence had set

his emotions whirling. He felt shaky and sick and had to clear his throat to go on. He had longed to say wonderful, loving things to her, but now he was clearing her out of his life, treating her as if she was nothing more than an employee. But he couldn't talk to her about the terrible event in the farmyard. It was too painful. He couldn't let her carry on working here. He couldn't bear to have her about the house. How would he operate around her? It was impossible. As his life was going to be from now on. 'I'll see that you have a generous severance. Plenty to tide you over until you find something else. And a good reference. I think it's best ... in all the circumstances. Mark will be taking over Rose Dew after the visit to Roskerne. I'm sure he'd be glad to have you keep house for him.' He thought he would choke on the bile rising in his throat as he said the dreaded words. 'Goodbye, Susan.'

Susan said nothing. She was too numb. At the beginning of the year her life had changed dramatically for the better, and now all the good things had crumbled away. Things would never be the same again – a new job, even if she got to work for Mark, wouldn't fix that. For the first time she had experienced proper family life, belonged to a group of people who had cared for and admired her. Now she was an outsider, and Maureen was too. Facing her across the massive desk and the chasm of their differences, she was hit by the realization that while she'd miss the family and this lovely house, she would miss him most. Her heart had received a mortal blow.

Somehow she had to make her legs move and leave. Somehow she must leave with dignity and not upset him further. Wetting her lips, she managed to mutter, 'Please tell Faye how sorry I am about Maureen's behaviour. I'll keep her off Tremore property. Goodbye, Mr Harvey.'

He listened to each of her slight steps as she went. When the final closing of the back door came it was as if everything vital had been cut off from his heart. He fell down in the chair and lowering his head, wept as he'd never wept before.

He wasn't sure if he could live here at Tremore any longer with Susan living just along the lanes. Perhaps Faye should sell up to Lottie after all, and he and the Smith children go away and start a new life with her and Simon – that was if Faye turned down Fergus Blair's marriage proposal. If not, then he could move away to be near to Jonny. Whatever happened, he was facing the bleakest and loneliest future.

Susan didn't remember walking along the lanes and reaching home. She felt unreal, as if a stranger to herself. She saw Tristan in a different light now, but it was too late. She had lost something more than her job. If not for the distrust she had refused to let go of and the guard she had put on her heart, she could have lived and loved with a man who would have filled every part of her being. The corner of her eye caught sight of a man standing further up the track. Instinctively she knew it wasn't Mark or any man belonging to this world. It was Jude Keast. Was he still looking for his lost loved ones? Since that terrible day they had vanished, he must have lived out the rest of his life breathing loneliness. Now, although having Maureen until she grew up, she must live that way too.

'Jude,' she whispered in despair, 'I'm as lost and as lonely as you are.'

Fifteen

The tide was coming in, gradually licking over the soft golden-white sand, an unstoppable force and a consuming entity. Yesterday there had been bright sunshine and a gorgeous blue, cloudless sky. Last night the wind had changed to the southwest, bringing with it showers of chilly rain. Early this morning, the cliff top house of Roskerne and every horizon had been drenched in a heavy mist, then it had cleared by breakfast, allowing a weak sun to show its face. Now the sky was clouding over with grey clouds that were growing ever heavier and darker. The weather mocked Faye's fluctuating thoughts. After another restless night, she was strolling along the beach alone. Once again mulling over the choice she should make for the future.

A final decision was almost impossible. 'It won't be as easy to leave as I'd thought when I got upset,' she'd told Fergus when he'd pressed her for her answer to his proposal prior to his return to Glenladen. They had taken a few moments to be alone in the summerhouse. 'The Smith children are every bit as much my responsibility as they are my uncle's. You've seen how they are. They witnessed my uncle being attacked, and then Mark punching the man who did it. This was supposed to be a happy holiday for them, but they're so miserable. Pearl is missing her little friend, Maureen. There was no choice but to punish Bob for what he did. But it's awful for a child to think he can't have an ice cream or join in late evening picnics on the beach for a whole week when he's on holiday. I couldn't believe my eyes when I saw the state of him, all scratched and bruised. If I'd been there things might not have got out of hand.'

'But you don't know that for sure, Faye.' Fergus had tried to take her hand, but she'd moved away from his reach. 'If you decide to marry me, it wouldn't have to be straight away. We could get engaged and allow the children time to get used to the idea. They're a nice bunch. They don't seem to hate me.'

'The children are confused.' So was she. When Fergus was stressing his promise of a good life for her and Simon she longed for the security and was drawn again to him, but she was not really in the position to reach for this easy option. 'They've had a stable life at Tremore with me and Uncle Tris since their parents died in the war; now it stands out that they're anxious and feel their security is under threat. How can I leave them? And how can I leave Uncle Tris? He's putting on a brave face for the children's sakes but he's distraught, he's heartbroken. I don't think he'll ever get over Susan.'

'I can understand that. When I saw her that one time I thought her a striking woman. They looked right together. It's a pity things have gone wrong. But Faye, you have to consider Simon and yourself.'

'Simon, yes. I'm not so concerned about myself. I've been selfish in the way I've let Susan down. I'd intended to make a close friend of her, but I all but ignored her when I left Tremore.'

'Why? Had she annoyed you? Been slack in her work?'

'No, I was just moody.' She couldn't tell Fergus about her feelings for Mark, that she'd been jealous he had seemed closer to Susan than to herself. 'And now I feel I've completely deserted her. She must be feeling wretched, and little Maureen too.'

'There is one answer to the whole situation. I had a chat with Tristan over drinks last night and he'd voiced the very thing.'

'What's that?' Faye had frowned. A magic wand couldn't be waved over the sorry mess.

'He's thinking of making a new start, moving away with Pearl and the twins. I don't think he'll be able to stand living with Susan Dowling close by. You could all come to

Scotland. I'll find a suitable house for Tristan and the children on the shores of the loch. The estate is just as much a beautiful and peaceful place for the children to grow up as here in Cornwall.'

It had been a tempting offer, and she had nearly said yes to it there and then. It seemed the right thing to do. Marriage to Fergus, to be wife of the laird, with Simon growing up in his father's home, accepted by his half-brothers and half-sister, and with Uncle Tris and the Smiths living close by, all of them mixing with the kindly people found there, seemed the perfect solution. Life with Fergus would be good. She liked him a lot. He made her smile. She had enjoyed him being here with her and Simon; building sand-castles, fishing in the rock pools, taking picnics on the sand and up on the cliffs. She had dined with Fergus at the hotel. She had taken comfort in his presence and the reminiscences of the time she'd spent on his estate. He had stayed at Roskerne for supper. Once he had stayed so late he had slept over. He would have slept with her if she'd allowed him to. He'd flirted with her all the time, reminded her, with silky looks and sultry tones, of the times they had made love. 'It had been wonderful, hadn't it, Faye? Darling?' He had smiled and smiled into her eyes. She had admitted he was right. She had lain in the next room and had nearly gone to him. Fergus was sensuous and could all too easily fill her with desire. The feel of his arms around her, to cling to his body through one lonely night, was a need she had nearly capitulated to. But she had stayed strong, not wanting to make more complications in her already difficult life.

Life at Glenladen for all her extended family beckoned strongly. But there was Mark, although it was silly to think about him. She had denied to herself that she loved him, yet when she had seen him again on his arrival, those old feelings had refused to stay buried. In the days apart he had become stronger and more vital, gaining a healthy colour. He had been cautious with her – probably wondering if she was going to be as cool with him as the day she'd suddenly left Tremore. He had taken her hand and kissed her on the cheek, the salute of a friend but nothing more. He didn't say much. He was just a quiet presence, a friend to everyone, there to give support to whoever needed him.

Sometimes she allowed herself a little hope with Mark. He was different with her. He'd gaze at her and each time he caught her eye he smiled a sad sort of smile, as if he was trying to convey something to her. Did he care for her? Had he missed her during her absence? Then she'd chide herself for being stupid. He would probably like to talk to her about someone who was a forbidden subject at Roskerne. Susan. She sensed he felt guilty for leaving Susan alone with her misery. The first thing he had done on arriving was to write to her, either to encourage her, or ... perhaps he had feelings for her. One thing was certain: she couldn't stay put and see Mark fall in love with someone else. He hadn't looked to phone or write to Justine, it seemed he was finally able to begin leaving her in the past.

Here on the north coast, the waves of the ocean often breached the shores as gigantic rollers, crashing their way inland and scattering loose shells and shingle, thundering against the granite rocks. Faye liked the sea to be wild, indomitable and brazen, with the tang of salt water sharp in her nose. She watched the soaring, foam-peaked waves curling up and up and then come roaring down, breaking up and splashing with gusto as they hit the rocks just feet away from her. They filled the pools and made wondrous music, gurgling and slapping, as if praising their Creator as they shifted the tiny pebbles. She was wetted with a wonderful bracing spray. She must go back before she was cut off and would have to climb the cliffs to safety. There were only a couple of places near this spot where it could be done, and even then it was a tricky operation.

She watched one more wave do its triumphant business and withdraw, the undertow, always a potential danger, drawing back the grey-green waters and forming retreating rivulets between the weather worn shapes of the hard dark rock and on the silvery sand. The sea didn't struggle. It just got on with what it had done for millions of years. She was here for just a blink of an eye in time and she was struggling to make the right decision for those she loved, except for Mark. Fergus had said he would return as soon as he could, and she would try to have a decision for him then.

'Faye!' It was Mark. He was hurrying towards her, waving his arms, clearly worried she was putting herself in danger.

She wasn't far from it. The sea never formed a straight line as the tide advanced, and water further along the sand was at least waist-deep. She knew this place and knew she had time enough to get off the beach without making a swim for it, but to ease Mark's concern she ran on her bare feet to meet him. What she would give to see his arms outstretched to her in love and to run into them, to be held fast by him. There was no use in dreaming. Even from a distance, she saw he felt no more for her than concern. And why should he feel more? His marriage had not long ended and it was too soon for him to consider anyone new in his life.

'You had me worried there for a minute,' he said, his hands now casually stuffed in his pockets. 'But I suppose you know what you're doing. The weather's changing again.' The run had made her complexion glow and he was admiring her gorgeous figure in a simple cotton sundress. She had Rita Hayworth hair and Betty Grable legs, but she was so much more than a glamour girl. Faye had an appealing fragility about her. She had a need to be loved and to give love, and she would give love in full measure, loyalty and passion to the right man. It was altogether a matchless combination. He admired her so much. He would have been willing to let that admiration bud and grow into love and desire if not for Fergus Blair's appearance. He had nothing against Blair. He seemed a competent, witty, genuine man, offering Faye an ideal life. There was a connection between them, a mutual respect. For himself, he had lost out on what might have been. He couldn't promise Faye anything. He wasn't ready for a new relationship yet.

Faye gazed at him. They had not had the chance to talk alone yet. What would he say? Had he sought her out, or had he simply been coming this way?

'There will be rain soon,' Faye said, breaking the silence 'I'll have to think of something to amuse the children with indoors. Is Simon all right with Mrs Loze?' They headed towards the steps that would take them up to the house.

'He's in the kitchen with her now. I've had him out in the garden. He tried to eat the rose petals. One or two wouldn't have hurt him. It's surprising how many different leaves and herbs and even flowers we can eat safely.'

'I suppose you had to resort to eating all sorts of awful things to stay alive.' She regretted saying that. Mark would hate to have his POW experiences brought up.

'Yes, I did.' He was thoughtful for a moment but not upset. The sea and fresh air had a cleansing effect on his mind. He lifted some sand with his toes. Once, sand was all he'd had to try to clean his ravaged body with. And he wouldn't mind the rain when it came. Chilly, ruin-a-fine-day English rain. It was bliss after suffering the hell of the monsoons, bringing with it poor vision and tortuous stifling heat, treacherous insects and blistering skin diseases.

'It's unusual to see you without Addi.'

'Occasionally he wanders off by himself. You were so still down on the shore. Were you thinking? Deeply, I mean?'

She stared at him. It was the first time Mark had asked her a personal question. 'Yes, about a lot of things.'

He strolled along silently for a moment, then said carefully, 'About anyone or anything particular, if I may ask?'

'Yes. Susan.' She thought it was probably Susan he wanted to talk about and not anyone else. 'I'm worried about her, actually. I think I should return to Hennaford for a few hours tomorrow and see her. It's cutting Uncle Tris up, letting her go like that. Goodness knows what she's going through. I was her employer too. I owe her my support. Have you heard from her?'

'Just a brief note through the post this morning thanking me for getting in touch. Faye, I hope you don't mind me mentioning this, I hope you consider me a close enough friend to get involved. Tristan has mentioned that he's thinking of moving away, perhaps with you and Simon up to Scotland. Have you made up your mind about Fergus Blair?'

What exactly made him ask this? Friendly interest, or something deeper? Must she always be tossed between hope and doubt like a scrap of driftwood on a mighty wave? 'No,' she replied, although she was veering towards accepting Fergus's proposal and the possibility of everyone moving up to Scotland.

'Faye, I know you must be thinking hard about it. I could see for myself that you and Blair had a connection, other than Simon, I mean. But please think very hard about what you should do. I'd hate to think you'd make the worst decision of your life. Please be sure he'd make you happy. And that you would rather be all those miles away than at Hennaford with your branch of the family.'

'Thank you for caring.' It must be all that it was to him.

'I care very much about you, Faye. You took me into your home and nursed me back to health. You're allowing me to live in one of your properties. I shall be eternally grateful to you.'

But not eternally in love, she thought sadly. 'It's been a pleasure.' A gust of wind suddenly tugged at her hair and a few spits of rain started to fall. 'Gosh, we'd better hurry back before we get soaked. The rain usually pelts down much quicker here on the coast.'

In the middle of the night a pair of tiny feet pattered across the few feet of landing at Little Dell and entered the second bedroom. 'Mummy...'

Susan was spending another sleepless night too. 'Come in here, my love.' She pushed back the bed covers and Maureen climbed in with her rag doll. They cuddled up tightly, as if all they had in the world was each other, which was more or less how it was.

They had not left home since the day of Maureen's scrap with Bob and Susan's dismissal by Tristan. Mark had called and offered to stay behind from Roskerne. 'No, you go,' Susan had stressed. 'We'll be fine.'

'But will you though? I'm surprised Tristan let you go so readily. You must be devastated.'

'Not really,' she lied, 'but he was. You know why. Please, Mark, I don't want to talk about it. After a few days, Maureen and I will go on as before.' No they wouldn't. Not when they had known a happier life and had found more than just good friends. In Susan's case something wonderful, the best thing likely to ever happen in her life, had been within her grasp and she had let it slip away.

'I miss Pearl,' Maureen whimpered through the dark, clutching Susan's nightdress.

'I know, sweetheart.' Susan stroked her hair, tangled on her pillow as she'd tossed about.

'And Mr Tris.'

After a moment, Susan said, 'Me too.' She would have cried over it when alone if not for feeling so numb.

'Sorry Mummy. I lost you your job. You were happy at Tremore. You won't be happy again now, will you?'

'I'm happy as long as I've got you, Maureen.' She squeezed her daughter tight. If she ever lost her ... She put on a bright voice. 'Anyway, I shall be cleaning and cooking for Mr Fuller when he moves in above us. It will be nice having him and Addi close by.'

'Mr Fuller's nice, but Mr Tris was special. Wasn't he?'

'Yes, Maureen.' If only she had realized earlier just how special.

'Will he ignore us when he gets back?'

'He'd never do something like that.'

'I miss him.'

'Yes Maureen, you've already said that.' *Please don't say it again, it's killing me.*

'I was so looking forward to going to the beach and paddling in the sea and playing rounders on the sand. I wonder if Pearl's having a good time.'

'I shouldn't think she's having as much fun without you.' Susan knew she had made a mistake with that remark.

Maureen started to sob, her little body shaking miserably. 'I've let everybody down.'

'Don't cry, sweetheart.' Susan wiped Maureen's tears away with the hem of the sheet. 'I'll make it all right.' She had to do something for her precious daughter. Maureen had lost her friends and her uncle, albeit Kenny was a nasty rogue, all in one day.

Maureen went quiet for a few seconds. 'How?'

'How what?'

'How will you make it all right, Mummy?'

'I...'

'Yes?'

The note of eagerness in Maureen's voice made Susan pluck something out of the air.

282

'I'll take you out to the beach tomorrow. We mustn't hide ourselves away at home. I'll pack up a picnic and we'll take the bus to Perranporth. It might rain again but we'll have to hope it will be mostly dry. I'll buy you a bucket and spade and a kite.'

Maureen hugged her. Then, 'Will it be as nice as Roskerne?'

'I'm sure it will be.' Susan felt a dreadful pull on her heart. If things hadn't gone wrong they would be at Roskerne now, enjoying their first holiday. Tristan would have been as attentive as always, and away from her usual restraints, by the romance of the sea she probably would have felt able to return his feelings. The chance was lost, gone forever. She sighed heavily.

Maureen entered another thoughtful silence. 'Are you wishing it was Roskerne instead, Mummy?'

'Yes.' *Yes, with all my heart.*

'Sorry.' Maureen's voice was small and crestfallen.

'It's not your fault, sweetheart.' If Tristan hadn't been humiliated in front of her he wouldn't have dismissed her over the matter of Maureen's behaviour. A trip to Perranporth wouldn't put things right as she'd promise. But just for once why didn't she do something out of character, something courageous? It was something she needed to do. After her horrible experiences with Lance,

283

she had never thought she'd fall in love, properly in love. But she had, with Tristan, and she had to give that love a chance. She sat forward suddenly, taking Maureen with her. 'I've got a better idea. We're not going to sleep now so we'll get up and dress and have an early breakfast. Then first thing we'll go down to the farm and ask Cyril Trewin if we can use the telephone. I'll call for a taxi. We can afford it with the generous wages Mr Tristan gave me. We'll go to Roskerne and hope they will agree to see us. You must apologize to Bob and to Miss Faye. I'll talk to Mr Tristan to ... well, I'll just talk to him. All we can do is to see what will happen.'

Maureen wriggled out of bed, dancing about with her rag doll. 'Oh, Mummy, that's wonderful! At least we'll get a look at the sea.'

Sixteen

At mid-morning Faye went to the hall to ring for a taxi to take her to Susan. It was a shock to see Susan and Maureen emerging from one themselves, the private car that the local bus company near Hennaford used to convey paying passengers. She hastened outside to meet them. 'I can't believe it! I was coming to see you today. I've been feeling guilty for not getting in touch.'

While Maureen's face was shining as brightly as the sun presently was, Susan was embarrassed and on edge. Susan was wearing her best summer frock, a pair of sandals kept for best occasions, she had pinned up her hair and arranged curls on the top, and had applied lipstick. 'I hope th – this is all right,' she stammered. 'Maureen wants to make things up to Bob, and to see Pearl and Len. I, um, want to talk to Mr Tristan. How is he?'

Faye thought that Susan had come carefully dressed to plead for her job back, but was elated to realize the truth. 'The children are down on the beach with Mark. Uncle

285

Tris is taking a walk along the cliff. He goes out every day on his own.' She whispered for Susan's ears alone, 'I'm so glad you've come. He really needs you.' Then in her usual tone, 'Come through the house. I'll take Maureen to join the others. Susan, you only have to go down over the terrace at the back and the lawn and follow the cliff path to find my uncle. He's gone up coast today, he doesn't usually go far. There's a natural grassy dip in the ground safely back from the edge. It's a nice private spot hidden by a high bank of grass. You can't miss it. There's a huge boulder at the side of the path and the dip is below it. He's probably gone there to linger and think.'

Hoping Pearl would be just as happy to see her, Maureen was glancing from woman to woman as they went through the house. They were passing secret messages to each other. She knew what it was all about. Her mother was studying her reflection in every mirror they came to, and she heard her ask Miss Faye, 'Do I look all right?'

'You look lovely,' Miss Faye said. 'Good luck, but I'm sure you won't need it.'

Maureen secretly put her hands together in prayer. 'Do your best, Mummy,' she whispered, more intent on that than the awesome sight of the sea through the large bay windows. 'We both need Mr Tris.'

Following the directions Faye had given

her, Susan quickly reached the fence near the cliff edge and hurried along beside it until she was on the cliff path. It was narrow and well trodden by generations of feet, with springy grass either side. There was no beach beneath the fifty-foot drop of cliff here. Having taken little notice of the sea until now, Susan found the magnificence of miles and miles of blue-green waters, the constantly undulating expanse, and the clouded horizon that stretched on and on in both directions and far away, thrilling and for a moment frightening. It took her breath away. With so much sky above she had never seen so much of creation before. She felt small and insignificant, yet this pressed on her the desire to seek her own happiness, to make whatever passage of time she had on the earth meaningful and fulfilling.

Careful not to snag her legs on prickly golden gorse, feasting on the sight of crops of pink and purple heather, she kept her eyes ahead, hoping to see Tristan. She had no idea what she would say to him, she hadn't rehearsed a word. She trusted her instinct that he'd immediately forget his humiliation in the farmyard and be glad to see her. After twenty minutes, she reached the boulder and saw the tiny trail bearing downward to the dip. Before she had completed the climb down to the dip, she was horribly disappointed to see Tristan wasn't there. A swallow was soaring high above and gulls were wheeling as if in some gleeful game over the heart of the ocean, but they and nothing here gave her a clue to whether he had been here today. It was a perfect place to come and think. The pale grass was pressed down in several places. Tristan had sat here often.

Surmising he must have walked further on today, she returned to the cliff path and carried on. She was bound to see him. He had to come back this way eventually. Looking out to sea, she saw the clouds that had once been far away had come closer. Before they had been fluffy and white sitting along the edge of the sea, but now they were a billowing mass, ominously dark in the middle. It unnerved her for a second. Everything on the coast seemed more powerful, with a sense of a sweeping immutable energy, and again she felt small and unimportant. But she had been important to Tristan. She had a tinge of doubt and prayed she still was, hoping those menacing clouds weren't mocking her and she had left things too late.

She went on for about a half mile and saw to her dismay the path divided, the second grassy track running inland amid dressings of brambles, gorse and fern. Which way had he taken? Climbing up on a bank she peered all around hoping to spot him, but the landscape was empty apart from the flora and some rabbits bobbing about. She hoped the other path came to a dead end. She'd stay here and wait. She became aware of a cool wind starting up and the sky darkening and she turned round to face the clouds. They were coming inland quickly. Bringing rain with them.

Tristan got back to Roskerne under the tempestuous sky. Any second now and the heavens would open up. He sighed. He had promised the children if it rained he'd watch a play they had made up. Mark would have brought them up from the beach and they were probably rehearsing up in the attic, where they liked to play. He wasn't in the mood. He wanted only to be alone. To think about Susan, even though he could never have her. He couldn't let her go out of his head yet. He'd steel himself for the children's performance. They needed lots of attention until they felt settled again. How was Maureen coping? He worried about her all the time. How was Susan? Would she speak to him if she saw him again? She must be feeling a terrible sense of rejection. He had been made to feel a fool, his heart had been crushed, but he had taken it out on her. Faye would be with her by now. How would Faye find her? What would she have to tell him? He pictured various scenarios, fretting about Susan and Maureen. He was such a fool, weak and pathetic. How could he have hurt the woman he loved? It should have been he who had gone to Little Dell today, to beg Susan to forgive his coldness at the very least.

He was climbing the steps up to the terrace and was surprised to see Maureen come running out of the house. 'Maureen! What are you doing here? Is something wrong? Is your mummy inside?'

'I saw you coming from the windows, Mr Tris. Mum went looking for you. Didn't you see her? Miss Faye told her where to find you.'

'I did a circular walk today. I didn't come back by the cliff path.'

'She's come to beg you to take us back. Don't go to Scotland, Mr Tris!' Maureen threw her hands about to emphasize everything she said. 'Stay at Tremore. Please! You like Mum, don't you? She likes you too. She told me so. She talked about you all last night. She said she misses you. She doesn't want to work for Mr Fuller. She wants to be with you at Tremore.'

Maureen was an imaginative child, and Tristan didn't dare allow himself any hopes that he might mean something to Susan. The reality must be that Susan had come to ask for her job back. Whatever the, outcome, at least he could be glad about that. 'You know it's wrong to tell lies, Maureen.'

'I'm not, Mr Tris! I swear.'

'Well, you go inside with the others and I'll go back and meet her.'

'She's been gone ages.' Maureen had been forgiven by Bob and allotted a part in the Smiths play, but she didn't think anything about acting out some drama now. She turned on the tears. 'What if she's got lost? What if she's fallen off the cliff? She might be hurt and scared.'

'I'm sure she's perfectly safe, Maureen. I'll make sure she is. Now I'm trusting you to be a good girl.' He dashed down the steps. The first fat drops of rain began to fall. He ran on. He wanted to get away from the house. Whatever Susan had come to say he wanted to hear it from her while they were alone.

As the rain hit her face, Susan decided she must hurry back to Roskerne. Keeping her head down as she went forward she turned often to see if Tristan was coming back and was behind her. Soon she was saturated, the wind buffeting her, occasionally threatening her balance. Her sandals were wet and muddy and her feet were sliding inside them. She was cold and hugged her body. She got as far as the place above the dip and looked back, rain dripping off her now-straggly hair and blinding her eyes. It was hard to see far into the distance but there was no sight of him. Where was he? Surely he wouldn't stay out in this weather? Perhaps

291

he was sheltering somewhere. That must be it. She hoped he was all right.

Tristan strode along as fast as he could, keeping a hand to his brow to keep raindrops out of his vision. He saw Susan with her back to him. She must be looking for him. His heart went the several hundred yards distance to her. She was huddled up and he wanted to wrap her up in his arms and protect her. Could it really be that Maureen had told him the truth? Why else was she staying out like this in the pouring rain? Had she actually realized she cared for him and wanted him? Any moment now and he would be sure. 'Susan!' he shouted loudly but his voice didn't reach her through the wind and the surge of the ocean.

She turned. Pushing her sodden hair back from her face she looked ahead and saw him. At last! She waved both of her arms with enthusiasm.

Tristan intended to wave back but instead his arms reached out to her. Susan really had come to him. Now his heart was soaring with everything beautiful. He could hardly believe it but it was fantastically true. 'Susan!'

Susan sidestepped the path and ran towards him on the spongy grass. He wanted her as much as before. Her hours of emotional agony were over. She had followed her instinct and her heart and had been gloriously rewarded. She heard him calling her name. She called back. 'Tristan!'

They quickly closed the gap on each other. When Susan almost reached him she slowed down, careful about his sore ribs, then she put herself into his open arms. He brought his arms around her and fastened her to him. They clung to each other, hugging tighter and tighter. He took her face inside his hands and lifted tendrils of dripping hair away from her lovely wet skin. 'I can't believe you're here like this, Susan, darling.'

'I've wanted to see you so much. I thought you wouldn't mind me coming,' she caressed his strong shoulders then ran a fingertip along his chin.

'I don't mind anything you do. I never shall. I love you, Susan.'

'And I love you, Tristan.'

They stood in the drenching weather pressed into each other. Tasting their first kiss of sweetness and promise and wonderful drops of rain.

Seventeen

'It's all been finished off beautifully, Tom,' Lottie said, after he had showed her over the renovations to his section of Ford Farm, all done to keep the olde-worlde personality of the farm's late eighteenth-century origins. They were sitting at the table of his sparkling kitchen, once the old play room, and which boasted a new Cornish range and tiled floor. Redundant furniture had been brought down from the attics, and with a couple of the Jack Russells padding about and some of the numerous cats cleaning themselves or dozing, slit-eyed, up on the window sill, it all looked familiar and cosy. 'Jim and Alan have done you proud. You and Jill must be thrilled.'

'We are. There's only the door at the foot of the old back stairs connecting us to Mum's wing now. There are two distinct homes. All we need now is three or four noisy brats running about.' Tom sighed wistfully over the mug of coffee he was nursing between his big rough hands.

'That will happen. Jill's not worrying about it, is she?'

'She's fretting a little. We've been married nearly two years and have never done anything to stop babies happening.' So as not to tempt fate, Tom and Jill had decided the room intended for a nursery was to be left undecorated for now. 'At Uncle Tris's wedding, Jill said he might be producing a baby now he's got a younger bride. All in good time for us, I suppose.'

'I hope there'll be good news soon. You'll make wonderful parents. Jill's a wonderful person. She's forgiven me for being so tiresome with her. I'm so pleased you're happy, Tom.'

'Thanks. And you, Lottie? We haven't really talked for ages. Are you and Nate getting along better now you're on your own? Do you regret giving up your share of the farm?'

'I miss it here a lot, but actually I'm quite enjoying running our temporary home. Deciding what we shall eat. Establishing our routine. Nate is good with Carl. They adore each other. Both Nate and I are making an effort to meet each other halfway. We're beginning to behave more like a proper little family. I feel a little more hopeful now.'

'I'm sure that once you get your own place everything will work out fine. Nate's a good bloke.'

'Yes, he is. I've never really doubted that. He's out scouring the land agents again today. He's so determined to find us the right farm. I'm leaving it to him. He says he won't insist on a place if I don't like it.' Nate was behaving strangely, but rather than being cross and suspicious about it, Lottie was thoughtful. He was kind and buoyant. He said he had made new friends and would be introducing them to her soon, promising her she'd eventually receive a wonderful surprise. He was meeting these friends at least twice a week, staying out for varying lengths of time. They were apparently heavy drinkers, for he always came back smelling strongly of alcohol. Once he had returned late, drunk and hardly able to climb the stairs. He'd been apologetic about his hangover the next morning, but light-hearted and bubbly too, and she had been intrigued and not angry at all. He was finding a way to settle down into his new life and she was content with this. He was secretive, making quiet phone calls and slipping luxury goods, which he could only have got off the black market, in and out of the house. It didn't worry her. None of the items were for women. He had even asked her to make a batch of yeast buns, explaining that they were a favourite of one of his friends. All this made Nate mysterious. It excited her. She liked that. She liked being with Nate. The spark of love they'd had seemed to be rekindling. She hoped.

She patted her swollen middle. 'I hope we

find somewhere before this one's born. At least I'm not torn about the future like poor Faye is. It's a pity Fergus Blair turned up. The children have been back at school for two weeks and she's still putting off a decision about Blair's proposal. I'd hate to have so many things to consider. I think she should face the small-minded gossips and damn them! It's awful that she feels she might have to give up her home, everything she's come to love. She and Susan have agreed on the way the house should be run. She could be enjoying life as one big happy family. Blair's coming down again soon. I hope he doesn't press her to make up her mind.'

'Me too. From Simon's point of view though, it's good for him to know his father is interested in him. He won't inherit anything from Fergus Blair except perhaps for some money, but if he was able to choose for himself he might like to grow under his father's roof.'

'But at the moment he's growing up in his mother's home and is set to inherit his grandfather's property. It's a hard choice for Faye. I don't envy her.' Lottie glanced up at Tom under her eyelashes and leaned closer to him. 'There is a complication.'

'Oh? What's that?'

'I wouldn't normally say anything, but as I'm not here to keep an eye on Faye, I think someone should know that she's in love with Mark Fuller. He's not returning her feelings, and I'm worried it might become a factor in Faye's final decision. It's a little easier now he's living at Rose Dew, but even so, he's too close by for her to simply forget him.'

'Poor Faye. I'll make a point of going over to see her, try to get her to open up to me.' Tom got up to go out to the yard. 'Well, I'd better join Jill. She's helping Tilda to bottle preserves at the moment. We're going to be clearing ditches and leats today.'

Lottie put the empty coffee mugs on the draining board. 'It's brilliant how you love doing so much together. Carl is out for a walk with Mum, Pappa and Paul. I think I'll take a stroll and call on a few people, starting with Elena Killigrew. She's due any day now. I've knitted a matinee jacket for her baby.'

'You knitting, Lottie!' Tom laughed. 'You'd better be careful, you're in danger of getting domesticated.'

Putting a light coat over her skirt, smock and cardigan, Lottie headed down the short hill to the ford, crossing over the few inches of water on the long slab of granite at its side. It was a cheery early autumn day, but suddenly she was feeling less optimistic. It hit her hard how she was missing the simple things that were so familiar to her. The trickles or the rushing of water, or the dry ground of the ford bed, depending on the weather. The contours of these hedgerows, the field gates she had climbed or vaulted over. The horse chestnut tree rich with shiny red-brown chestnuts for conker contests, which would be presently fought hotly by Hennaford's children. She had not thought it all through at the time she had forsaken all this for her marriage. There was still a lot to be resolved between her and Nate. They were trying hard to make their marriage work, making compromises, mainly putting the other's needs first, but there was still that underlying tugging apart. They were shielding themselves. Both were careful not to talk in depth. Neither had said sorry for their previous selfish behaviour. She wondered how much they were kidding themselves they could stay together forever. If it went wrong it was going to be awful spending the rest of her life with him. They might end up being counted in the soaring divorce rate.

The road forked to the left leading to the village. She took the right-hand fork, soon rounding a tight bend to begin the short distance up the steep hill to Ford House. The closer she got to the large white-painted house, set behind a grassy verge and a dry stone wall, the more edgy she became. She was nervous to face the heavily pregnant Elena Killigrew. It would be an uncomfortable reminder that she herself was to give birth in about four months. But Elena, with her tranquil, God-trusting ways, was just the person she needed to talk to. She was nursing the hope that some of the peace Elena always managed to retain would rub off on her, and subsequently her own labour and delivery wouldn't be so painful and frightening this time round. She needed a way to stay calm if she wasn't going to succumb to panic when her pains started. She couldn't help herself, but if she heard horror stories about women having harrowing childbirth experiences she went over and over them in her mind, and every old wives' tale she knew. About women who had suffered debilitating post-natal depression. Labour that went on for days and trauma to the body, and women and babies who had even died. The majority of women were safely delivered of live, healthy babies, and she had to fight to keep this fact in her head.

A dry brown oak leaf floated down off a tree behind the hedge and she caught it. It was fragile and rustled in her hand. She squeezed it and it disintegrated. It was silly to compare herself to the natural fate of a dead leaf, but she felt it was a premonition. What if giving birth to this baby destroyed her? She couldn't bear the thought of leaving Carl motherless. Of never seeing Nate again. She had known that terrible fear throughout his war service, acutely so when, not so many miles away on the River Fal, he had left on a troop ship for the Normandy landings. She was transported back, caught up in her first love for Nate. She loved him and she needed him, needed to be with him and it didn't matter where. She wanted a happy marriage, a wonderful life with him, just like Tom and Jill had together, and she was terrified of being incapable of providing the loving self-sacrifice he deserved.

Besieged with panic, her heart thumping madly with the desire to flee, she shot off in a run, clutching her tummy to support her bump, puffing with the effort of the sharp climb. She wasn't the praying sort, but she'd ask Elena to put her hands together for her, to ask the Almighty to show her a way to save her marriage. She heard what sounded like a feral cat howling, and it made her insides leap and she burst into tears. She was praying now, praying that Elena was home and was alone. She needed Elena's support and the understanding Elena would surely offer as much as she needed the breath in her body.

It was only a short distance but it took what seemed an interminable length of time to reach the carved wooden gate with the words Ford House burnt into it. Fumbling with the spring latch she leapt down the steps, threatening her balance. Whipping round to the back door, she knocked once and tried the handle, relieved to find the door unlocked. Shaking with nerves, inhaling deep breaths to calm herself, wiping her eyes on her sleeves, she went in through the back kitchen and into the kitchen. It was empty. Some breakfast dishes were washed and stacked on the rack, waiting to be dried and put away. The remains of a single breakfast, presumably Elena's, were left on the table. She went to the door that led to the passage. 'Hello! Elena!'

There came a strange groan and then the animal noise again. Lottie listened. Apprehension settled on her like a morbid, weighty cloak. Something was wrong. 'Elena, where are you? Elena!'

'Oh, is that you, Lottie? I need help. I'm in the bathroom.' Elena's voice, dry and strained, filtered down the stairs.

Forgetting her problems Lottie hurried up the stairs. 'I'm coming, Elena. Don't worry.'

Elena groaned, and Lottie rushed to the smallest room on the landing. She pushed the door open and gasped to see Elena sitting with her back against the porcelain bath, knees up, and gripping her enormous stomach. 'What happened? Did you fall?'

'Yes,' Elena wailed. Her face was white and spotted with red blotches. 'I came up to spend a penny and then got this terrible pain. I don't know how it happened but suddenly I was on the floor. I've tried to get up but I just can't. I think I've sprained my wrist. The baby must be on the way.'

'OK, OK, no need to panic.' Some sort of power kicked in inside Lottie. A strange calm spread through her and all tension left her in a whoosh. She felt light and agile, strong and able, totally in control. 'I'll help you into the bedroom. Have you been down there since breakfast?'

'Yes, I'm afraid so. Jim wanted to stay home today with me being due tomorrow, but I was so sure nothing was about to happen. Ow, ah, ah, ah!'

Lottie knelt and held her hand until the contraction had passed. Elena's pains were only five minutes apart. The midwife was needed urgently. 'I take it Jim's working on one of Faye's properties today. I'll phone Tremore and get someone to fetch him home, and I'll ring for the midwife. Before the next pain comes, I'll haul you up. As soon as you can, put your good hand on the side of the bath.'

After a struggle to get Elena upright and a cautious walk across the landing, Elena was sitting in a chair while Lottie whizzed about and prepared the bed with the draw sheets and maternity things already waiting for this event. As soon as Elena had changed into a nightdress and bed jacket and was propped up against the pillows, her next pain came, a forceful one. Lottie held her hand and encouraged her to breathe deeply throughout. 'I'll fetch a damp flannel for your face. You've got the fire lit. I'll build it up with logs then I'll slip downstairs to make those calls. I could ring for my mother, but I'm afraid she's out.'

'Thanks, Lottie.' Elena smiled. 'I knew someone would be sent to help me.'

By the time Lottie had completed the phone calls and was returning upstairs, Elena was moaning softly through another contraction. Lottie hadn't been at all quiet during her labour with Carl and had yelled all the way through the last hours, sometimes cursing Nate for her pain and distress. Was this one reason for the resentment she'd had for him? Right now she was at ease and even enjoying looking after Elena. 'We're in luck,' she said breezily. 'Nurse Stevens is in the village. She's just finished a call on old Mrs Maker and will be here soon. Uncle Tris is fetching Jim. I've phoned the farm and Tilda's popping down to take charge of the kitchen. I can stay until late. Someone will take me home. So there's no need to worry, you've got plenty of support.'

'Thanks, Lottie.' Elena sipped from the glass of water left on the bedside cabinet. 'But I'm not worried.'

'I can see that.' Lottie was gazing at the cradle and baby clothes and other nursery items in the room.

'I'm not superstitious that something bad

will happen if everything is ready before-hand. I made up my mind that even if the worst was to happen, I would enjoy making things for my baby, imagining what he will look like in the cradle, wrapped in the shawl that was once mine. And the Lord has a purpose for everything.'

Lottie nodded, going quickly to the bed as Elena grimaced as the next pain started building up. After it had subsided, 'Aren't you at all afraid?'

'I'm nervous, of course. Are you afraid of something, Lottie? I sensed unease in you when you asked that, and when you entered the bathroom you looked as if you'd been crying.'

'I'm afraid to give birth to my baby!' she blurted out, regretting it immediately. What a thing to say to a woman soon to give birth herself. 'I'm sorry.'

'It's all right.' Now it was Elena reaching for her hand. 'Most of us are afraid of some-thing. We all need someone to see us through the rigours of life. You haven't told anyone about this before, have you? The fears we hold in our minds tend to grow out of con-trol when we keep them hidden. Don't be afraid to bring it out in the light, Lottie. Tell Nate and tell your mother. They'll under-stand. They love you. Their love will see you through.'

Having someone to understand her and

offer just the right words brought on a rush of tears. Lottie felt an enormous release of fear, sorrow and self-pity. 'It's not a good idea to worry about something until it happens, is it? I got myself into a right state when I was having Carl. I thought that after seeing so many animal young born, giving birth would be easy. I was my usual wilful self throughout my pregnancy and early labour, refusing to take advice and rest, and it all became a terrible trial.'

'I'm sure all will go well the next time.' Elena squeezed her hand, then she was pressing harder as the next pain contracted her body. This time she made a lot of noise. 'Ohh, that really hurt, but it's one more over with.'

'That's the spirit, think positively. I will too from now on. And I will stop being so selfish. I was a spoiled brat, always demanding my own way.'

'Don't lose your vitality, Lottie. It's what makes you who you are. Nate fell in love with every part of you.'

'But he didn't know everything about me when we got married. I'm sure there's a lot he doesn't like.'

'Maybe there's a little, but that's natural. I'm sure he's also finding it exciting to discover your hidden qualities. You and Nate have spent more time apart than together. Now you've got the joy of finding out more and more about him. It took me a while to get used to Jim's stubbornness, but I was thrilled to discover he wanted to occasionally cook us romantic dinners.'

'Yes, I see what you mean.' Lottie recalled Nate's new, spirited sense of purpose. He was also being patient and understanding, because she didn't often feel like making love and there had been no intimacy for weeks.

'Lottie, the last pain was over five minutes ago. Do you think the labour's easing off?'

'Probably not. Your body might be taking a little break. I remember that happening to me.'

The midwife arrived and the journey of Elena's child into the world started again. It was evening before Lottie left to walk up to the farm and it was growing dark. Her steps were light and her mind uplifted. While Jim had paced up and down outside the bedroom, smoking endlessly, joined after work by his adopted son Alan, and adopted daughter Martha, Lottie had stayed in the bedroom with Elena, supporting her through the final stages of labour. Watching as the baby emerged from Elena's body and was placed on her tummy, hearing its first cry, had reached a place in Lottie's soul she'd had no idea was there. To see the joy on Elena's, and then Jim's face, as Nurse Stevens declared the baby to be perfect, was something she would never forget, an experience she felt honoured to have shared in.

She burst into her mother's kitchen in her old exuberant manner. Everyone was gathered there and they all looked at her expectantly. 'It's a boy! A healthy seven pounds and eight ounces. Elena had quite an easy time of it. He's to be named James after his father, and Timothy. Elena asked me if I would like to add a name for him and I chose John. He's absolutely beautiful. It was the most moving thing I've ever seen.'

'Well done, my love.' Emilia smiled at Lottie and then to herself. 'Thank goodness you happened to call on Elena.' Thank goodness for more than one reason. Lottie had found no comfort in anything she or anyone had said to her. It seemed someone kind and gentle outside the family had been just what Lottie needed to prepare her for her next childbirth.

Carl toddled to her and Lottie swept him up in her arms. She was now looking forward to her new child. She was surrounded by excited people all wanting to know more details.

Tom encircled Jill's hand with his. 'Our turn will come, darling.'

'Come and take a seat, Lottie,' Emilia fussed in maternal mode. 'Tilda cooked a meal for Jim, Alan and Martha. Did you have anything to eat?' When Lottie smilingly shook her head, she went on, 'I'll get you something. You sit and take it easy. Nate phoned. He was worried about returning to an empty house, but when I explained where you were and why, he suggested that as you'll probably miss the last bus back, which you have, and as the time factor couldn't be judged, you might as well stay over for the night.'

'I'd love that.' Love being cosseted in the heart of her family. Feeling weepy and emotional, she picked Carl up and hid her face against his sturdy little body.

With the night to himself, Nate ordered a taxicab to take him back to where he had been for most of the day. Coose-Craze Farm. Nearly a dozen times he had called on the rancorous major, subjecting himself to insult and ridicule, and threats that Lofty, the bull terrier, would be set on him. Lofty was not a problem. Nate had learned on his second visit that the dog could easily be bribed with biscuits and was soft and playful. And he realized early on that Randolph Gibbons was more bluster than antagonism. He was costing Nate a small fortune in gin, cigars and other inducements, but Nate thoroughly enjoyed playing mind battles with the old boy and matching him drink for drink. It was a mercy that Lottie didn't seem to mind him coming home pie-eyed.

'Show me a photo of the little woman,' the major demanded on one occasion. Nate had discovered him out for a stroll, leaning his arms on a field gate – a gate that needed replacing, for its five bars of wood were rotting – gazing across the stubbled land shorn of its crops. The view glided down to the meadow and the woods that framed and protected the farmstead. The banks at the sides of the gate were littered with rain-squashed blackberries.

Nate had shown him the picture he kept of Lottie and Carl in his wallet. The major had put his horn-rimmed spectacles on and stared at it from the distance necessary for the long-sighted. 'A fine-looking boy. So this is she who you want to push me out of my retirement home for, eh? Very, very nice. Lottie, you say? She looks too good for you. Made a huge mistake marrying a damned foreigner. Why are you so certain she'd be eager to have Coose-Craze?'

'She wanted us to buy it when it was up for sale, but I was in Texas then and I refused to let her to go ahead alone with an offer. Lottie wants to stay close to her family in nearby Hennaford. I want only to make her happy. Now I've seen the place I very much want it too.'

'Close to her family, eh?'

It was all that the major said for a long time. Nate cottoned on that he was off brooding, as he often did. Another time, when the old man was snoozing, he'd gone to Violet Treloar in the kitchen, where he had learned much about his background. 'I think he came down here because none of his relatives, cousins mainly, I think, wanted him near them. I get the impression he's moved around a lot in the last fifteen years. He's lonely. That's what makes him so grumpy,' she chattered while ploughing through an overflowing basket of ironing. There were a lot of shirts and collars, all stiffly starched. Not only was the major sloppy with his drinking habits; he was a fastidious dresser. The plain and purely functional women's clothes he saw in the basket pointed to Violet living in at the house.

Nate enjoyed being in Violet's company. She was hospitable and jolly, attractive in a pagan way. She was in a long-standing engagement with the cowman, Howard Hayes, who, like Nate, was a D-Day veteran, and whom Nate had met and found to be an amiable sort. The workforce was mainly like that of Ford Farm and Tremore Farm. Ordinary, honest, hard-working men and women, eager to do well by their employers, families and the tiny community in which they lived. There was only a dozen homes, all tied to Coose-Craze, in the hamlet, and most were inhabited by Treloars and the Hayes. Nate thought Howard Hayes a very lucky man to be marrying Violet.

'That's kinda sad,' he said. 'I hear he takes little notice of how the farm is run.'

'You're right there. 'Tis a good thing we've got a good foreman in Howard's father, Morley. Major could be robbed blind and know nothing about it. Still, we all know our jobs and are happy just to get on with it. His solicitor and the auctioneer see to everything else for him. When I first met you, Mr Harmon, I thought it would be wonderful if you bought the place, but part of me don't want to see the major packing up and ending up somewhere else where he's not wanted. He's just a sad old man with not much to show for his life. He tolerates your visits because he's desperate for company. You show an interest in him, even though it's really for your own ends.'

'I must say I've enjoyed my times here. I wouldn't want to see the old boy out in the cold either. I've got fond of him. Do you think he'll give way to the pressure I'm putting on him?' While Violet welded the heavy hot irons, which she heated on the range, he watched the lithe movements of her body. She was wearing a shapeless green and white frock, but it didn't disguise her fully feminine figure. She had strong arms and rather big hands but her legs were well shaped. Her thick, unruly hair only saw a quick rake through with a comb and it had grown down in varying lengths. It was a mess, but like the white cotton socks and ankle boots she was wearing, it somehow added to her appeal. She didn't know fashion or make-up and likely didn't care to, and it didn't matter one bit. Nate wondered if it was the fact that he was presently sex-starved that was making him see Violet in sensual terms. Partly maybe, but there was something beguiling about her. Strange that he should be looking at her with base thoughts; he'd never taken any notice if one of the guys from his army unit had pointed out a pretty girl. From the familiar way Hayes moved about her, it was obvious they were lovers. Nate envied the farmhand.

Violet caught him staring at her. 'Did you want something, Mr Harmon? A drink? Something to eat?'

'What?' He shook his mind clear. He had no right to be eyeing up another woman. It wasn't fair on Lottie or Violet. 'Oh, no, thanks. I wouldn't dream of stopping you from your work, Vi. Call me Nate.' He needed to keep his distance from her, but he had just suggested a less formal footing. He mustn't flirt with a woman he hoped would become his future employee.

She had given him a close lingering look. 'I will. Nate.'

Had he been dreaming or did she pout her lips at him? He had thought about Violet a lot since then, and he had spent a lot of time with her alone. The major dozed each afternoon and Nate always made straight for the kitchen. Violet didn't seem to mind. She had started staying on when it was her afternoon off. 'To hear about your life in Texas and in the army,' she'd said this afternoon. 'Nothing exciting's ever happened to me. To talk to you is like going to the pictures. I want to hear about it first-hand.' He was happy to tell her anything. 'You're just like John Wayne,' she'd said, then, lifting her eyes to him, added, 'but much better looking.'

Now he was going back to Coose-Craze because thinking over all Violet had told him about the major he had an idea that made him fairly confident he could clinch a deal with the old boy to sell up to him. It couldn't wait until tomorrow. He told himself this second visit was only to see the major.

Night had laid a dark velvety carpet over the landscape of Coose-Craze and the only light came from a crescent moon and a lantern hanging outside the farmhouse back door. His arrival started up the poultry cackling and the young collie barked and ran at him. He quieted Flash, but Lofty had been disturbed inside the house and was butting the back door. The door was thrown open and in the dim electric light the outline of the major appeared. 'Who's there?' he roared. 'Speak up, damn your eyes or I'll

314

blast your head off!'

'It's OK, Major.' Nate thought it wise to put his hands up high above his head as he approached the door. 'It only me. Nate Harmon.'

'OK! You think it's OK to disturb a chap's home on a cold dark night, Harmon? No manners, you Yanks. Don't you know it's the done thing to phone first? Do you fancy having your head blown off?'

'No, Major.' Nate was contrite and sounded it. He was also worried the major, unsteady and perhaps confused after all the gin he had consumed this afternoon, might accidentally press the trigger of the shotgun. He had hoped the major was warming to him, and that his eagerness to come back tonight hadn't ruined his chances. If the old boy was offended and dug his heels in, it might be difficult or impossible to shift him. 'I'm sorry I've alarmed you. Forgive me, I should have rung. Please let me in. I've got something to say which I think you'll like to hear.'

'Go on, Major, let him in.' Violet's voice came from behind him. 'Now he's here you might as well listen to what he's got to say. Mr Harmon's mentioned he plays chess. You could have a game afterward. I'm sure you can give him a thorough thrashing.'

The major lowered the shotgun. 'Well, all right. Come in, Harmon, but don't forget to wipe your bally feet!'

The quickness with which the major had given in offered Nate hope that he was actually welcome here. When they got to the front room, he saw that Violet had been sitting in with her knitting. The wireless was on and she and the major had been listening to Tommy Trinder cracking jokes. The old boy was lonely enough to seek the company of his housekeeper, a young woman he had nothing in common with. Violet set up the chessboard, the pieces carved from ivory as Chinese peasant figures. She grinned at Nate before withdrawing, whispering, 'Don't worry, the gun wasn't loaded. It would be too dangerous to let him charge about with it like that.'

'Before we get down to a game...' The major eyed the chessboard with relish – he obviously had not been challenged to a game for some time. Then he looked at Nate squarely, although Nate was sure he also saw a hint of fear in his watery old eyes. 'Why have you come back? Let's get that out of the way first. I'm not selling up! You might as well accept it. I'm not up to another move. If that means you'll bugger off and I'll never see you again, so be it.'

Nate returned with a smile. Part of him wanted to give the major a son-to-father type embrace. It was amazing how fond he'd got of the old boy. 'First let me say I consider you a friend, Major. I hope you feel the same. I've come up with an offer I hope you won't find offensive or patronizing. I want this farm, another wouldn't do. The thing is, to coin a British phrase, I see you as part of the set-up here, you, Violet and all the hands. I'd very much like to buy the farm with you in residence. It wouldn't be the same without you. I'd like to update and enlarge the house, of course, but although it would mean some inconvenience for you, you would end up with your own private rooms. You'd be welcome to join my family as much as you'd like.'

The major looked shocked beyond words. His proud shoulders sagged and all the blustering energy seemed to have deserted him. Bent over, he trudged to the club chair and flopped down in it. 'I – I don't know what to say.'

'You'd like time to think about it, of course.' Nate went close to him, his eye on the gin bottle in case he needed a stiffener.

'It's not that.' The major looked up with tears falling unashamedly down his face. 'It's to think someone actually wants me with them, even to include me in their family life. I know I can be difficult and too regimental...'

'But you're also great fun and you're kind when you let your guard down. Violet sees that in you.'

'It's a tempting offer, Nate. To have someone around me as I slip into my dotage, and to watch kiddies growing up. Believe it or not, I like the sound of children running about. I wouldn't have to worry about the responsibilities of the farm and the staff. But what will your wife think about it? Lottie might not care to have a doddering old fool cluttering up the place.'

'I've a hunch Lottie will adore you. She's used to having lots of people around her, an extended family. You're a character, and so is she when she's got her fighting spirit, although she hasn't had much of that lately. She had her heart set on this place before. I'm confident that you agreeing to sell Coose-Craze to us will bring her spirit back. I can just picture her here, preparing for the birth of our second child, making plans, enjoying her life. So is it a deal, Major? Do you want to think about it?'

The major proffered a hand shaking with emotion. 'Think? No. I feel I've just won some sort of battle. Call me Randolph, no one's called me that in years. A deal it is.'

Nate held on to his worn old hand for a long time. They celebrated with a drink, then Randolph said, 'Nate, would you mind if I retired? I haven't slept well for years nor had an early night. I'm pleasantly tired for a change and would relish lying in my bed early tonight. Your wife's with her family, you say? You're welcome to stay. Rooms are a bit basic but I'm sure Violet could sort you out a bed. You're a former soldier, used to roughing it. Will you tell your wife first thing in the morning?'

'I sure will. Why don't you come with me, Randolph? I'm sure she'd love to meet you.'

'Thanks, old chap, but it's not my place. Why not bring her and your boy here, spring a pleasant surprise on her.'

Nate pictured Lottie being introduced to Randolph, looking about the farm for a brief time, puzzled why he had brought her here, and then he telling her it was theirs. He could see her jumping up and down in elation, back to the same precious, vivacious Lottie. 'I'll do just that.'

Violet tapped and peeped round the door. ''Scuse me for butting in. Is everything all right? It's so quiet.'

'Ah, Violet, dear.' For the first time in years the major's raddled face broke into an affectionate smile. 'Nate will tell you. I'm off to bed. See you both at breakfast. Goodnight to you.'

Violet's mouth gaped open for some time after Randolph had left. 'What's going on? What did you say to him?'

Nate explained.

'That's marvellous!' She ran to Nate and took his hand. 'You deserve a medal for that. You're a very wonderful man to keep the major on. He can die happy now. Howard

319

and the others will be so pleased you're to be our new boss.'

She didn't take her hand away and he didn't let it go. 'I hope you'll continue working here, Vi. Are you planning to get married soon and becoming a housewife?'

'Howard and I are happy plodding along as we are.' She gazed up into Nate's eyes. 'And I'll never be the housewife type.'

'Good. Good.' He stared down on her.

'So you're sleeping here. I'd better air you a bed then.'

He nodded, and although he knew it was wrong and foolish, he reached for her other hand. Then worried about complicating and perhaps destroying his married life, which was about to finally begin properly, he backed away. 'Sorry. I had no right to get familiar. I think I should leave.' He couldn't stop himself from saying, 'I love my wife, but I like you very much, Vi. Goodnight.'

She went after him. 'I'm glad you love your wife, Nate. It's not love I'm after. I'm quite content being Howard's intended and one day to marry him.' Her face turned to fire and she swallowed hard. 'It's excitement I want. I've spent almost every minute of my life on the farm and in Taldrea. I want to do something bold and daring for once. I want to taste forbidden fruit. It makes me wicked, but just once I want to know what being really wicked feels like. I want you, Nate. I know it's bad and cheap of me, but I want you. Am I making a fool of myself?'

'You're not cheap, Vi, or a fool.' The way she was gazing at her, with desire and pleas, made her irresistible. He wanted to taste wickedness too. His eyes fell on her parted full lips. She was feline and raw and he wanted to taste every unrefined part of her. 'I don't want to wreck anything for either of us, but I want you too, Vi. It's a long time since I've had any excitement. But if we spend the night together, just once, could we live and work together successfully afterward? We might give it away and bring our lives and those we love crashing down.'

'I've only lived in since the major came here. He demanded it, said he wanted someone at his beck and call, but I think he was too scared to stay here on his own. I'll move out as soon as you and your family move in. I prefer being at home with my family and having Howard only next door.' She was watching Nate's mouth. Wondering what it would be like to be kissed by another man, and this man, coming from another country, smart and sleek and more sophisticated than the men she knew, held a powerful attraction. Howard satisfied her when they made love, but she longed to know if there was more to experience. The forbidden aspect alone was a powerful aphrodisiac. Her womanly regions were crying out for pleasure. She couldn't stop herself touching Nate. 'We'll put it behind us tomorrow. Carry on as boss and employee. It'll be easy if we try.'

He had gone without sex a long time and there was no passion promised for several months. Violet was too mesmerizing for him to hold out. The need in his loins, that had been growing for her all day, flamed into lust. He grabbed her, hauling her against his body and used his mouth and tongue on hers. Violet kissed him back with a sort of madness. She clung to him, clawed him, and made herself familiar with his arousal, then letting him go, she tugged off her cardigan and pulled open the buttons down the front of her frock. They separated long enough for him to throw off his jacket and for them to pull up clothes and push others down. With frantic hands on each other they fell down on the day bed, and soon Nate was pushing inside her. They made love as if fighting a war, but already knowing they would emerge as victors. It was delicious and exquisite and utterly wicked. Every sense in them was heightened to intense pain and ecstasy. Nate held on to the furniture and pummeled and pounded away at her. Violet moved with him like a crazed athlete. They were shouting and crying out. He climaxed first but managed to hang on for Violet. Panting like old dogs as he lay on top her, they both laughed hysterically. It was some time before the madness left them and their breathing settled down.

'Was that wicked enough for you, Vi?' He put a gentle peck on her fiercely burning cheek.

She teased a lock of his thick sandy hair. 'Totally. For you too?'

He kissed her breasts, the heat coming back in force. 'Too right. Let's go upstairs. I want to do more.'

They snatched up their clothes and went up the creaking old stairs hand in hand. 'Heck,' Violet giggled on the worn linoleum on the landing. 'I forgot about the major. Do you think he heard?' She was too far in a state of bliss to be worried about it.

They listened. From behind the door next to them came sounds of snuffly, contented snoring. 'Guess he didn't. Where's your room?'

'Down the end. We can be as noisy as we like in there.'

The wickedness was on Nate again. He pulled Violet's clothes from her grasp and, with his own, threw them on the floor. He eased her back against the wall. 'Let's start here.'

'Outside the major's room?' Violet shuddered with the thrill of possible discovery and renewed hunger for him. She grabbed him, hooking her leg up around his body, demanding more and more excitement.

Eighteen

Faye helped Simon pull on his wellington boots to go outside and play with the other children. The air was brisk, the sun was shining weakly and the ground was wet and leaf-strewn. The Smiths and Maureen wanted to be outside in all but the most extreme weather, and Simon now fussed to go with them. The girls had promised to look after him and ensure he stayed in the garden. Faye eyed the twins, who were tossing a football between them. 'Don't play too roughly for Simon, boys.'

'Auntie Faye,' Bob said, and with his twin synchronized a pained face. 'He'll grow up to be a sissy if he doesn't go through a bit of rough and tumble.'

'We'll be careful not to hurt him,' Len muttered, shaking his head. 'Come on, Simon. Never mind the girls. If you go with them you'll have to play mothers and fathers and you'll definitely end up a sissy.'

Faye was amused at the twins' scathing sagacity and matter-of-factness. They were growing up fast now they had started at the grammar school in Truro. 'I'll call you in when it's time for milk and biscuits.' Moments later she was watching them from the window. Simon had the Harvey height and was striding along between the brothers, nearly keeping up with their longer stride. She laughed when he treated the girls, who were playing hopscotch on the terrace, to a scornful look. 'What's the best thing for me to do for you, my son? If I take you away from here you'll miss your playmates.' If only something easy and obvious would happen to help her in her dilemma. Fergus had been patient and understanding. He was travelling down on the overnight train and would be here fairly soon, and she couldn't really allow him go back home again without an answer. She spent little time thinking about what she wanted. She couldn't have Mark, so it didn't really matter.

The telephone rang. 'I'll get it, Uncle Tris!' Tristan was in the kitchen, taking his morning coffee with Susan. A new housekeeper wasn't going to be engaged until Faye had decided what to do about the future, and she and Susan were sharing the housework.

'Hello, is that Faye? This is Justine Fuller,' said the voice at the other end of the line.

'Oh. Hello Justine. How are you?' Faye frowned. The exuberance she was used to hearing from Justine was missing.

'Faye, can I ask how Mark is? Is he quite

settled now he's in his own little place?'

'Yes. He seems fine there with his dog.' Faye raised her brows over the question. Justine was speaking with emotion and unease. 'We're keeping an eye on him. As far as we know, he hasn't had a flashback or gone into a trance for weeks. A new farm worker and his family have moved into the cottage below him, so he's not isolated. The wife cleans for him twice a week. He comes here once or twice a week, and for lunch on Sundays. Is everything all right, Justine? You sound anxious.'

'Faye, I need to ask you a great favour. I need to see Mark, but I need you to be there. Can you fetch him to your house, please?'

'You mean now? Are you in Cornwall?'

'Yes. Truro railway station. I won't say why I've come. It's terribly complicated. You'll see for yourself when I arrive. It might be best if you kept the children out of the way.'

'Very well, it all sounds very mysterious and worrying but I'll do as you request. I'll ask my uncle to take the children over to the farm. Have you been in touch with Mark lately?'

'No.'

'So he's no idea what this is about?'

'No, none. This is pretty serious, Faye. Mark's in for a shock. I'll appreciate it if you are there to support him. Look, I've got to go. I'm about to jump into a taxi. See you in about half an hour.'

Justine rang off before Faye could ask anything more. Sighing, rubbing her brow, she set about doing what Justine wanted. What on earth could be a shock for Mark, she pondered while hurrying along the lane. Could it be something to do with the divorce? That was supposed to be over and done with next year. Justine could have become penniless. Perhaps she'd had to sell her house and wanted to come to live with Mark. But that would hardly give him a shock. If she had realized she still loved him and wanted him back, she wouldn't need to be this dramatic. The only other thing Faye could think of was illness. Justine could have developed a dreadful condition or be terminally ill; that would be an awful shock to Mark.

He speculated over all the same things as they walked back along the wintry lanes, with Addi, as ever, his faithful shadow. 'Thanks for coming to fetch me, Faye. You do so much for me.' He would like to do a lot for her, but that would be impossible unless Fergus Blair was pushed out of the picture. 'I hope Justine isn't ill. I can't think of anything else that would bring her down in the state you described.'

'It won't be long until you find out.' Faye wanted to tell him that whatever the reason was behind Justine's unexpected arrival, she would be there for him, but she couldn't actually promise that. Mark seemed content living on his own with Addi, and he was now considering what to do to earn a living. There had been mention, because he had enjoyed rebuilding Rose Dew, of him setting up a business along those lines. The nation was in the throes of constructing much-needed new homes, so there was plenty of opportunity. She hoped his confidence and good health weren't about to be knocked down. Witnessing Mark becoming unnerved now made her see how restless she was herself over her own future, and how those at Tremore wouldn't be able to live at ease until she made up her mind if she was staying or leaving. Her decision was simple: it was what was best for Simon, and she had known the answer to that for some time.

With Addi shut in the kitchen, they waited in the porch for Justine's taxi to pull up. Susan was with them. Faye had asked her to join them. Mark had needed the support of them both on the day they had first confronted him, and he might need them again. Long minutes ticked by. Tense, silent minutes in which the three were lost in private speculation. Susan, so happy and secure in her new life and the constancy of Tristan's adoring love and eager arms, thought it most probable that Justine had some sort of bad news. They all started, as if coming alive from stone statues, as a taxi crunched over the drive and they went out into the cold air. They watched quietly as Justine and another, older woman, thick-bodied in a grey utility suit and high-crowned felt hat and carrying a large hand woollen muff, got out.

'Wait here, please. We won't be staying long,' Justine said to the driver, in a tone that lacked energy.

'You're off almost straight away, Justine?' Mark said. He didn't offer her a kiss on the cheek, for her stance was remote. He received an unpleasant shock. She was pale and thin, and looked tired. Illness it was, then. She had come with a friend because she was too weak to travel alone.

Faye and Susan exchanged glances over Justine's haggard appearance. 'You'd both better come inside,' Faye said.

The group made their way to the drawing room. Mark ushered Justine to the fireside chair so she could warm up beside the crackling logs. Justine motioned for her friend to sit there instead, and stayed on her feet. The others did also.

'What is it, Justine? What's wrong? You're clearly not well,' Mark said. Faye noticed his face was creased with concern, but the old affection he'd showered Justine with before was largely gone.

Justine was distant and clearly uncomfortable. She licked her lips, swallowed, and cleared her throat. 'This lady is a colleague of mine from the hospital, Maudie Oliver. She kindly offered to accompany me today. I don't think any of you have noticed what she's holding in her arms.'

Faye, Mark and Susan all peered at the object Maudie Oliver had. She carefully tilted her light burden, not a muff, and they distinguished the face of a baby. It was a tiny baby, swaddled in a white shawl. Obviously not Maudie Oliver's child: she was past childbearing age.

'You've brought a baby with you, Justine?' Mark asked, shrugging his shoulders in perplexity. 'Why? What's this all about?'

Justine turned to Susan. 'Would you like to hold her? Maudie, give her to Mrs Harvey.'

Maudie Oliver obeyed quickly, giving Susan no choice but to take the baby. Susan wrapped it in a secure hold. 'She weighs nothing at all. She was obviously premature. Her skin's very dry and she hasn't got any eyebrows yet.'

Mark shot Faye a worried glance then turned to his wife. He gestured with outspread hands. 'Justine, what's this all about? Whose baby is this? Why have you brought her here?'

Faye realized the truth of the situation – it wasn't only Mark about to receive a tremendous shock. She understood why the baby had been offloaded on to Susan. She felt her body stiffen as Justine said, in a dry quivering voice, 'She's ours, Mark. Yours and mine.'

'What?' Mark gasped. 'Did I hear right?'

'Afraid so.' Justine's gaze hit the floor.

Mark wasn't sure if this was actually happening. He shut his eyes, but when he opened them again everything was in the same place. He paced up and down the room with his hand rubbing the back of his neck. He glanced at the baby, then at Faye, who was rigid in expression. Then he marched up to Justine. 'Why on earth didn't you tell me you were pregnant? This changes everything.'

'No, it doesn't.' She met his horror with resolution.

'Of course it does. We can't go through with the divorce now.'

'Mark, please listen to me and take this in. I didn't tell you because rearing a child is not what I want. You were still recovering from your ordeal, but I knew you'd insist on doing the decent thing. I was going to have the baby adopted, but at the last moment I couldn't bring myself to go through with it. You're her father. You have the right to decide if you want to bring her up.'

Mark referred to Faye again. She tossed her head away. It wasn't really her business, but it hurt to learn he had made love to Justine under her roof. And now Justine was here in her home, giving her baby away, already cutting herself off from the poor, helpless, tiny thing, and it sickened her. Suddenly, Faye was furious this had been brought to her door. Did these people think she had no feelings? She was weary and angry at being used.

Her grimness unsettled Mark, and he too was angry with Justine. 'You just can't walk away from your own child! You're her mother, for goodness sake.'

'I'm sorry, Mark, I really am, please believe that. But I just can't do it. I've tried to love her, to bond with her, but I feel nothing. I've not got a maternal bone in my body. She was born six weeks premature and she's now four weeks old. I haven't given her a name. I didn't want to think of her with an identity. If you decide to take her you can register her with the names you choose. I'm so sorry about all this Mark. It's better that I never see her again.'

'Of course I'll take her!' Mark pointed at Justine in accusation. 'I'd never turn my back on my responsibilities. I'm sure I'll soon learn to love her. I'll have to make a lot of changes in my life. Dear God, I can't believe this is happening. You'll help me, of course, won't you, Faye?'

He'd flung the question over his shoulder and it made Faye fume. Mark seemed to think she was nothing more than a stopgap. How dare he take her for granted! He had not even bothered to look at her and enter a discussion. 'No! No, I won't. I've got my own son to think about. I'm not just good old Faye, reliable and easy to put upon. Justine, you're a selfish bitch. Mark, you can work out things for yourself. Excuse me.' With her head up, she stalked out of the room.

She strode through the house and out of the back door. Coming towards her was Fergus, and he was holding Simon's hand and chatting to him. Simon was gazing up at him keenly. Their mutual affection was distinct. 'Oh, look, it's Mummy come to meet us. Hello, Faye,' Fergus called to her. 'I saw Simon in the farmyard and thought you wouldn't mind me bringing him to you.' He saw her dark anguished expression and, picking Simon up, hurried to her. 'Are you all right?'

Fergus cared how she was. She ran to him and Simon. 'No, I'm not, but I'm all the better for seeing you.'

Nineteen

Mark walked home finding it hard to believe he was pushing a pram – Simon's old carriage pram; Faye had at least loaned him this – and that his own baby was tucked up in it. He was afraid, in a cold sweat, and he felt so alone. This morning he had woken up with a purposeful future to look forward to. Last week he had asked Jim Killigrew to meet him in the pub for a drink. He had bought two whiskies and led the way to a quiet corner. Took out his cigarettes, offered one to Jim and lit them both. 'I'd like to talk to you about your business, Jim,' he'd said.

'Oh?' Jim had come back cautiously. It was in his nature to be wary and sometimes surly.

'I'll come straight to the point. Please hear me out. I enjoyed doing the renovations on Rose Dew, and now I'm planning to do something in the building world, not in opposition to you, I hasten to add. You've mentioned you've got more work than you can handle and are thinking of taking on more men. Your business is thriving and you have a respected reputation, and I'm hoping you might consider allowing me to put money into it, to form a partnership with me. If you want to expand and be competitive you'll achieve it better that way, without a bank loan. I think we could work well together. OK, you'd have a partner, but you would make much more profit and there would be even more for your children to inherit. Will you at least consider it?'

Jim had stared at him then stared into space as if picturing the benefits and the disadvantages of the proposition. He drew in on his cigarette and blew out the smoke. 'So you're staying on in Hennaford for good.'

'That is my intention. I feel I belong here.'

Jim narrowed his eyes. 'And if I'm not interested you definitely wouldn't set up in opposition?'

'You have my word. I'd look further afield.'

'If you hadn't said that I would have told you to go to hell. As it is, I'll say it's worth thinking about. I'll talk to Alan. It concerns him too. And let Martha have her say. My wife will want to pray on it. I'll also consult Tristan Harvey. He's always been good enough to advise me. I'll get back to you in a few days.'

Jim had kept his word, and on his way to Coose-Craze this morning he had stopped off and said the partnership could go ahead. Mark had been about to go to Tremore to pass on the good news, when Faye had turned up saying Justine was to arrive. His prospects had been raised, and then his world turned upside down in a few short hours. The business partnership might have to be put on hold. At the very least he had to sort out care for his baby.

My baby. My daughter. It sounded so strange. He had got used to having young children around him, but he was a stranger to the care of babies. He was scared. She was tiny. He might hurt her. He had stayed in Tremore House long enough for Susan to show him how to make up a bottle of babies National Dried milk and give the baby a feed. Then how to change her nappy and undress and dress her in some of the clothes from the holdall Justine had brought with her. Susan had written out a list of a baby's routine and the things it was vital he should do, to boil the bottles to ensure they were sterile and soak the nappies, and so much more. He beat down the panic rising inside him. What if he did everything wrong and the baby got sick? What if he couldn't stop her from crying? Seeking reassurance, he halted to pat Addi, dutifully close at his side. 'How on earth are we going to manage, boy?'

Susan had said she would call later in the day and that gave him some encouragement, and tomorrow she was going to Truro to buy all the things the baby would need, but it hurt him that Faye had refused his request to stay at Tremore at least for tonight. She'd said a baby in the house would unsettle the children. He had seen that it certainly would have unsettled her. He was cross with himself for not realizing she had been in some sort of turmoil, making her snap and storm out of her house. He had presumed too much. It had been wrong of him, but it still hurt that she could reject him so easily.

It was hard pushing the pram up the uneven track towards home. The baby started to cry. Mark's guts twisted in painful knots. What was the matter with her? What should he do? 'Shush, shush there.'

His new neighbour in Little Dell, Valerie Pascoe, a young mother, who cleaned for him twice a week, paused while picking her washing off the line and stared at him in astonishment. Here could be the answer to some of his problems. 'Mrs Pascoe! Could you help me, please?'

She came hurrying. 'Have you really got a baby in there, Mr Fuller? Upon my word, you have! How come?' Her friendly peasant face gleamed with amazement. She pulled at the line of curls on her homely brow while he explained. Valerie, in paisley apron and turban, declared, 'Well, finding out you're a father is wonderful, isn't it? I can see it's left you in a bit of a predicament. I'll carry her up to the house for you. She didn't like the bumping she was getting, bless her dear little soul. No wonder she's bawling her little lungs out. I'll stay and get her settled.'

'Thanks, Mrs Pascoe, you're a godsend.' The baby fell quiet when Valerie was cradling her and rocking her gently in her able arms. 'I'd be very grateful if you could come in every day from now on, except for weekends, of course, and care for her when I go out.'

'I'd be delighted to.'

Mark expelled deep breath after deep breath. 'I'll always be in your debt. I'm sure I'll be turning to you regularly for advice.' He found it easier to drag the pram up the slope rather than push it. He gazed across at the tiny features of his child, his daughter. She was making faces and bubbles were forming on her bow lips. Words drifted into his mind. Fairy child. Angel. Cherub. A miracle. And she was his. He had held her in his arms at Tremore, clumsily holding the curved glass bottle of warm milk to her lips in a state of disbelief and terror at how insubstantial she was. Justine didn't love her. Couldn't love her. Could he? A new emotion began to build up inside him. A fierce desire to nurture and protect her. It reassured him he had made the right decision to take her on. He was going to get the help he needed, but he had a few nerve-wracking days ahead.

'Are you all right, darling?' Fergus asked from the doorway of Faye's bedroom. She was sitting on the double bed, her hands stretched out either side of her and pressed down on the eiderdown, her head hung over.

She looked up. 'Just a bit deflated. Silly, really. Come in, Fergus.'

He did so, standing about with his hands in his pockets so as not to crowd her. The events of the day had brought her down, leached her confidence, which, except for the happy times she had spent with him at Glenladen, she had never known in abundance. He was a heel for sending her away, letting her cope with motherhood alone. Every time he thought about Simon, he thanked God she'd had the courage to keep him. Faye was wonderful and amazing. She should have every blessing there was to be had. But life had served her another rotten trick. He could tell she was now racked with guilt for refusing to support Mark Fuller, even though everyone had stressed they understood her point of view and that Fuller hadn't been left to cope alone. It was tough and unfair that the gorgeous woman he loved was suffering because of the selfishness of others yet again. He must try to get her to open up to him. 'Are the children all asleep?'

'Yes. The girls chattered on as usual but I've haven't heard a squeak out of them for about ten minutes.' Faye was weary and drained and wanted only to curl up and sleep.

'Tristan and Susan have taken a walk over to Ford Farm. Would you like to do anything in particular?'

'Not really.'

'You look so miserable, darling.' He went close to her, resisting the urge to touch her, which he longed to do. 'Are you regretting agreeing to become my wife? You seemed eager about it this afternoon. Have you changed your mind about having the wedding in Glenladen's kirk? We can do anything you say. I only want you to be happy. I hope you know that.' If she asked him to, he'd give up Glenladen and pass it on to his son, Donald. He would tell her this, but he was afraid it might put more pressure on her.

'I know, Fergus,' she sighed. 'It's nothing to do with you.'

He was heartily relieved to hear that. Carefully, he sat down beside her. 'This business with Mark Fuller has upset you.'

'I shouldn't have been so hard. I saw red and took it out on him. He must have had a terrible shock and been frightened by his sudden new responsibility. Of course he would ask for my help. I'll go and see him tomorrow and explain. Mark's a really good person, I'm sure he'll understand.' Fergus put his arm round her and she leaned

340

against him, needing his closeness. 'The thing was, I felt he and Justine were thinking, "Good old Faye, she'll come to the rescue." I wasn't asked for my opinion. I felt unimportant. And I'd like my little boy to be important to others. Simon has been shunned and overlooked because I'm not married. I know I'm being oversensitive, but I can't wait for us to get away from here.'

'I'm sorry you're had a bad time, darling. You and Simon are very important to me, everything, in fact.' Fergus hugged her tightly, wanting to erase all her painful memories.

Although the full meaning behind his words were lost to her, it meant everything to her to hear them. He comforted her in a way no one else could. She needed him as much as Simon needed to have his father in his life. If Fergus hadn't come when he did, the future would be empty and frightening for both of them. As for Mark, she finally had her feelings for him in perspective. Today's happening had wiped out all her hopes for him. Rescuing him and nursing him had filled her with romantic notions. She had been looking for someone to love and to have love her back. It had been just infatuation, leaving her feeling stupid to have been hankering after him. 'Knowing you care about us is what's kept me going. Simon will love Glenladen. I was worried about taking him away from his playmates here, but children adapt quickly wherever they are as long as they feel secure. The twins and Pearl will be fine with Uncle Tris and Susan and Maureen, my going won't make much difference to them really, so I can leave here without regret. We'll all have a good life together, Fergus. I'm so glad you came.' She held on to him and buried her face in his shoulder. Fergus made her feel safe and wanted. She was confident he would help her forget all the awful things that had ever happened, and create the better ways that would enable her to go on.

They stayed quietly for some time. She felt warm and cared for. One of the best things about Fergus was how sensitive he was. He was good company, the best of company. She couldn't imagine now why she had left it so long to decide to marry him. He had his head leaning lightly on hers and was tracing gentle fingertips on her upper arm. She closed her eyes to enjoy the soft, pleasurable sensations. It was a pleasure being with him; it always was. She had been too absorbed in her worries for Simon, how her leaving would affect the Smiths, and her yearning and disappointment over Mark, to concentrate how it was with Fergus. He was a wonderful man, and except for laying his priority to duty when she had told him she was having his baby, he had not hurt her in any other way. He adored Simon and gave him all his attention, as he did to her. He was sensuous in his powerful masculinity and his tactile loving ways and his sense of fun, and in these quiet moments, she was moved by him as strongly as when they had formed their deep attraction and need for each other in his draughty old castle.

He kissed her silky black hair in several places. 'I can't wait to take you and Simon up to Glenladen and introduce you to the estate as my future wife and Simon to his brothers and sister. I'll make sure you have a contented family life, darling Faye.'

'I know you will,' she sighed dreamily, easing into a soothing sense of security, something she had not known since she'd had to leave him. She trusted Fergus. Only he could make her feel this way.

'I brought something down with me in the hope you'd say yes, darling. My great-grand-mother's engagement ring. You admired it in her portrait, and it will be perfect for you.' While keeping her in his arms, he produced a tiny dark blue velvet box and lifted up the lid. 'I hope it's a good fit.'

Faye gazed at the square-cut sapphire and diamond cluster ring. How wonderful he was to remember this detail. During their affair she had dreamed she might become his wife, but now it was to be a reality. She grew as excited as any other young woman to be getting engaged, and she was thrilled to be feeling this normal reaction. 'You put it on my finger, Fergus.'

When he had done so he kissed the ring, kissed her hand, then kissed her lips. 'I'll make you happy, darling, I promise.' He wanted to tell her he was in love with her, but sensed it wasn't the right time, and he left her to her simple joy.

'The three of us will be happy,' she said. 'And I'm looking forward to serving those on the estate. The first people I will call on are Mr and Mrs McPherson.' She stroked Fergus's face. 'Thank you.'

'What for?'

'For coming down to us. For giving Simon and me a worthwhile future. For being you,' she whispered softly.

'I'll never let you go again, Faye.' He lowered his head to kiss her lips.

He kissed her warmly and tenderly, then couldn't help himself and ran away with a little passion. He pulled back, afraid to rush her. But Faye had enjoyed all the amazing sensations of the kiss and wanted more. It was easy to give way to desire with Fergus, and she'd no longer deny herself the joys and ecstasy of being with him. She sought his lips with hunger. Sighing for her, he let himself go over her eager mouth, and all their old ardour fired into life, and they gave themselves over to a blissful journey of rediscovery. 'Don't worry about being careful,' she whispered. 'What does it matter if we have another baby now?'

The struggles of the last few years were over for her. When replete and exhausted in his arms, she had the contentment of knowing she was doing the right thing for Simon, and for herself.

Twenty

'I understand Mark is coping well with his baby,' Lottie remarked to Faye. They were putting up new curtains in Coose-Craze's front room, the only room Lottie was going to have decorated until the overhaul and extensions were completed. Lottie had chosen pale blue brocade, which lightened the room considerably, for the major's archaic furniture was being used for the time being. It was Faye who was up on the stepladder threading the brass curtain rings on to the rail. Lottie was being careful for a change, and was placing the matching re-covered long cushion pad in the window seat.

Faye peered down on her. 'He's a natural. He adores her. I think it's the best thing that could have happened to him. Everyone's rallying round him. He's still finding it hard to come to terms with Justine abandoning the baby. He's written to her, but his letters have been returned unopened. He got in touch with a neighbour and was told she'd sold up and moved months ago, obviously as soon as she knew she was pregnant.'

'So she's quite determined to never have contact with the baby.' Lottie made a disapproving face.

'I was so angry with her that day. After all I'd gone through, I couldn't understand how a woman in her position could give up her child. She wasn't some young girl in a fix. The baby wasn't a lover's child. Mark was willing to give their marriage another try. She didn't want to know. I suppose I should feel sorry for her. She might come to realize one day she's made the biggest mistake of her life.'

'She probably will.' Lottie remembered how she had not wanted the baby that was growing inside her. Thank God, through Elena Killigrew that had all changed. She smoothed her hands affectionately over her protruding middle.

'I shouldn't have sent Mark away with the baby. He's been very sweet about it, and he's apologized to me too. He's asked me, Uncle Tris and Susan to be her godparents. The ceremony's on Sunday. He's named the baby Jana.'

'The old Cornish form of Jane. What about you, Faye?' Lottie tilted her head to get a good view of Faye's face. 'Are you really able to leave Mark behind in your heart and mind? Are you sure you're doing the right thing in marrying Fergus Blair? And going all the way up to Scotland?'

'I've worked out my feelings for Mark. He's nothing more to me now than a friend. I'm absolutely sure I've made the right decision about my future, Lottie. I'd made up my mind to marry Fergus just before Justine turned up with the baby. There, the curtains are up. They look lovely. You're going to have a wonderful time making this place your own. And I like the major. He's a sweetie. I think Nate was very clever, arranging things the way he did.'

'I'll never forget the moment I realized where Nate was taking us. I was dizzy with hope, and the instant I saw Randolph's beaming face I knew the wonderful truth. He and Nate kept passing these silly looks and I knew they'd made an agreement. I pretended I didn't, of course. I didn't want to spoil their big surprise for me.'

'You already know most of the people of Taldrea. What's your housekeeper like? I haven't met her yet.'

'Oh, Violet Treloar. She's nice. Down to earth. I've always liked her. I'm afraid she's missed her monthly and has scuttled off to marry her cowman fiancé. Nate was devastated. He'd got quite fond of her, as he did the old boy during all the time he'd spent trying to buy the place. I'm interviewing three women for her replacement tomorrow. I'll choose someone older. Don't want to risk another young woman leaving because she's in the family way.' Lottie parked her heavy body on the sofa bed and put her feet up. 'Make yourself comfy. I'm in no rush to get things in order. I learned my lesson the hard way during Carl's pregnancy. It's enough for me at the moment to keep up with listening to Nate's excited ideas. He's busy rebuilding the outhouses. Jim and Mark and their workforce will be building us a sitting room, dining room, office and kitchen, four bedrooms and a bathroom. Then we'll all move in while this part is modernized for the dear old major. New and old together. And young and older generations together. Just like at my old home.'

'It's good to see you happy again, Lottie.'

'Well, we've all got to grow up some time. Now, back to Fergus Blair. Are you absolutely sure about him? Sorry to rabbit on, but you haven't got your mother handy to shell out advice.'

'I care a lot about Fergus. He might not be the love of my life – I might never meet him, whoever he may be – but Fergus will make me a good husband. He's been really good to us, and Simon's already bonded with him, he's a great father, and that's what matters most. To be honest, I'm looking forward to the peace and quiet of Glenladen after this muddled year. The twins and Pearl are quite happy knowing Susan's there to replace me. They're looking forward to travelling up to

Scotland for holidays. With me gone there will be more room for Uncle Tris and Susan. I'm glad about selling Tremore to Uncle Tris. It never brought my father happiness and I don't want it for Simon. I'll put the money in a trust fund for him, and he can decide what he wants to do with it when he's old enough.'

Lottie nodded, satisfied not so much with Faye's words as with her look of content. 'Whatever you do, don't become soft again. You'll be enjoying your new life by Christmas. Do you want any more children?'

'We'd both like another child.' Faye laughed. 'Actually, it might already be on the cards.'

'You naughty girl.' Lottie grinned. 'Can't say I blame you. Fergus is a very attractive man.'

'Yes, he is.' Faye dwelt on Fergus for some moments. She had not glossed over the truth about him to Lottie. Now she was sleeping with Fergus again she found herself eager to be alone with him, while looking forward to seeing him again when he wasn't there. The plans she was making for the future with him were happy ones. 'Well, Lottie, everything seems to be working out for us at last. Hopefully, there will be no storm clouds ahead.'

'You bet. I won't let anything spoil things for me. You think like that too and everything will be fine.'

* * *

Mark was sitting on his bed, once Susan's; he had bought Little Dell's furniture from her. He was holding his sleeping daughter. He did almost everything for her and loved doing it. 'Jana.' He placed a tender kiss on her soft pink cheek. 'You're so beautiful. Daddy loves you and I'm going to do everything in my power to give you a happy life.'

The padre in the labour camp had preached that everything happened for a purpose. He had often wondered why he should have survived the horrors, and now he knew: to give life and love to Jana. He would not let her or God down.

'I like this little cottage, darling,' he whispered, 'but I want you to grow up somewhere with a bigger garden. Jim Killigrew and I are going to build us a fine new house on a piece of land Emilia Harvey has agreed to sell me. So we'll be moving across to the other side of the village.' The new business contracts had been signed, and Mark was to work part of the week until Jana was three months old, to give them time to settle together. Tomorrow he would go over to Coose-Craze and begin his first day. 'Daddy will miss you but I'll be straight home afterward, darling, I promise. We'll have a good life together. I'll never let anyone hurt you. Now you'd better go down in the cradle and sleep or Mrs Pascoe will be telling me off for spoiling you. I'll go for a walk with Addi, but I'll be back in time for your next feed.' He laid her down in the cradle and covered her warmly, rocking her for a few moments until she was asleep. It was minutes before he could tear himself away.

Maureen, the Smiths, and Valerie Pascoe's four children were playing hide and seek on Tremore land. Maureen had run off on her own and was up above Rose Dew and Little Dell. She crouched down behind a beech tree and pulled off her red woollen hat and scarf so she wouldn't easily be spotted. As fidgety as ever, she turned to look down at the two cottages. It seemed ages since she had lived in Little Dell. It was still a thrill to be sharing Pearl's room at the big house. To be where there was so much space and a proper bathroom and so many fine things. It was fantastic to see her mother happy, and to have gained a stepfather who doted on her. She now called Mr Tris Daddy, and he had begun the procedure to adopt her, and her name would be changed to Harvey. Maureen Harvey – she was going to be so proud when she could tell people it was her name.

Mark had planted the garden at Rose Dew, and cabbages and brussel sprouts, the greens she hated having to eat, were stretched out in uniform rows. Snow-white nappies and tiny baby clothes flapped in the wind on the washing line. She took to wondering about the baby. People were saying Jana Fuller was like a porcelain doll and looked a lot like Mr Fuller. Maureen was curious to know if both counts were true. She missed Mr Fuller. She'd only caught glimpses of him lately. Her mother called on him, but wouldn't allow her to go. 'Wait until the baby's older,' she'd said firmly. 'Give Mr Fuller time to get used to being a father.' He'd had the baby a couple of weeks. Surely that was time enough. He was her friend, and friends called on each other. She'd ask if she could go to Rose Dew tomorrow to see the baby. Take Jana a present; she could have the doll nasty Uncle Kenny had given her. She didn't want anything to remind her of the man who had hurt her wonderful new father. Never patient for long, curiosity got the better of her and she decided to go down to Rose Dew right now. Len was the 'seeker' in the game and he always peeped to see where his playmates were. From the distant sound of his voice – 'Ready or not, here I come!' – he was heading in the opposite direction, where the others must have gone. Perfect. She had time to slip away, and they'd never know she had disobeyed her mother.

With Mark in residence, and the trees that had loomed over the cottage cut down and stacked as logs against the new wooden shed to season for firewood, and smoke coming out of the two chimney pots, she wasn't scared the ghost would be there. Intent on her mission, she didn't see she wasn't alone until a figure appeared in front of her. 'Hello, Mo.'

'Uncle Kenny!' She froze even though he was smiling down at her. His small eyes were like marbles. His hands were rammed inside the pockets of his camel coat.

'I was about to knock on your door in case your mother hadn't gone to work, but I noticed the place had different curtains up and other stuff. I thought she'd moved away. Then I saw you up here. You look nice, Mo. Got new clothes, I see. How's that then?'

Rallying her feisty spirit, her little features drawn and dark, Maureen hissed, 'Why are you here?'

'Now that's not very friendly, is it?' He leaned forward from the waist and brought his sneering face close to hers. 'Or the proper way to speak to an elder and better. You're asking for a cuff round the lughole. So why are you all togged up? Has the Harvey toff set your mother up somewhere nice? Is she milking him for treats for the both of you?'

'It's none of your business. Mum doesn't want anything to do with you any more. Go away!'

Kenny scowled and cuffed her ear hard and she shrieked in pain and temper. 'Watch your lip when you're talking to me. Where can I find your mother?'

Bringing her hand to her stinging ear, Maureen shouted, 'I won't tell you anything.' Then, quick on her nimble feet, she sped off. 'I'm getting Mr Fuller! He'll set his dog on you!'

'I don't think so.' Kenny laughed mockingly as she headed for the cottage wall, chasing after her. 'I saw him walking through a field with his mutt when I drove here. He's on his way back, which is good, because he's just one of the rotten blighters I've come to settle a score with. No one lays into me and gets away with it. And you're for it now, girl!'

Maureen was scared. She knew she would not reach the door in time to hammer on it and get inside safely, but as she reached the wall she picked up a big stone and turned round to face him. 'Mrs Pascoe! Mrs Pascoe!' she screamed, while praying the other children would come this way and see what was happening and run for help.

'Got a fancy woman, has he?' Again came his evil laugh. 'I'll soon flush her out.' Kenny stooped, swept up two hefty stones and lobbed one over the wall to smash through a window. The glass exploded in splinters and there was a crash and a scream from inside. He pulled his arm back ready to throw the second stone.

'Don't, Uncle Kenny!' Maureen screamed. 'There's a baby inside!'

'I'm not bothered about some brat. Either you come here to me now or I chuck this one too.'

He passed the stone menacingly from hand to hand.

'A – all right. Just don't hurt the baby.' Frightened by his violence, shaking all over, she took a small step forward.

'That's better. Now tell me what I want to—' A movement in front the broken window caught his attention. He thought the woman had come outside, but it was a man who was there, an old man, not very distinct, in dark clothes and cap. He couldn't distinguish the man's eyes, but they held him fast and chills rode up his back.

The door was opened a crack, a hand beckoned and a woman called out, 'Quick Maureen, get inside!'

Maureen didn't stop to wonder why her uncle was suddenly mesmerized and staring into space. She scrambled over the wall and fled up the path and Valerie Pascoe's cardiganed arm shot out and pulled her inside. 'It's all right, my handsome.' She turned the key and hit home the bolts. 'Thank God I got you in safe and sound. Do you know who he is?'

'He's my uncle. He's beastly. He hurt my daddy.' Maureen's eyes were wide in fright and she had a hand over her pounding heart.

'I heard about that. Well, he won't easily

get the better of me. Come upstairs, we'll barricade ourselves inside Mr Fuller's bedroom with the baby. Mr Fuller keeps his Army handgun up there. If that bloke tries to break in I'll threaten him with it.' Valerie Pascoe was well built and strong, and although nervous, she was determined to protect her charge and Maureen.

'Come out, Maureen, or I'll come in and get you!' Kenny bawled. He had blinked and the man had disappeared. He could only reason he had seen a ghost, but the fear was superseded by his anger with his sister's child. He had come for revenge on Susan for rejecting him, and on Tristan Harvey for treating him like dirt, and on Mark Fuller for making him look a fool. He never forgot a grudge, and today it had spilled over into a boiling rage and the need for revenge. He threw the other stone, breaking another window.

Maureen screamed. Valerie grabbed her hand and rushed her up the narrow, carpeted stairs. Maureen helped her to push a chest of drawers against the door in the bedroom. The baby was stretching in the cradle. Valerie lifted up the cradle and put it down in the corner furthest from the window in case the villain threw missiles at it. 'Here, maid, you rock little Jana and keep her asleep.' Valerie thought it best to keep Maureen occupied. She fetched the handgun from a high shelf in the wardrobe and un-wrapped it from its protective oiled cloth. It wasn't loaded. But if the man hammering on the door and shouting abuse managed to break his way in he wouldn't know that.

Mark was watching Addi belt down the valley just yards from home to fetch a stick he had thrown. He'd recently encountered the hide-and-seekers, and they'd asked him if he had seen Maureen. 'Sorry. So you can't find her?'

'She's probably sneaked off thinking she's clever.' Len had been unimpressed. 'Come on you lot, let's go and play in the farmyard. She can stay hidden for as long as she likes.'

Mark had smiled to himself. Maureen was as mischievous as ever.

He felt a touch on his arm and got a shiver down the back of his neck. Looking round, he saw Jude Keast an inch away from him. There was such a look of anguish in his heavily lined old features. Then Jude was yards away, and further away still, in the direction Mark was aiming for. He knew what Jude was trying to tell him. Something was wrong at home. 'Addi! Here! We have to go now!'

After cycling back from Coose-Craze, Faye thought she'd call on Mark. She would be leaving for Scotland in a few days and she wanted to talk to him about Jana's baptism. She left her bicycle at the entrance to the track and heard shouting. It was aggressive and abusive, and she crept cautiously upwards to see what it was all about. Little Dell seemed deserted, but a stranger was battering on Rose Dew's door with his shoulder. To her horror, she could hear him yelling threats to Maureen. Faye turned tail and raced back before the man spotted her. Scrabbling on to the bike she sped off to get help. She hadn't met Kenny Locke, but in view of the threats he had made in the farmyard she assumed it was him. Maureen must have gone to see Mark and the baby. Mark couldn't be there or he'd be confronting Locke.

Turning at the crossroads she was relieved to see Fergus and Simon coming her way. 'Fergus!' Urgently, she explained the danger to those inside Rose Dew.

'Take Simon, run to the farm and call the police,' Fergus said, taking the bicycle from her. 'Don't worry. I'll sort this chap out.' He was away in a blink.

'Be careful!' Faye shouted after him, before picking Simon up and running on. Fergus was hardy and powerful, but she was afraid for him. Someone of Kenny Locke's background might have a gun, or was likely to wield some other deadly weapon. She could not bear the thought of Fergus getting hurt. Fearing for his safety, it seemed as if scales were falling off her eyes and the wall of over-cautious reserve she had built around her heart was dissolving. Suddenly she knew the difference between thinking she was in love to knowing she was. She knew the sun rose in the sky in the morning and the moon was there at night, and she knew she was in love with Fergus. It was liberating; her mind had never been so clear, her heart so free. And never was she more scared for him. As she pounded along with their son in her arms, she pleaded, 'For goodness sake, Fergus, be careful.'

Mark and Fergus closed in on Rose Dew at about the same time and saw Kenny Locke battering on the door with a log. 'Locke, get away from there!' Mark screamed. 'Addi, get him!'

The dog was already racing ahead, barking fiercely. Kenny swung round and saw Addi bearing down on him. He was too set on violence to be scared of Addi this time and swung the log back ready to lash out at him. Addi leapt over the wall and he was on Kenny so quickly he didn't get the chance to use the log to ward him off. Addi brought him hurtling down with his back hitting the door, pinning him down with his heavy front paws on the chest, his teeth bared while snarling into his face. 'Get him off! Get him off!' Kenny was scared now; scared his face would be ripped off.

Mark didn't slow down until he had

stormed up the front path to Kenny Locke. He kicked him in the side. 'I'll tear you apart if you've hurt my daughter!' He kicked him again. 'Bastard!'

Fergus, who'd had the longer run, reached them, disappointed not to have tackled Locke himself. 'Maureen's in there! Maureen, are you all right?'

'So this is where she is. Keep your eyes on this piece of scum, Blair.' With Addi still forcing Kenny down, he called through a broken window. 'Valerie, it's Mark! There's no need to be afraid. Locke's been brought under control. I'm coming inside.'

The bedroom window above was unlatched and pushed up and he stepped back to look up. ''Tis all right, we're all safe and sound up here,' Valerie called down.

'Thank God!'

'Faye was on her way here and saw what was happening. She's phoning the police,' Fergus said, glaring down at the cowering Kenny. 'It's a long stretch in prison for him.'

'If I ever see him again he'll end up six feet under,' Mark promised, balling his fists.

Minutes later, Maureen was running down the track into the arms of Susan and Tristan, who had been rallied by Faye. Susan did not bother to face her half-brother. He was nothing to her. It was enough to know Maureen had bravely stood up to him and he would get the punishment he deserved. The little family went home.

Faye had left Simon with Eliza Shore at the farm. She hurried up to the cottage with trepidation. No one had been hurt except for Kenny Locke, and although she knew it was silly, she was so afraid for Fergus that she wouldn't rest until she saw for herself that he was unscathed. All she wanted was to be with him.

She dashed inside the cottage, ignoring the danger of the damage and splintered glass, her eyes searching for him. Strong and resolute, he was guarding Kenny Locke, who was tied to a chair, with Addi flanking the other side. 'Fergus! Thank goodness you're all right.'

She went straight to him and his arms reached out to her. 'Of course, I am, darling. It was Addi who brought him down, but Mark would have flayed him with just a single look.' Seeing her concern, knowing her first thought was for him, he crushed her to him and showered her with kisses.

She gloried in his reaction to her. Whenever she went near him he responded to her instantly. It spoke loudly of how much he cared for her, that he really did want her. Why else had he come down to her, risking a cold rejection? Why else had he come back and stayed for so long and been so patient with her? She wrapped him up and kissed him kiss for kiss.

He whispered in her ear, 'I have to say this, darling. I love you.'

She smiled up into his eyes with all her new love. 'Me too. I love you, Fergus. I wish I'd realized it before. I wouldn't have kept you waiting for your answer.'

Mark was standing in a clear spot in the middle of his broken home holding his daughter. Faye had not even noticed him. He was sad there would never be a chance for him with Faye, but she and Blair looked absolutely right together. He had Jana, and she was enough for him for now.

Valerie came through from the kitchen with a tray of cups and the teapot. 'Thanks Valerie,' he said. 'I'll never be able to thank you enough for taking care of Jana and Maureen.' He owed his thanks to Jude as well. There was always the sense of Jude's presence here, but he couldn't detect it any more. Then somehow he knew what had happened. Jude had felt guilty for not protecting his own family, but now he had saved Jana and the others, he had allowed himself to go on to the next world. Mark smiled, he also knew that Jude had been met by his wife and child. And that for him at last the mystery of what had happened to them was revealed and he was at peace.

'Well, it'll give something for Mrs Moses and the others to talk about,' Valerie replied, pouring out milk. 'Miss Faye, have you seen my young 'uns? I'm glad they weren't around earlier.'

'They're playing at the farm with the Smiths. I told them to stay there until I got back.' Faye left Fergus and moved to Mark and gazed at Jana. She was sleeping contentedly, undisturbed by the drama. 'You can't stay here until the windows are repaired and this mess is cleared up. You're very welcome to stay at Tremore. We can all comfortably squeeze in together. It's officially my uncle's house now, but I'd love for you to be there until I leave so we can see a lot of each other. Can I hold Jana?'

'Of course.'

After the police had taken Kenny Locke away, she carried Jana all the way to Tremore, with Mark and Fergus on either side of her.

'Tell me, darling,' Fergus said much later, when they were alone. 'Did you have a bit of a thing about Mark? There were times when I was sure your thoughts were centred on him.'

'Yes, I did,' she replied, snuggling into his arms. 'Back in the days, not so long ago, when I was confused. I was only chasing a dream. I'm glad to have met him. My life is richer for it. And now I know what real love is like, that I love you very much, I shall never have to chase dreams again.'